To Mum + —

Acts of Destruction

love Mat

Mat Coward

Alia Mondo Press

ISBN: 978-0-9558686-1-0

Printed in Great Britain by the MPG Books Group,
Bodmin and King's Lynn

Cover design and layout by Dean Harkness

Typeset by Andrew Hook

Published by:
Alia Mondo Press
c/o 85 Gertrude Road
Norwich
NR3 4SG

AliaMondo@phonecoop.coop

www.matcoward.com

CHAPTER ONE

It's often been noted, down the centuries and across the world, that a man who has something to smoke and something to read can survive almost anything.

Detective Constable Thom of the North London Serious Crime Squad had the sports pages and he had his pipe - burning home-grown today, admittedly, his ration of imported tobacco having run out some days earlier, but at least burning something - and he was surviving his sixth hour of keeping watch on a rooftop garden full of nectarines quite happily, when his mobile rang.

It was the control room, telling him that what seemed to be a dead body had been found in suspicious circumstances in a suburban street not far from where he now sat. Since his blipper showed him as the nearest detective to the scene, was he available to attend? Obviously, he wasn't; obviously, he could not abandon his fruit surveillance, and once he'd explained the nature of his current assignment, the woman in the control room understood that entirely. She apologised for disturbing him, and called the squad's main office instead.

Within ten minutes of the dead body being uncovered, therefore, two officers were hurrying to view it, having caught a bus from directly outside their Kentish Town headquarters which would take them to within a two-minute walk of the putative crime scene.

There were other factors - food production, wildlife habitats and so on - but it was mainly because of their contribution to flooding that paved-over front gardens were now illegal. Fifteen square metres of hard-standing could produce a hundred litres of run-off per minute during a half-decent storm. The legislation had allowed for a two-year grace period, during which householders could re-green their gardens themselves, or get the neighbourhood committee to organise a work gang to do it, or get a grant from the community council to pay someone to do it ... and still some people's front windows looked out onto tarmac instead of grass. Some were lazy or disorganised, some were privacy rebels.

"There's a bloke down my road," Catherine told Greg as they turned into the murder street, their strides lengthening, "refuses to dig up his drive because if he did he'd have nowhere to keep his car."

"What is he, a doctor?"

She shook her head. "He's got no exemptions at all, hasn't driven the bloody thing in years, he just keeps it standing there. Polishes it with a clean rag once a week."

"Can't bear to part with it?"

"Last Christmas, my husband said he should sell it to the Re, use the money to get his garden done, and he'd still have enough to take the kids to the seaside for a week. They give you a decent price at Recycling, they don't cheat you. He hasn't spoken to either of us since."

"So what does he do for a living?"

She snorted. "Bus conductor, of all things."

A uniformed cop stood four-square outside their destination, keeping back a crowd of gawpers which existed, as yet, largely in his imagination.

"DI Greg Wallace, DS Catherine Blake," said Greg, flipping his wallet ID at the constable. Catherine blipped hers - from her pocket blipper to the PC's shoulder unit - as she usually did, and Greg wondered (as he often did) why he was a flipper and she was a blipper. It wasn't a matter of age; she was in her mid-fifties, at least ten years older than him. He'd been in the job longer than her, though - maybe that was it. He'd always been a copper. She'd worked in sales as a young woman - a field which no longer really existed, hence her current calling - so perhaps it was inevitable that her rituals wouldn't match his. "You've got a dead body for us?"

"Over here, sir." The PC led the way towards the far end of the drive, nearest the garage. "Direct Works had a court order for a compulsory re-green. We've had quite a few round here the last month or so, the street committees are getting a bit bored waiting for the anti-social minority to comply voluntarily. But they'd only just started digging, when they found that."

Greg crouched by the trench dug in the paving. "That's a dead body, that is," he said, standing and nodding to Catherine to take his place.

"Is it murder?" asked the constable.

"Well, it's a crime," said Catherine, "if only illegal disposal of a body. Someone knew he was there."

"Constable, can you call Scientific for me? And tell them to use motor vehicles, on my authority. I want the evidence made safe as soon as possible."

"Are they at home," Catherine asked, "the occupants of the house?"

"That's a slightly odd thing," said the PC. "I've only had a look through the windows, but as far as I can see, the place is unoccupied."

Greg frowned. "Unoccupied? When was the last time you saw an unoccupied house?"

"Must've only just happened," Catherine said, "otherwise the street committee would've reallocated it. Or the community council, or Displaced Persons. Bit of a coincidence, though. Rather suggests that whoever lives here didn't want to be around when the paving came up."

"Maybe it's moving day," Greg suggested. "You'd better call in, try and find out. We don't want some poor bloody family turning up at their new home to find it crawling with corpses and cops. And while we're waiting for Scientific, I'll get someone started on the door-to-door. Now, who's the best tea-drinker in the squad?" The question was rhetorical to the point of ritual, so Catherine only smiled as Greg made a show of scratching his head before answering his own question. "Ah, I know! This is a job for Bob Lemon."

*

A mixed vegetable garden this time, rather than an orchard of dwarf fruit trees, but the same crime: crop theft. On the roof of a quadcycle factory only about half a mile from where Ginger Thom had been fruit-watching. How annoying. But how like life.

"DC Thom, Serious Crime Squad." He nodded to the nervous-looking management bloke, and the nervous-looking management bloke - a Mr Doyle - nodded back. They were both wearing gloves, as it happened, but the thing was to get into the *habit* of not shaking hands. "Much missing?"

"The lot. Well - everything that was ready to pick. Sugar snap peas, early potatoes, celtuce ... all sorts. The canteen's had to go out and buy a load of veg to keep them going for the rest of the week."

Doesn't sound like kids, thought Ginger. "I'd like to talk to your nightwatchman, please."

Mr Doyle winced, and looked even more nervous. "Haven't got one. We had one, but a couple of weeks ago he left us to go and work in a coalmine."

"What was he, scared of heights?"

"His father and his grandfather had both been miners, apparently. Granddad was blacklisted after the big strike back in the - 1990s, was it? Anyway, he saw all the fuss on telly the other month, and seemingly suffered an attack of nostalgia. Applied for a job, and as soon as a vacancy came up, he was off."

The manager sounded deeply disapproving - of nostalgia, or people changing their jobs, or miners' sons in general, Ginger couldn't say. "You have to admit it's an impressive show, when they return to work at the re-patriotised pits."

"If you like that sort of thing, I suppose."

"All the miners marching up to the gate behind the brass bands, and the banners flying, and the Minister of Energy ceremonially handing over the keys to the chairman of the joint union committee." He was putting it on a bit thick, now, he knew that. But on the other hand, he was enjoying it. "And the old ex-colliers from the strike generation, and their wives and widows, lining the route, holding up pictures of the ones who've died. All a bit romantic, if you ask me."

Doyle's nervousness was fighting with irritation now. "What does he know about coal-mining? Born and bred in bloody London." He took his hat off, scratched his head, and replaced the hat.

"Preferable to working nights, I suppose," said Ginger.

Doyle sighed. "Well, this is it. It isn't a popular job. In theory, we're supposed to have two on watch, but we could never recruit more than one, despite the pay. And since the boyo marched off, we can't even manage that. We're going to have to ask a neighbourhood committee to allocate someone soon, which is never satisfactory. We'll end up with a villain on community service, or some poor old sod with a gammy leg."

Ginger looked around the garden. It was similar to those found on the roofs of most workplaces, public buildings, and other large structures: raised beds of crops growing in light compost, windproof fencing around the edges, a couple of small sheds for the tools, and dotted here and there the infrastructure - water-trappers, solars and mills. One thing missing, though. "Can't see any security cameras. Are they invisible?"

"Our efficiency audit told us they'd be a waste of resources, as long as we had two nightwatchmen." Doyle added embarrassment to his repertoire. "And of course, as long as we had *one* man, we were always trying to hire a second. And currently, of course we're still trying to hire a second - it's just that now we also need a first. So in the meantime - "

"You haven't got any cameras."

Mr Doyle nodded, then shrugged. "Of course, as things turned out ... "

"Ah, that's the thing about things, isn't it?" said Ginger. "They always bloody do turn out, just when you don't want them. So, as things stand, anyone can wander up here and help themselves at night?"

Ginger's empathetic remarks about things turning out seemed to have defrosted Doyle a little. "Not far off, I'm afraid. I know it's absurd, but it's a situation that is proving ridiculously difficult to put right."

"Your workforce are local?"

"Within the guidelines, certainly." The thaw was over; Doyle was sounding distinctly defensive, now.

Ginger took a note of the ex-nightwatchman's name, in case he needed to contact him. "You're not a co-operative, I understand?"

"We're still privately owned, that's right. We're just about small enough to be exempt."

"But presumably the roof garden *is* classed as a co-op? So, until you manage to hire a watchman, can't you get a voluntary rota going among your employees?"

And now, Ginger noticed with interest, defensive was replaced by just-a-little-bit evasive. "As I say, there's not many of them, and they're all busy people. We wouldn't really want to impose on them."

DC Thom didn't reckon he'd ever heard of an entire workforce being too busy to safeguard a pile of spuds destined for their own families' bellies. He was still a relatively young man, true, but he'd definitely lived long enough to have never heard of that. But that wasn't what he said. What he said was: "Just to mention - they're not actually guidelines, sir. It is a legal requirement under the Agreement of the People that all enterprises, with very few exceptions, employ a specific, agreed proportion of their workforce from within a specific, agreed radius of the workplace."

"Oh, of course, Detective Constable: there's a bloody law for everything, these days," said the voice of the private sector.

At the murder scene in Sudbury - he was already thinking of it as a murder scene, though of course Catherine was right, there were other crimes which might have resulted in this body under this hard-standing - Greg was nodding at, and being nodded to by, a cheerful young woman carrying a sleeping baby: the secretary of the Beech Lane street committee. The woman, of course; not the baby, even if it'd been awake.

He thought the secretary of the street committee was right to be cheerful, present circumstances notwithstanding; it was a pleasant street, in what used to be a suburb, when things were a bit more centralised in that way, before what most people called "the Process" began smoothing and stretching the cities at least somewhat. The 1930s houses were solid, and set in decent-sized plots. When Greg was a kid, you'd have had thousands and thousands of these houses, ringing every city in the country, with often only one or two people living in each one. And all those nice big gardens, with hardly a vegetable amongst them.

The road curved gently, and he could see, just about at the bend, a group of young children squatting in the middle of the road intensely concentrated on some sort of game. He wondered if, when these houses were first occupied, the traffic had been light enough for children to play in the road; in the 1930s? Perhaps. And then there'd have followed decades when you could barely cross the road, let alone play in it, and so to now: a fair amount of traffic, these days, but nowhere near as much as twenty years ago, and very little of it motor traffic. Not much of it so fast that a kid couldn't get out of its way. All the same, there'd been a death not far from where his mother lived, just before Christmas, of a nine-year-old girl by a pony and trap. The driver hadn't been drunk but, unbelievably, the pony had, and the driver would spend at least the next ten years doing community service.

"I'm DI Greg Wallace," he told her. "You're Nesta Popperwell?"

"Pleased to meet you. Someone said a *body*? Can that really be right?"

"I'm afraid it is, yes. A dead body has been found under the paving. Nesta, it would have been your committee's responsibility to call in a compulsory re-green, yes?"

"No, in fact that's done at community council level. Once it gets to compulsion, you see, it's taken away from the street committees - the idea being not to lead to bad feeling between neighbours."

"Ah, right. Thank you: I should have known that."

She returned his smile. "It's all still a bit new, isn't it? And a bit complicated."

"Well, and I'm old enough to remember the old system: if you wanted to get anything done, you went to the town hall, filled in a form ... "

"And ... ?"

Greg shook his head. "No - no *and*, that was it. You just filled in a form, and six months later nothing happened. Happy days. Just out of sheer nosy curiosity, how do Direct Works leave the garden, once they've dug up the drive? Do they leave the householder with naked earth, or what?"

"No, they put it all down to lawn. Obviously, the hope is that people will grow a bit of food eventually, but given that you're talking about people who've had to receive a compulsory in the first place, you can't be too confident."

"So, grass isn't ideal, but at least it lets the rain drain away."

"That, and also lawns are more valuable than people think. They're extremely useful to various birds, mammals, invertebrates, and of course the mowings go into the compost. And if the householder ever does get up off his bum, it's pretty easy to convert a bit of lawn, or a whole lawn, for fruit and veg."

"Listen, Nesta, we're a bit puzzled to find this place empty - such a nice house, such a desirable street. Has it - "

She shook her head. "No, no, it's not - "

He held up a placating hand. "I'm not suggesting your committee has been in any way - "

"No, no - it's not empty." Her interruption was more determined this time. "The couple who live here, they're just on holiday. They've got relatives in - Cornwall, I think it is."

"On holiday?"

"They were leaving at the weekend, I think it was."

"Well, that is very odd, Nesta. Because if they're on holiday, it appears they've taken the furniture with them."

"The *furniture?*"

"The place is mostly empty, as far as we can see. We haven't been inside yet, but we've looked through the windows."

The secretary of the street committee was clearly astonished. She was so astonished, her baby woke up. Or else the baby was so astonished, it woke itself up. Greg couldn't really tell. He didn't know an enormous amount about babies. "I don't know what to say," the young mother said. "I've no explanation."

"Will the - what's their name?"

"Nottle."

"Will the Nottles have left their contact details with the street committee's crime prevention person? Or maybe with their next-door neighbours?"

She waggled her hand. "It's quite likely they won't have, to be honest. It's not compulsory, you know."

"Sure. Most people do it, though, in case anything happens."

For the first time, Nesta looked a little uncomfortable. The baby was all right; it had gone back to sleep, callous as all its kind. "The Nottles are a bit ... what could I say?"

"A bit private?" Greg suggested.

She nodded. "Yes, a bit private. They don't come to meetings much, you don't see them in the pub, or street events, or sports or clubs. Keep themselves to themselves."

Greg smiled at her tone. When he was a lad, keeping yourself to yourself had been considered one of the great suburban virtues.

There were two Loftys. At the moment, they were in a quadcycle, just passing Trafalgar Square. They were on their way back from something and on their way to something else, as people so often are.

There were always two Loftys; this had been decided a good

while previously, at Detective Inspector level. One Lofty was in his late twenties, the other in his early sixties. One was called Lofty because he was short, and the other was called Lofty because he was tall. One, in other words, was what might be called a "natural" Lofty, while the other could be described as an "ironic" Lofty.

As luck would have it - and luck would, no matter anyone else's feelings on the subject - both Loftys arrived in the Squad on the same Tuesday. Neither, it quickly became apparent, was willing to answer to anything other than Lofty - both having held the nickname since childhood, and neither feeling they should be the one to relinquish it - and so it had been decided that they should be known in the office as Big Lofty and Little Lofty respectively.

It was the *respectively* bit that didn't work. No-one, least of all the Loftys themselves, could ever quite remember - or quite agree - whether the Big and the Little had been applied naturally or ironically. Half the squad took it that Little Lofty was the shorter of the two - and the other half didn't. Confusion over trivial matters can be very close to disastrous in a setting such as a Serious Crime Squad.

And so (at least, this was how the story went), DI Wallace ruled that the two Loftys should permanently and invariably be paired together, as unbreakable working partners. That way, it couldn't matter which one was which: whenever you asked after them or sent for them, you'd get both, so the one you wanted - if you happened to know which one you wanted - would reliably be included in the package. The Loftys, to use a slightly old-fashioned phrase, came bundled.

This didn't work badly. The apparent loathing between the two detective constables was, most of their colleagues believed, largely indulged in for recreational purposes.

For the record, the young one was short and the old one was tall.

"Are you pedalling, you lazy old sod, or am I doing it all?"

"The exercise'll do you good, kidda. Look, are those evangelists?"

"Where?" The young one slowed the quadcycle, and looked where his colleague was pointing. "Oh, yeah, could be."

"Shall we have a look, then?"

The young one made a squeaky noise between his teeth. "It's not my idea of Serious Crimes. We're supposed to be on our way to a murder."

"It's against the law," said the old one. "It's not up to policemen to pick and choose which laws they enforce."

"Pompous old toss," replied the young one, bringing the quad to a halt. "Anyway, I've heard on Radio Free Europe that *enforcing* the Privatisation of Faith laws is against *international* law. So we could end up being done for doing it. It's against human rights, you see."

The old one sneered, using his whole body for full effect. "Yeah, well, I've heard on Radio Free Europe that the moon's made of foie gras."

"Yeah, well, you *haven't*, in fact, because you never bloody listen to Radio Free Europe. You don't listen to or watch or read anything you don't agree with. Your mind is completely blocked against anything that goes against your precious Process."

"So why did you stop the quad, then?" The old one knew the answer to his question: Lofty had stopped the quad because - for all his disdain for modern Britain, and the Process, and for all his passionate, if sometimes not overly knowledgeable advocacy of a return to the good old days of free enterprise and individualism and the never-failing, self-regulatory perfection of the unflawed market - he was still an honest, loyal and ambitious police officer. He did not pick and choose which laws he enforced, and preaching in public was, undeniably, a crime; to be precise it was an Action Considered Injurious to Unity as laid down by the Agreement of the People. Freedom of religion was absolute in modern Britain, legally guaranteed, for the first time in the nation's history, so long as that religion was practised behind closed doors, in the home or in registered places of worship. Secularism in public - a term which included schools and workplaces, streets and parks - was, likewise, absolute; and, likewise, guaranteed by law for the first time. This was a country which had had enough of divisions caused by faith. It might be thought that it should have had enough some hundreds of years previously, but, at any rate, it had certainly had enough now.

"Tell you what, if you like, why don't you call the local uniforms? Report an offence Injurious to Unity, let them deal with it."

The old one held no principled objection to compromise. "Go on, then, kidda," he said, "but you make the call while I pedal."

You could go quite fast in a quadcycle when both passengers were pedalling (less fast, in truth, when the two Loftys were on board since it was rare for both of them to be pedalling simultaneously) and being that the vehicle was, on such a calm day, roofless, conversation required raised voices against the noises of travel. Luckily, neither Lofty was a quiet speaker, either by nature or choice.

A mile or so further northwards, the old one said, loudly: "That was an odd business this morning."

"Why odd? Yobs chucking stuff into ponds. Or did you think vandalism wasn't going to exist in your shiny utopia?"

The accusation of utopianism was too soft and stale to require a reply. So the old one gave the young one a five-minute ear-bashing on the subject, in his finest Black Country monotone, and then carried on. "I don't reckon that stuff was chucked in. Not at random. It looked methodical to me."

The young one couldn't be bothered to argue for long against a proposition that was so evidently true. "All right, then - what for?"

"Only two motives I can think of. To get rid of the stuff that was chucked - or else to ruin the flood pond. If the former, we can tell the DI it's a routine matter and he can hand it over to another section. If the latter, it most surely comes under Serious Crime."

After a few moments' thought, the young one said: "He won't take us off the murder to investigate the pond, though, will he? I've never done a murder before."

CHAPTER TWO

The examiners from Scientific had arrived in their van, siren screaming - unnecessarily, in Greg's view, and very probably illegally - much to the delight of the local kids. Round here, Greg supposed, they probably didn't see a motor vehicle as often as once a week. The Commonwealth of Britain's fuel shortage was not as extreme as in some of those countries which had failed, as yet, to make the kind of structural changes which Britain had made; even so, the exemptions which allowed petrol and its analogues to be used for various categories of person or purpose were becoming fewer all the time. They were becoming more precise, too; doctors could still drive to visit patients, for instance, but could not drive between their own homes and their surgeries. Greg's son's rugby team was no longer allowed to use a minibus to attend away fixtures which would take less than ninety minutes by public transport.

"Greg - there you are." DS Phil Kale leapt off his racing bike and marched over to the section of garden wall which Greg had chosen as his leaning post. He'd been leaning against it, smoking a roll-up, and running through checklists in his head. He stifled a sigh, now. The DI tried not to sigh every time Phil Kale marched up to him, because it really wasn't fair: Phil was a decent bloke and an assiduous detective. It was just that bloody *marching* - his wiry limbs swinging, his scraggly, reddish beard bristling, his teeth grinding. Phil was a decade younger than Greg, but he had the worry-lines of a man two decades older. The marching always signified bees in bonnets. One bee in particular.

"All right, Phil. You come to join the to-do?"

The DS took his pipe out of his trouser pocket and rammed it into his mouth. Greg had hardly ever seen him smoke it, but he sucked it at every opportunity, and with the kind of ferocity other men reserved for tug-of-war contests. "What? What to-do?"

"The murder, Phil. Have you come to help me with my murder? Because if so, I could do with you on the - "

"No, no!" The pipe went back into the pocket. "I haven't got time for that, I'm afraid. I've come straight from the office. Listen: it looks like there's been a rescue in Muswell Hill."

"A rescue?"

Phil shook his head, impatiently. Rattled it, really, more than shook it. "You know, you know - a child's been reported missing, and the mother thinks - "

"Oh, I see," said Greg, stubbing out his cigarette and putting the dog-end into the little enamelled dog-end box his ex-wife had given him last Christmas.

"Yes, please don't say *I see*, as if I'm making this up, Greg!"

"No, of course not, nothing of the kind, it's just - "

"Sarla Brown, aged seven next week," Phil read from his notebook. "Went off to visit her friend, two doors down, ten o'clock this morning, never arrived at the friend's, not seen since." Greg glanced at his watch. Phil saw the glance, and rolled his eyes. "Yes, yes! Not long ago, sure. But she's *seven* next week, Greg. 'Give us a child before it's seven ... '"

"You've started the search?"

"Everything's being done by the book, I assure you of - "

"I don't doubt it for a minute, mate - I'm not questioning - "

"But we need to get moving. I don't think she is 'missing'. I think she's been taken."

"So, why do you call it a rescue? On what evidential basis?"

"The *mother's* calling it that, Greg."

"OK, same question."

"She heard - "

"She *says* she heard, yeah? Same as the neighbours *say* the little girl never arrived at their house. You don't take things for granted in cases like this, you know that."

Phil took his pipe out of his pocket, tapped it against his knuckles, and put it back. "She says she heard - and I believe her -

14

North American voices through the open kitchen window just after the little girl left the house."

"Did she have a look?"

"She couldn't, she was doing something at the stove."

"What does she say they said, these voices?"

Phil shook his head. "Just voices. Talking to someone."

"Each other probably. And they were North American? She doesn't say Yank?"

"Two women's voices, Greg." He treated the DI to a significant look. In the stories, it was always two Yank women, never two men or one of each. "And, yes, she says North American, not Yank. That's why I believe her - she's not hysterical, she's not running round the place saying *My baby's been kidnapped by Yank missionaries!* She's saying what she heard and what she saw. She's a good witness."

Greg took the time afforded by rolling and lighting another smoke to pre-edit what he was about to say. It was still going to come out wrong, but at least he'd have made the effort. When DS Kale was in one of these moods, that was about all you could do. "Look, Phil, you and I are never going to agree on this."

"God's sake, Inspector - clock's ticking!"

"Philosophically, if you like, you and I are never going to agree. You believe that Christian missionaries from the US and the former US kidnap British children, and smuggle them back to America, to save them from growing up in a secular society."

"Atheist communist society - that's what it says on their websites. Exact words."

"And you believe these 'rescues' are actually happening, and I don't. I think they're urban myths, and that the nutters on the websites are just fantasising. I have never heard of one single, confirmed case, and neither have you - because if you had, you'd have told me about it. You haven't given me one piece of evidence today that you yourself would take seriously if this was any other kind of case. And I need you on this murder."

"Murder?" Phil's expression of amazement suggested that the DI had said he needed him to help set up the trestle tables for a street party. "Surely you've got Catherine on that?"

"I need two sergeants on this one, Phil. One back at the office, and one - "

"I can't believe what you're saying! Surely a missing child is more urgent than someone who's already dead?"

Well, you could hardly argue with that. "All right, look. I'm not calling in the Foreign Office, or whoever you've got your heart set on." He held up a silencing palm. "No, I'm not, forget it. Not unless you've got something a bit more than two Canadian tourists strolling down a London street chatting about the weather. But you can continue with the case for the moment, and we'll manage without you here."

Phil muttered something that sounded suspiciously unlike a thank you, and turned towards his bike. Greg called him back.

"Just a second. You can work on this as long as it looks like a possible kidnapping. All right? As soon as it begins to look like a false alarm, or a domestic, I need you straight back here. Evidence-based decisions only, please, Phil. No crusading, you understand?"

"Can I go now?"

"Go on, keep me informed."

Catherine Blake had heard the last few exchanges of the conversation; enough to be a little surprised at its outcome. Greg saw that on her face, and shrugged. "He won't be much use here if his mind's elsewhere, he'll only sulk. Anyway, if it really is a missing child case, he'd be my first choice to handle it. I just wish I could get my squad to take murder seriously!"

"You think it is a murder, then?"

"Like you said, it's a something; you don't bury bodies under drives for no reason. Any idea yet when the paving went down?"

"I've got Bob Lemon on that, he's asking the neighbours. And Gerard is on file searches back at the office."

"In that case," said Greg, "while we wait for Scientific to do their doings, we might as well go and find ourselves some lunch."

"The local's just round that corner." Catherine pointed, and they set off pubwards.

"So what do you reckon?" Greg asked. "Are Yanks kidnapping our kiddies?"

Catherine lit her pipe. "Got problems enough of their own to be going on with, haven't they?"

Everyone liked talking to DC Bob Lemon - just about everyone he'd ever met - which worked out pretty well, because Bob liked talking to everyone. Drinking tea, eating biscuits, and talking. He had to eat the biscuits, because he needed to be a bit tubby; he was a baby-faced, brown-skinned man in his forties, and if it hadn't been for the slight tubbiness he'd have looked far too young, he reckoned, for people to feel happy about confiding in him. Tubbiness aged a man subtly and in a pleasing way. Anyway, that worked out pretty well, too, because he liked eating biscuits. His Nan's home-made, by preference, with anything chocolate and/or ginger in close second place. Some years ago, Bob Lemon had sat in an interview room in a police station in Birmingham eating his Nan's chocolate and ginger chip biscuits while the chap sitting opposite him had told him, in detail, how and where he had disposed of the corpses of the three young girls he had raped and murdered. Bob had chomped and nodded and sipped at his tea, and afterwards his then boss had told him "You are a fucking hard bastard, Orangey, and I mean that as the deepest of compliments."

Everyone liked talking to Bob Lemon, but nobody liked it quite as much as old women did.

"People don't move home so much, these days, do they?" said Mrs Denmark, a widow who lived in a house ten doors down from the assumed murder scene. "Not like they used to, years ago. Not voluntarily, I mean."

"That's true," said Bob. "Are these home-made? They're fantastic."

"I've never had a shop-bought biscuit in the house, my love, and that is the truth."

"Why would you? You can't buy quality like this."

"Have you tried the shortbread?"

"Don't worry, Mrs Denmark, I'm getting to that next."

"Of course, there's floods and so on, so people have to move, but I can remember when young people used to change houses every few years. The property ladder, they called it."

"But you've always lived here, you say?"

"I was born here," she said proudly, "and I was married here, and I fully intend to die here. But not quite yet."

Bob wondered why having spent an entire life at one address was something people felt proud about. It sounded like a neutral thing to him, deserving neither pride nor shame. "And do you remember when it was that the front garden at number nineteen was paved over for parking?"

"Well, you see, that's happened more than once, to my knowledge. It was first done in the late 1970s, I should think, because the couple who lived there had two cars - which was quite unusual in those days, but the wife did those Tupperware demonstrations, you see - and then in the 80s it was turned back into a garden, because the bloke who lived there wanted to grow veg, he was into self-sufficiency."

"Did he?" Bob smiled. "There's nothing new under the sun, is there?"

"Oh, I hope you're wrong, dear, I really do. It wouldn't be much of a life without something new. Anyway, that didn't last long, because the next family had four cars: his, hers, and the two teenage girls. So it was all tarmac then."

"Four cars? Amazing. Hard to imagine now, isn't it?"

"To be fair," said Mrs Denmark, "people worked so far flung back then, and you couldn't trust public transport, not like now with a bus stop on every corner and a railway station in every village, and who knows what else. We didn't have any of that when I was young, you had to fend for yourself in those days. Yes, you did."

And another thing Bob wondered: why did old people always sound so disappointed when they talked about something being better now than it had been in the past? Was it because it undermined their nostalgia?

They were both smoking their pipes now - home-grown, not proper imported tobacco; it was a long time since Christmas - and sipping their tea, Bob having eaten as many of the old widow's biscuits as he felt decently able to.

"After the four-car family, there was an old widow - she wasn't there long, she died, but she did have a little lawn, and some flower beds, I remember that. Pansies in winter, and wallflowers in spring. Then I think there was a young guy on his own, he was there briefly. It might have been him that did the last lot of paving." She shook her head. "I don't think I ever knew any of their names, to be honest. It wasn't that sort of area, in those days. You just nodded in the street, sort of thing, that was about as far as it went."

"Do you know the couple who live there now? The Nottles?"

"Not really, love. They're not very social. Been there a good while, mind. They were quite young when they moved in, they must be in their fifties now, I should imagine. He teaches food preservation at the community school."

"See, that's already something we didn't know. Does he teach adults or children?"

"Both, I think - they mostly teach both now, don't they? He specialises in jams, I do know that." She frowned. "Or maybe jams and pickles. I know I asked him to look at my tomato solar when it went wrong and he said he hadn't a clue, so he obviously knows nothing about food dehydration."

"What does Mrs Nottle do, do you know?"

"Scientist, I think, or a researcher of some sort. So which one have you dug up, then? Him or her?"

"It's a him, we reckon," said Bob, "but we don't think it's Mr or Mrs Nottle. Been there too long, you see; probably been there since the hard-standing went down."

"First, second or third lot?"

"Presumably the most recent."

Mrs Denmark tapped her pipe against her teeth. It was moderately unusual to see an old woman smoking a pipe - it was more of a young woman's fashion. Old women associated it with their great-great-grandmothers; young women associated it with something their mothers would never have dared do. Perhaps Mrs Denmark had been a non-smoker until the flu scares, Bob thought, and had chosen a pipe because you didn't have to inhale. "Well, either way," she said, after a while, "I can't think of who it might be."

"No-one who vanished from the scene suddenly, or went missing?"

"No-one comes to mind. You see, we didn't think of it as vanishing, back then - it was just moving on, perfectly routine. Here today, there tomorrow. But if I think of anyone I'll call you."

"As long as you've been baking," said Bob.

He sat and talked to her for a while longer because that was what he was good at, and every boss he'd ever had bar one had understood that Bob chatting to people was never a waste of time, even when - as in this case - it was basically a waste of time.

As he was leaving, Mrs Denmark told him: "They had a caravan, too. Can you believe it!"

"Who, the Nottles?"

She shook her head. "The family with four cars. Not like the modern ones, I mean, not horse-drawn - a great big motor home, out there on the drive."

"Four cars and a caravan?" Bob popped his eyes. "It's a wonder they didn't tarmac over the house, never mind the garden."

"You useless sod," said one of the Loftys to the other, as they entered the briefing room.

"I've been promoted," the other Lofty told DC Gerard Cochrane, who was setting out chairs.

"You been promoted, Lofty?" said Gerard.

"Definitely. I was only a useless bugger, yesterday."

"Your turn to buy the cakes, then." Having placed seventeen chairs facing the dais, Gerard now began placing briefing notes on them. He'd been hard at it on the typewriter, and then on the hand-cranked duplicating machine, the last few hours; everyone attending the briefing would have whatever information they needed, assuming it was yet available. DC Cochrane was an acknowledged master of the organisational aspects of police work, and it was a mastery he was proud of. This was a craft he had studied and honed over decades, but there was another reason why he wanted his colleagues to know how good at it he was: he didn't want them thinking that he did so much office work because, at the age of seventy-three, that was all he could do.

A seventeen-year-old girl had asked him, that very afternoon, why he'd stayed on in the police, and he'd replied as he always did: "There's no reason why I've stayed. It's just that there hasn't been a reason, yet, for me to go."

Under the Agreement of the People retirement was available to everyone - including the self-employed - at the age of fifty, without loss of income. But it was not compulsory, and many people (though not all that many detective constables, it had to be said) chose to continue working. Workers could be compulsorily retired, from any job or calling, but only by a tribunal finding that they'd become unable to perform their tasks "solely or chiefly by reason of age." No-one was going to say Gerard Cochrane couldn't perform his tasks, from age or any other cause. He intended to keep working in the Squad until he was eighty-five, and then have a look around and see what he might fancy doing next. As no previous male member of his family had ever, as far as Gerard knew, survived beyond seventy, he reckoned he was doing all right.

He'd joined the then Metropolitan Police in Hackney, in the 1970s. Some of the youngsters more or less fainted when he said that. They thought the 1970s, maybe, was when Queen Victoria died. Gerard missed almost nothing from those days, apart from striptease. In the pub they'd used as their local in the days when he'd first made plainclothes, there used to be strippers on at lunchtime. As a young near-virgin, he'd thought that was just about wonderful: for the price of a pint and a pork pie, bosoms and bottoms closer to your eyes than the dartboard was. You never saw strippers nowadays. It wasn't that there was no demand, Gerard was pretty sure of that; more likely, there was no supply. The bosoms and bottoms of today had better things to do with their time.

He didn't ask what one of the Loftys was being useless about. He had no objection to their double act, but he reckoned they could manage it without him. Instead, seeing Bob Lemon had turned up, he took him over a cup of tea and told him there was someone he ought to meet.

Sitting in the nearest thing to a corner that this largely non-angular room possessed, was a girl, or young woman - Gerard hadn't decided yet - reading one of the duplicated bundles of briefing notes with great attention, and wearing a big windcheater which she showed no inclination to remove or even to unzip. She had very black skin, was a bit blushy and very pretty, and healthily plump.

"Erin, this is another of our team - DC Bob Lemon. Bob, Erin Smee." They nodded. Bob's generation - not to mention Gerard's - tended to keep their hands in their pockets to remind them not to offer them for shaking, but to Erin it came naturally: the germ-free nod, the smile, the nod again. "Erin's just left school, and she's doing her work-sampling. She'll be attached to the Squad for the next three months. I've been asked to be her main supervisor, which I consider an honour and a pleasure - "

She smiled again. "Thank you, Gerard."

" - but the idea is that she should spend a bit of time with everyone, eventually. Get an all-round picture. I'll be sorting out a preliminary rota in the next couple of days."

"Work-sampling, eh?" Bob gave her a big smile. He liked teenage girls. He'd got three of his own; two daughters, and a second wife. "Wish they'd had that when I left school, I wouldn't have ended up doing this!"

Erin laughed, and beyond Bob's eye line, Gerard winked, approvingly. She didn't look like a girl who minded laughing politely, or found it difficult, but her potential embarrassment must surely have been increased by the fact that this was the third time she had heard the same joke within Gerard's hearing. "Are most of the school-leavers in your year doing work-sampling, Erin?" he asked now.

"About half and half," she replied, her London accent strong, and her voice pleasantly deep. "A lot of them know exactly what they want to do, so they're going straight to it - or filling in with something else while they wait for a vacancy. Or doing courses, obviously."

"It lasts a year, does it?" Bob asked. "So what other samples are you doing?"

"Farriery, potato breeding, and bar work."

"Now, that is what I call a range of interests! What attracts you to detective work, Erin?"

"Honestly?" She grinned. "Over-glamorised fictional presentations of policing in radio, TV, films and books."

"Honestly?" Bob's round face lit up with delight.

"I said, honestly."

"That's *precisely* what got me into it," said Bob. "I saw the detectives on TV, and I thought - that is so cool."

"And is real-life detective work anything like the fiction?"

Bob nodded. "Exactly like it."

"What - honestly?"

"Exactly like it," said Bob. "I mean, totally different in every way, obviously - but *exactly* like it, if you know what I mean."

Erin smiled, shyly. "I think I do, yeah."

"Right," said DI Wallace, "thanks, everyone. We'll get started." The Squad's permanent strength was twenty-one full-time positions, police and civilian, some of those being made up of two or even three part-timers. Attendance at this evening's all-staff briefing - allowing for annual leave, sick leave, and those busy on assignment elsewhere or off-duty - was fifteen. Greg looked at the briefing sheet. "OK, I'll go through the cases in the order that Gerard's listed them. As ever, feel free to interrupt if you suspect I've lost my way or nodded off. Now then, we'll - oh, sorry! Didn't see your hand up. Yes, Jade?"

The detective inspector yielded the floor to the glamorously grandmotherly civilian who had worked as the Squad's office manager for more than a decade. "Do you want a bit of cake with that tea?" she asked.

"Thank you, Jade," said Greg, "that's an excellent question. And I shall give it the full and honest answer it deserves: yes, I certainly do, I am bloody starving. Thank you." He took a bite and a swig. "Right. The corpse found at nineteen, Beech Lane, is that of an adult male. Scientific are doing their doings right now, so we hope to know more tonight or in the morning. But for now, that's it, except that there are no screamingly obvious signs of violence to the body, and that they are as sure as they can be at this early stage that the body went down at the same time as the paving. Which according to a neighbour was ... ?"

"Some time in the mid-to-late 90s," said Bob Lemon. "That's about as near as we've got at the moment. I think Gerard was ... ?"

"Nothing in the records yet," Gerard said. "We'll carry on looking, but I'm not hopeful. Everyone was doing it back then."

"Are the current occupants suspects?" asked Ginger Thom.

"The current owners," said Greg, "Bradley and Kim Nottle, are a bit of a puzzle altogether. In answer to your question, Ginger - no, our working assumption is that they're probably not directly linked to the body, assuming it was buried before they moved in. However, we'd obviously like to speak to them, and at the moment that's proving difficult." He explained about the almost empty house - since confirmed by an entry team - and the Nottles' apparent trip to

Cornwall. "Our early attempts to locate them have been fruitless. DS Blake will be assigning officers to that aspect of the investigation shortly. The Nottles appear to have no siblings, and only one surviving parent between the pair of them: Bradley Nottle's mother lives in a care home near Swansea, and an informal word with the matron there classes her as unfit to interview."

"They've not told anyone where they're going on holiday?" said Ginger. "Are they privacy freaks?"

Greg finished his cake, and washed it down. "Not particularly social, from what we've heard - and of course they've ended up having their front garden re-greened compulsorily - but on the other hand, the husband, Bradley Nottle, is a teacher at the local school. That's not normally the sort of job that would go to an individualist, is it?"

"What does Kim Nottle do?" asked a DC.

"Some sort of research scientist, apparently. We're checking that."

"Should we be worried for their safety?" asked Gerard. "Do we consider them missing?"

"Good question, Gerard. The house is being checked right now as if it were a crime scene, but if that doesn't turn anything up then I think we'd have to say the only way we'll know whether or not the Nottles are safe is to find them." Greg checked his notes. "And I don't think we know anything more than that at this stage. As I said, Catherine will be sorting out three teams to cover our three main priorities: identify the dead body; establish the whereabouts of the Nottles; and thirdly, identify and trace all previous occupants of the house from about 1990 onwards." He frowned at his notes for a moment, looked over at Gerard and then clicked his fingers as his face cleared. "Of course, yes - I'd forgotten to say hello to Erin Smee, who's joining us for a three-month work-sampling. I don't think we've ever had a work-sampler on this squad before, so this is very exciting for us, and you're very welcome."

"Thank you, sir."

"You've joined us on a busy day, as you can tell, so you might not get quite the measured induction we would normally aim for - but you'll certainly get a fair idea of what we're all about." Greg glanced at Catherine; she nodded. "DS Blake will find you an assignment. You won't be a spare part around here, I can promise you that."

"Thanks," said Erin. "I'm loving it already."

Greg paused, and looked at the girl properly for the first time. "Are you really?"

"Yeah. Sir."

He reckoned she was, and all. *Well, well* ... "You hear that, folks? She's one of us."

"Poor mite," Jade called out. "She looked such a sensible girl, too."

"Now then, next on the list," said Greg. "Obviously, a lot of us will be working full-time on the unlawful burial - especially if, as we're rather assuming it will, it turns into an unlawful killing. Most of the rest of you will probably be involved to some degree as and when. But we've also got a couple of other investigations which we all need to be aware of. Lofty? Anything in this pond business?"

"No, nothing," said one of the Loftys, as the other one said "Could be, yes."

Greg's face clouded. "Could you decide which it is, please, and then get back to me?"

"Sir," muttered both Loftys, in perfect sync.

"Next: Ginger, how are your missing veg going?"

Ginger stood up, notebook in hand. Dark-haired (he'd been "Tabby Thom" at school, but he preferred Ginger, given a choice), slight, and in his twenties, he was amongst Serious Crime's most recent recruits. He'd known exactly what the work-sample girl had meant when she said she was already loving it: he'd felt the same way, right from his first hour. He'd hated being a uniformed cop so much he'd almost packed it in several times, and now thanked his luck daily that he'd held on long enough to find himself, for the first time in his life, doing something he was good at. "There's been one more raid," he said, and told them about the quadcycle factory's unguarded rooftop garden. "It's in the same area as the others, but as you'll see from the briefing sheet, it doesn't really fit the pattern - if there is a pattern."

"Are you thinking it might be a one-off?" Greg asked.

"I think it could be. The fact that the place has no security - it could just be opportunist. To be honest, I think they could *all* be one-offs."

"You're not convinced by the pattern that Uniform thought they saw?"

Ginger shrugged. "It's there if you look for it. But it's just as easily not there. People nick food, don't they? That's human nature. In World War Two it was endemic. The courts used to give people hard labour for it."

Out of the corner of his eye, Greg saw a pipe-fill of tobacco change hands between two DCs. He tried not to smile; evidently someone had just won top prize in tonight's Blitz Bingo, correctly guessing how soon into his contribution the young detective would make a comparison between present day difficulties and those of the 1940s. For his part, Greg was all in favour of his officers harbouring healthy obsessions: he reckoned they demonstrated keenness, connectedness, imagination. Unhealthy obsessions were a different matter, obviously. Speaking of which ... he looked around the room. *Ah yes*: over there by the door. Looking impatient, as usual ...

"OK, Ginger, thanks for that very balanced report. I think for the time being, I'm going to ask DS Blake to assign you on the tarmac case, and see what happens. Naturally, if we start getting indications that there is more to this than a series of unconnected raids, you'll be reassigned. Organised food theft would clearly have to take priority over a long-dead body. So keep an eye on it, will you? Right, finally for now - DS Kale has been monitoring a missing child." Phil took a step forward, and Greg was quick to continue speaking. He had one or two things to get clear before he gave Phil the floor. "Let me stress that this is not as yet a Squad case. As well all know, most missing children turn up. Phil has merely been liasing with the local police, in case we're called in later. Phil? What's the latest?"

"Right," said Phil Kale, who was never at his best addressing meetings. He took a piece of paper out of his pocket, read through it, then put it back and got another one out. He read through that one and nodded to himself. "Right, as the DI says, we seem to have a missing child in Muswell Hill. A little girl, she'll be seven next week, her name's Sarla Brown. She set off from home to visit a close neighbour at ten-hundred, that's over eight hours ago, and has not been seen since. Her parents live together, and all other relatives and friends are being contacted, so far without any news. Uniformed and volunteer search teams, likewise, have reported nothing so far. The parents are convinced she's been taken, and - "

He met Greg's eyes, and the DI knew what was coming next.

" - the mother reports hearing North American voices in her front garden at the time of Sarla's disappearance." Phil didn't notice the gentle eye-rolling of a number of his colleagues. To be fair to the man, though, he also didn't notice the significant glances exchanged between a few others. "Sir," said Phil, addressing Greg directly, "the uniform Superintendent on the scene is formally requesting at this time that the investigation be led by this squad."

"Is he indeed?" Greg was angry, and he didn't especially care if it showed. He could just about guess where the local Super had got *that* idea from. "Very well, then. Though I'm not entirely sure what we might do that his own detectives couldn't do just as well. But if that's what he wants ... Phil, you and one other officer get back over there."

"One officer?"

"For now. Catherine'll assign you someone. Obviously, if you find you really need more bodies, you can have them - at Catherine's discretion."

"Right," said Phil, shoving his notes into his pocket, and ramming his unlit pipe between his teeth.

"And that's about it, if there's no other business? Thank you, everyone - there's sandwiches in the pub for those who don't have to rush off."

One Lofty wouldn't drink at the Crown, because it was privately owned. The other Lofty wouldn't drink at the Ernesto Lynch because it was a co-op. No-one seriously believed that these were stances born of genuine principle - apart from anything, no-one seriously believed that either Lofty was that bloody stupid - but in the interests of a quiet life, the Squad drank at the Coach, because nobody knew who owned it and, so far, no-one had been daft enough to ask.

The sandwiches laid out in the smoking room, ordered in advance by Jade, came in three flavours: mutton and mustard; cheese and sweet pickle; vegetable slice. Ginger Thom - who wasn't nearly as obsessed with the Home Front during World War Two as his colleagues believed, but was in fact a passionate reader of *anything* written in or concerning Britain in the 1940s - always referred to the latter as "Victory Spread." Catherine Blake, apparently the only member of the Squad who caught the reference, said it didn't work as a joke, because the vegetable slice was in fact very tasty. It was certainly true that those sandwiches went first, but that was at least partly because few people under the age of twenty could get used to eating mutton. The cheese was good, but the pickle was pretty awful. There was an art to making pickles, as well as a science, which was why it formed part of the core curriculum in all schools. In the days of food shortages, Catherine had been the mother of two teenagers. Like so many, she had quickly relearned the skills of her grandmother's time. Making sub-standard pickle - let alone having the nerve to sell it - was unforgivable, and she would make sure Jade put in a complaint.

The mutton wasn't going to waste, though. Erin Smee - being the sole present representative of a generation which considered it to be a food fit for humans - was tipping the sheep sandwiches down her throat in the way that only seventeen-year-olds can.

"Was it a carp pond?" Ginger asked the Loftys.

The young one shook his head, and spoke around a mouthful of cheese-and-scraped-off-pickle. "Flood pond. No fish."

"Not that it would make much more sense if it was a carp pond. Why would anyone want to kill a load of carp?"

"Because they're disgusting, perhaps?" suggested Bob Lemon.

Over the last few years, farmed carp had become one of Britain's main sources of meat. Being low in their food chain, carp were highly efficient producers of protein: their output to input ratio was guaranteed to put a smile on any agronomist's face. But the fish was a taste which many struggled to acquire. Carp farming had been very widespread in Britain in the middle ages, but the coming of the railways had meant that more palatable, salt-water fish could be sold across the country without going off, or needing preserving. But now - with falling sea stocks, the general unreliability of imports, and the fact that most other farmed fish were fed on fish - carp's unfashionable status had been repealed.

Ginger laughed. "You miss your beefburgers, Bob?"

"No, as matter of fact I was a vegetarian for years. Lived on a diet of cheese sandwiches and soya steaks."

"You're not a stickie, though?" asked Erin.

"No. I'm not saying anything against those who have stuck to it, but personally, I was convinced by the arguments." Bob grimaced. "If not the flavour."

Unproductive land was unimaginable, when you lived on an island in a world of unpredictable international trade and frequent global shortages. Meat-eating on the grand scale was clearly an unsustainable bad habit, best left behind in the twentieth century, but there were areas of Britain where the only crop that could be realistically raised was sheep. Beef had been banned by national referendum some years earlier: cow meat was not cost-effective to produce, and was highly polluting. Dairy herds were being slowly phased out, and in the meantime cow's milk was rationed to the point of rarity. Cheese was considered an essential food - but cow's cheese was rationed, while that from ewes and goats was not. Goat milk in particular was a ubiquitous food, goats being relatively low polluters, willing tenants of sub-prime land, and good recyclers of vegetable waste.

Food and land: even more than energy and water, these were the two great British preoccupations of the age.

Before the Process began, almost all British arable land was used to grow feed for livestock, not for humans; and even then, huge amounts of animal feed had to be imported, much of it from countries that were unable to feed their own human populations.

Now, people were encouraged to keep chickens and pigs privately - as their ancestors would have done, a century earlier - and Backyard Husbandry was another compulsory school subject, from which only vegetarian children could opt out on grounds of conscience. Anything home-grown was completely off-ration: meat, fruit, veg, honey, eggs, anything. If you grew it yourself, you could eat it until you exploded - and if you chose to sell your surplus, the resulting income was untaxed. It was a modified version of a system pioneered in Latin America at the turn of the century.

"I admire the old vegetarians," said Erin, halfway through the last of the mutton. "You lot were like pioneers."

"I don't get the stickies, though," said Ginger. "OK, like Erin says, the old vegetarians were pioneers - they caught on before everyone else did. But now that the whole country is virtually vegetarian, I don't see any sense in people insisting on being a hundred per cent about it. Surely it's much more efficient to raise a certain amount of animal protein locally, than to try and import great piles of soya and pulses and what have you?"

Erin nodded. "It is weird - it's like they've gone from being ahead of everyone else to being behind."

"I think," said Catherine, realising that this might be a generation gap too far for a simple explanation around a pub table to bridge, "that stickies are probably people who've become vegetarian for moral reasons, rather than efficiency ones. Isn't that right, Bob?"

"Yeah, some people feel it's wrong to kill - simple as that. There've always been a few people who thought that, as far back as you want to go in history. Ancient Greeks, even. They're one of history's perennial minorities. But a lot of people, like me, figure that we've achieved eighty, ninety per cent of what we dreamed of - so we'll settle for consolidating that."

"Is it odd, though," Ginger asked, "eating meat again, after years of not eating it?"

Bob took a long pull on his beer before answering. "Odd is a good enough word for it, yeah."

"In World War Two," Ginger added, "vegetarians used to get extra cheese ration."

"Well," said Erin, lighting up a dainty, fashionably-painted pipe, "I'll tell you what, though - there were kids at my school who went vegetarian, just to be rebels, you know?"

Bob's gaze met Catherine's. He closed his eyes for a second and gave a bemused shake of the head. She smiled back at him, and shrugged. At the end of a long day, neither of them had the energy left to untangle the concept of existential teenagers giving up meat in order to demonstrate their alienation from their elders' attempts to save the planet.

"It's only a return to the traditional British diet," said Gerard. "My great-granny told my mum that when she was young, the only meat they ate from one week to the next was a lump off their annual, home-cured pig, stuck in the pot to give the stew a bit of flavour. If great-granddad happened to be earning well, they might possibly get a bit of beef for Christmas dinner. And they weren't poor people, though - just ordinary village folk. That period of a generation or three when normal people ate meat every day - that was just a brief blip in history. As, indeed, is everything else in human life, a thought from which much comfort might be taken." He finished his pint, and pointed to the middle of the table. "Now then, Greg's obviously not going to join us, so I vote we drink his beer."

*

Greg could just about taste that pint, but Phil Kale was not an easy man to shake off when he was trying to make amends through small talk. It was one of his more endearing - and more irritating - habits. If he thought he'd rubbed you up the wrong way, he'd seek you out at the first opportunity and talk to you about the weather, or the football, until he was confident that you'd been smoothed down again.

"You haven't got an allotment, have you?"

"I haven't quite got round to it, Phil, no." It wasn't only his thirst that was worrying Greg; if he didn't get to the pub soon, he knew perfectly well that the only sandwiches left would be mutton.

"You're automatically entitled to one, you know, now that you - ah - now that you're ... well, while you're currently living in a solo unit." He took his pipe out of his pocket and tapped its stem against his teeth.

Greg had never heard Phil use the word 'divorce.' Perhaps he feared that his DI would break down in tears if he did. "I've got Havana window-boxes front and back," he said, trying to enter into the spirit of the conversation - or, more truthfully, trying to pretend to. "I do all right for salads."

"Oh, well - that's nice," said Phil, giving him an encouraging smile.

Greg couldn't resist. "I don't really like salads."

"Oh dear. Well, you might think you're better off without a veg patch this year. Here we are, second week of July, and there's been no serious rain other than storms since February." He put his pipe back in his pocket and pulled out his pocket barometer. Everyone Greg knew seemed to carry one of these bloody things these days. Except Greg. Phil tapped the dial. "There you are, no change. Plenty of floods, no rain! Typical."

Greg feared the DS was getting himself upset again, so he decided to send him on his way before he started blaming the weather on the Yanks. At least he'd stopped calling them 'subbies' since his official warning on Language Injurious to Unity. "You'd best get back to your child-hunt, Phil. Keep me in touch with that, won't you?"

He was finally, almost, on his way out of the door, on his way towards a pint of beer and a sit-down, when Jade called to him from her office. "Greg! You still there?"

He stuck his head around her door. "Yes, Jade? Is there more cake needs eating?"

"I'll wrap a bit up for you. Scientific just phoned from Beech Lane."

Greg felt the tiredness in his knees, quite suddenly, and in his shoulders - though that wasn't sudden, he'd had that all day. "It's not going to be good news, is it?"

"They've got another body."

"Oh, shit." He accepted her offer of a cigarette - a defiant non-smoker, she always collected her ration - and a light. "That isn't good news."

"But apparently, that's not the bad news."

Greg stared at her for a moment, as if she was mad, but then remembered that - mad or otherwise - she was only the messenger. "What is the bad news, then?"

Jade shrugged. "The woman from Scientific says she'll tell you that when you get there."

CHAPTER THREE

DC Dahlia Kotane - short and round, and in her late twenties - sat in an electric two-seater, with DS Phil Kale, outside a terraced house in Muswell Hill, doing some wondering.

The big wonder was: how do you make off with a struggling child, in a car-less world?

In the old days, you could grab a kid, and within seconds, if you've done it right, she's inside a car from which little sound escapes, and which can be miles away in minutes. But today's post-petroleum personal transport options were slower to accelerate. Bundle little Sarla Brown into a pony-and-trap, for instance, and people would be able to hear her screaming all the way down the street.

"In which case," said Dahlia, "various possibilities."

"She wasn't struggling," Phil suggested, "so it was someone she knew. Or she *was* taken in a motor vehicle - which should be easy to establish."

Dahlia made a note on her notepad: *Ask MV Control check all movements MVs this area between relevant times.* "Or she was sedated," she offered, when she'd finished jotting. "Or she wasn't taken at all; she left of her own accord, under her own steam, or is still here, dead or alive." Corpse dogs and body-finder technology had already searched the parents' home and garden, and the neighbours', and those of other near-by relatives and friends, all with no result. Human searches for the girl continued, likewise without fruit thus far.

Phil shook his head. "No, she's gone. We won't find her here. Someone's got her - she's been taken."

Dahlia was inclined to agree that the poor girl had gone, but she was not so certain that she'd been taken. Or not originally, anyway. She could have wandered off for some reason of her own - some reason that made sense to a child - and then met with an accident.

But from the moment DS Blake's clipboard had paired her with DS Kale, the latter had been predictably adamant that little Sarla had been kidnapped. Means and motive unknown - and he was scrupulously, painfully careful not to mention the word "rescue" to DC Kotane - but the girl was missing, and her parents lived together so there was no custody horror going on, so that sounded like a kidnapping to him.

Dahlia wasn't keen to argue. For one thing, she hardly knew Phil Kale (this was the first time they'd been co-assigned since she'd joined), other than by daunting reputation. A bit obsessed, a bit intense, a bit po-faced. Those were just some of the things his colleagues didn't say about him. In a unit as tight and interdependent as Serious Crimes, you didn't say unkind or unprofessional things about your colleagues; certainly not behind their backs and, if you could possibly resist it, not to their faces either. But there were ways of not saying things that let them be heard, and those were the things that Dahlia had heard about Phil when his colleagues were describing him as "An exceptionally committed detective," "a total terrier," and "a very bright bloke indeed."

For another thing, Dahlia didn't actually have any facts as yet which either supported or undermined Phil's conclusions. And it did rather seem to her, the DS's certainties notwithstanding, that it might be a good idea to remedy that lack before doing any arguing.

If you weren't a gardener, it was a lovely evening. Greg arrived back in Beech Lane at around 7.30pm, riding pillion on a police courier's electric bike. It was a perfect summer's evening; warm after the heat, a little breeze, fragrant air and a calm sky. It was the sort of evening that made him think of cricket - actually, to *long* for cricket, on a mole-hilled green across the road from a tumbledown pub. He pictured himself as a spectator - feeling too lazy to clap a wicket, or even to lift his pint to his lips - or maybe, even, as one of the middle-aged men panting around on the field, trying to avoid the ball. One of his grandfathers was born in Yorkshire, the other in Somerset, so

Greg had been raised in the religion of willow and leather, and sometimes it still called to him, on summer evenings or in the gloomiest murk of winter.

He remembered unpleasantly hot London evenings from his early summers as a policeman, back before the Process began, when cities were effectively huge radiators, their concrete and tarmac and steel soaking up the day's sun only to leak it out again long into the night.

'The woman from Scientific' turned out to be, as Greg had rather hoped, the fabled Head of Central Police Scientific Unit Three. Doctor Minto - her first name was "Doctor," as far as Greg knew - was a tall, broad, black woman, significantly taller than Greg himself, looking immense and solid in her forensic coveralls, with no hair visible beneath what looked to him like a cricket umpire's hat.

They exchanged nods, professional insults, and words about the weather, and then she took him to view the second corpse. A picket fence of anti-contamination tape surrounded a turned over patch of ground near the bottom of the long, narrow garden. Greg stood next to the grave, and looked around at the sightlines: a hazel hedge on one side, and an apple tree on another, meant that the only direction from which the burial could easily have been overlooked was that of the house itself.

"Much more recent, this one," Minto told him, though he could see that for himself. The naked body was fresh, for want of a less stomach-cramping term; fresh enough to tell that it had once belonged to a middle-aged white man. He appeared to have died from some sort of stomach wound.

"No identification, I suppose?"

"Nothing on the body," Minto confirmed, "unless he was in the habit of carrying his ration card up his bum for safekeeping. Full set of teeth, though, showing recent dental work, so we should have a name as soon as we get him back to the lab."

"Are there any more, Doctor Minto?"

She shook her head. "We've looked everywhere, Greg, inside and out. Nothing else. We'll double check the entire plot, obviously, before handing it over. I'll put the cadaver dogs to work, in case the technology's overlooked anything. But we don't expect to find anything else. We don't often miss bodies."

"So what's the bad news? You told Jade this wasn't it."

Minto grimaced. "It's not. Greg, the bad news is this guy was shot - "

"Shit," said Greg; and then, as he realised that he'd interrupted her, he added: "Oh, shit. There's more?"

"Our gun-bloke can tell by the wound - we'll check all this back at base, but he's completely sure already - that the gun was a Spitfire."

Without knowing he was doing it, Greg reached into his pocket and brought out his tobacco and papers. He was halfway through rolling a thick, much-needed fag when he realised that he was standing in the middle of an active crime scene. He put the makings back in his pocket, rubbed the back of his neck, and said: "Shit."

As far as Greg was aware, there were no Spitfires - the patriotically-named, patriotically-employed "slow-shot" rifle - in private hands anywhere in the world. They were made in Luton, Bedfordshire, for only one customer: the Ministry of Defence and Public Safety. They weren't military weapons, though. Professional soldiers would laugh at them. The Spitfire fired one round at a time, and four separate manual actions were needed to achieve even that; it was a militia rifle, deliberately slow in its working so as to reduce the likelihood of accidental discharge in the hands of amateurs.

The Spitfire rifle was designed to be used by citizens to harry invaders. Every neighbourhood committee in the country was required by law to keep a number of them in a local armoury. Greg had encountered firearm killings before, but he had never even heard of one involving a Spitfire.

"I guessed you'd rather I told you that face-to-face," said Minto, "rather than over the air."

"Indeed. Thank you, Doctor. Look, is it all right with you if I take a wander down the garden?"

"Help yourself. If you find any more bodies, give us a shout and we'll come over and take the credit."

Greg had been looking at the mixed hedge which ran along the bottom of the garden, and wondering what was behind it. In the far corner, he found a gate and beyond the gate a piece of rough-grassed common land surrounded by tall trees - a place for kids to play and adults to picnic, he presumed. A pale strip of informal path led off to another far corner, and presumably, eventually, to a road. As far as he could see the common wasn't much overlooked by domestic windows. So, possibly, that was one little mystery half-solved. And a much bigger one left intact.

Local police were conducting the routine work of the search for Sarla Brown, leaving Phil and Dahlia free to concentrate on more strategic interviews. Phil wanted to chase the overheard Americans: he hadn't said as much, but Dahlia could feel that desire steaming off him like heat. "You'll want to start with the parents, Sarge?" she said, making her question sound so unlike anything that could possibly elicit a negative reply that it would, she hoped, be too embarrassing for him to do anything but agree.

"Parents," said Phil. "Right. Yes, I think we'd better, don't you?"

John and Chloe Brown sat on opposite sides of their bright, crowded front room, not attempting to comfort each other or even, as far as Dahlia could see, to look at each other. There were lights on everywhere - every room and hallway in the house seemed to be lit up - and Dahlia fancied it took all of Phil Kale's twitchy self-control not to go around switching them off. To be honest, she was finding it a bit distracting, herself. Her mother was always going on about how she missed what she called 'feminine' lighting. "When I was a little girl," she'd say, "you'd have lots of small, soft lamps lit all around the edges of the room, on little tables and shelves. It was only where a man lived on his own that you'd see the overhead light switched on. Now, it's all so brutal and masculine and harsh - one light per room, no shadows." Dahlia found her mother's constant complaints about the masculinity of modern life almost inexpressibly annoying - mainly because they seemed so toweringly trivial - but she did have to admit, the room looked prettier this way. Lots of shadows, though. She wouldn't have wanted that, herself, under present circumstances.

As well as light, the house was full of people - friends, relatives, neighbours - coming and going, milling, whispering. People were making tea that other people weren't drinking, or leaning against walls looking worried and ready for action, or dabbing at their eyes or scratching at their scalps. Small units of the volunteer search team were departing or returning. Doors slammed constantly, and phones never stopped ringing, but when people needed to cough they tried to do so quietly.

Phil cleared the room - with more firmness than tact, but with enough of both to get the job done - of all but Sarla's parents, while Dahlia sat herself between them and asked the first questions.

"You work full-time as a parent, Mrs Brown?"

Chloe Brown needed a bit of time to answer. First she had to wait for the words to crawl in through her ears and into her mind, and then she had to blink and swallow for a while, and then she had to search the small room to find who had spoken, and then she had to remember the question and work out what it meant. And then she had to speak, which was pointless because her daughter had been taken.

"Are you the police?" she said, at last.

"I'm Detective Constable Dahlia Kotane," Dahlia told her for the third time in as many minutes, "and this is Detective Sergeant Phil Kale. We're here to help you find Sarla."

"Thank you," said Chloe.

A woman who looked like an older, less sad and more angry, version of Chloe stuck her head and shoulders around the door. "Can I get you anything, darling? Do you need anything?"

"She's talking to the police," said John Brown, without looking at the woman. "Please don't interrupt."

The woman didn't look at John Brown. "If you need anything, sweetheart, just call me. I'll be right outside." Chloe looked at Dahlia for a while, wondering if the speech was coming from her, but eventually found its true source. She smiled politely, like a tourist, but didn't otherwise reply.

Phil managed to close the door without chopping off the interrupter's head, which Dahlia thought showed finesse and sensitivity, and then took up position with his back against the door, preventing any further incursions.

"My wife's mother," John explained. "To answer your question, Constable, you're correct - my wife doesn't go out to work at the moment. She gets the carer's wage to look after me and our daughter."

"Thank you, Mr Brown," said Dahlia. "And I believe you work in recycling?"

"I'm a spotter," he replied.

"Oh, I see," said Dahlia, a hint of apology in her smile. Saying a spotter "worked in recycling" was like calling a brain surgeon a designated first-aider. "Do you or your wife have any idea at all why someone might have taken Sarla?"

"Random," said John. "A pervert or a childless madwoman. Just random." He nodded, and tapped his fingers against his knees. "Has to be, mustn't it? Some random thing."

Dahlia heard Phil's quiet cough, and turned to see his sharp nod towards Chloe Brown. She felt herself redden, just a little. Phil was quite right; she had stopped talking to the mother - had even, slightly but literally, turned her back towards her - because it was so much easier talking to the father. That was bad technique. It wasn't especially good humanity, either.

"Mrs Brown? Do you have any idea who might - "

"Subbies." Chloe growled the word, her throat sounding as if it felt like sandpaper. "I heard them - subbies took her, I've told you and *told* you all and you won't listen! I heard them."

Dahlia was careful not to wince. It was a horrible word: to damn a whole race as sub-human was not, surely, understandable even when grief or terror made it forgivable. "You said that you heard two *North American* accents, Mrs Brown, from your open kitchen window, passing by in the street, shortly before Sarla went missing. Couldn't they have been Canadian tourists, or - "

Chloe shook her head. "So what? Canadians are just subbies with posh accents, aren't they?"

Her tone was insistent, but something beneath it made Dahlia think that she was speaking from distress more than conviction; fixating on the accents for want of something that made sense of the worst day of her life, rather than out of any real belief that her daughter was the victim of a religious crime.

Dahlia was careful not to meet Phil Kale's eyes just now; she didn't want to embarrass him or herself by seeing the triumph which, she suspected, they must contain.

In her own mind, she found herself siding with the oddly calm father: she had a horrible feeling that this girl had been stolen from an older motive.

"They could have brought the Nottles' furniture out through the back garden. At night, maybe, bit by bit. Through this gate ... "

DS Catherine Blake nodded. "And then along the path across the common, and presumably they've got a pedal tractor waiting out on the road there. Or a donkey and trap, or whatever." She looked back through the gate, towards the house. "Still a hell of an effort, isn't it? Manhandling a chest of drawers, for instance, out of the French windows, across the lawn."

"I know," said Greg. "They must have had a bloody good reason for doing it. Meanwhile ... "

"Meanwhile, the Spitfire. Yes." She took out her phone and did some work with her thumb. "Have you eaten anything tonight?"

"I had some cake."

She showed him the phone. "According to this thing, there's a National Cafe about ten minutes' walk the other side of the common. It won't be busy this time of night, will it? We can find a private corner. We can talk over a gravy pie and chips, green peas and treacle pudding."

"I thought you'd had sandwiches at the pub?"

"I'll just have a cup of tea. And a few of your chips."

Greg didn't take much persuasion. He loved National Cafes - they dis-reminded him of his youth. The rugged simplicity of their decor, service and menus was as unlike the choice-crazed, brand-maddened, design-obsessed world he'd grown up in as could be. In a National Cafe, you sat at a recycled plastic table on recycled plastic chairs and ate your meals from utilitarian plates and mugs with ditto cutlery. Everything in the place was comfortable and functional, and unremarkable. Not the sort of place you'd go on a romantic date. Restful, Greg found it. There were two choices in seating - smoking or non-smoking - and not many more on the menu.

The strategically-located Nationals were open twenty-four hours every day and intended primarily to cater for workers on meal breaks, especially shift workers. For this reason, the big, filling meals - which tended to be combinations of big, filling ingredients - were served with little regard for the nominal time of day: gravy pies at eight in the morning, fried eggs on fried bread at eight in the evening. Everything - including the meat dishes - came in two flavours: vegetarian and not vegetarian. Beyond that, fussy was not encouraged. And everything came with tea.

It was the sort of food - the sort of view of the world - which had been fiercely frowned on for most of Greg's life; women frowned on it, was Greg's remembered impression, and men frowned along for a quiet life. To be fair, his parents' generation had not led such physical lives - they'd travelled everywhere by car, for one thing, and shopped at giant supermarkets - so perhaps meals devoted to energy and stamina wouldn't have been appropriate. But there was an ideological aspect to this, too. Greg's generation was consciously turning away from all forms of superstition and anti-scientific belief; from the self-punishing, contradictory, fashion-driven myths of healthy lifestyling, every bit as much as from the gods and their warrior-priests. They were determined never again to allow a ruling class to cow them with nurtured fears and fads, making them view their own bodies as fifth columnists. No more imaginary illnesses; no more imaginary enemies. No more made-up terrorists, internal or external. (Though quite how that fitted in with Phil Kale and his Yank kidnapper hiding behind every pillar box, Greg couldn't honestly say. Change comes quickly, but it stays slowly; perhaps that was it.)

In short, Greg saw the Nationals as symbols of all that was best about the changes. Except that they weren't symbols, they were better than symbols because you could sit in them, out of the weather, and fill yourself up. Greg's brother-in-law - whose work on the canals was relentlessly physical - also approved of them, but his summary of their virtues was less philosophical: solid grub, fair price, always open.

Halfway through his pie, and with Catherine halfway through his chips, in the half-empty cafe, Greg slowed in his eating sufficiently to begin talking.

"I've never heard of anything like it before, have you?"

Catherine shook her head. "I simply don't understand it. Does this mean a rifle's been stolen from a citizens' armoury? Surely that's impossible."

"Could the murder have been committed when the gun was out legitimately?" Greg waved his fork, searching for an unfamiliar word. "On manoeuvres, or whatever it is they do?".

"Equally hard to imagine, isn't it? You'd think they probably count the bullets at the end of the evening, wouldn't you?"

Catherine's tone was a little sharp, and Greg smiled, knowing that she held strong opinions on the matter of citizens' armouries.

Every neighbourhood - a few streets, in a suburban context - maintained a local armoury of Spitfire rifles, for street-to-street resistance against invaders. Two residents were elected as key-holders to each armoury; elected at in-the-flesh meetings, in this case, since it was felt that electronic voting was inappropriate. There was a general sense that one needed to physically see and hear the candidates for such a post, to minimise the danger of electing loonies.

In the event of invasion, the Ministry of Defence would electronically unlock all armouries nationwide - Greg imagined some grim-faced bloke with a big hat on, ceremoniously pressing a red button in a central location - and each individual armoury would then be able to be opened by the two local keys. All three "keys" were needed, though if the system broke down at local level, the ministry could trigger an override procedure.

It all sounded perfectly sensible to Greg, inasmuch as he thought about it at all, which was very little. Catherine, however, had a principled objection to the Ministry's involvement: it meant, she argued, that the people's local armouries weren't, ultimately, under the control of the local people at all. In a society where absolute democracy was considered desirable for justice and necessary for survival, this struck DS Blake as a significant anomaly.

She was an active supporter of the Two Keys Only movement, and had been, for months, collecting signatures to trigger a formal "great debate." One million signatures were needed, and the word was that they were almost there.

The last great debate had been the one about beef. Greg had found the whole thing rather impressive, even exciting, though he'd not really found himself passionately on one side or the other of that particular fence. Months of discussion in all media, electronic and print, began the process: debates between opposing experts or advocates, as well as question and answer sessions, and both partisan and objective documentary reporting. Alongside that, ran public meetings from street level to national, while all civic organisations, from the WI to the Food Workers Union to the schools, were encouraged to formulate their own positions based on consultation of their members.

The culmination of a great debate was either legislation being introduced in parliament, or, less often, a national referendum - depending on the nature of the subject and whether the question which arose at the end was a simple yes/no, suitable for direct democracy, or something more subtle, requiring the finesse of representative democracy.

"After all," said Catherine, still attacking leftover chips in a ruthless mopping-up operation, "what are the chances of *two* freely elected armoury deputies being corrupt or mad or stoned off their heads at the same time in the same neighbourhood?"

"So two keys are enough? You don't need the third."

"Not only don't need it, but the existence of that central override makes a military coup very easy." She held up both palms. "OK, sure, that sounds melodramatic, and I know that democratising the armed forces was tackled very early on, for obvious reasons, but even so ... "

She paused for another chip. Greg quite fancied one himself, but had half a fear that she would slap his fingers if he reached for one now. "Even so?"

"In an army, you've got to have a chain of command, people have still got to say 'Yes, sir,' when they're told to open fire. Otherwise you haven't got an army. And I've read my history, Greg. I know how many revolutions - "

"You're not supposed to say revolution," Greg interrupted. "It causes embarrassment to sensitive souls."

She smiled. "Yes, dear, thank you - I know how many *democratic processes* around the world over the last hundred years have made fantastic progress until they were crushed by the army rescuing the nation from that word that nobody mentions."

She went up to the counter to fetch two more teas. They smoked and drank in silence for a moment or two, before she asked: "So, back to more immediate concerns - what do we do first?"

"I'll call Minto, ask her to get her 'gun-bloke' to help us check the local armoury. First priority, quite apart from our murder investigation, is we need to know if the gun's still loose."

"Or - shit, I've only just thought of that - are there *more* guns loose?"

"Indeed. While I'm doing that, you see if you can find out when the armoury was last unlocked for practice drill, and who the armoury deputies are for this neighbourhood. I'm afraid we're going to have to ruin their evening."

Greg and Catherine walked briskly back to Beech Lane, the DI feeling revitalised from the food, or perhaps just from the sit down. It'd been a long day, far from over.

"You all right to carry on?" he asked. "Have you rung home to say you'll be late?"

"That's fine," Catherine replied, "not necessary."

She always used to phone home, Greg thought, but he didn't pry, and it was while he wasn't prying that his phone rang.

"It's Ginger, boss."

"All right, Ginger? You had any luck tracing Kim Nottle?"

"No, it's nothing like that, I'm afraid. I knocked off about an hour ago, I'm actually calling from home. Just had a shout from Uniform about another rooftop garden getting raided. They logged it, and saw that I was down on the computer as TBI. No details yet, but I'm quite happy to attend, if you want me to."

"Yes, please do attend, Ginger, and keep me informed. If there is anything going on with these rooftops, we want to make sure we don't miss it."

After hanging up, he told Catherine to see about removing Ginger's To Be Informed status on rooftop garden thefts. "Otherwise, every time a biscuit goes missing from an old folk's tea party, those lazy sods in Uniform are going to shove it over onto us." He chewed over his words for a few paces. "Or, I could be being unfair. It could be that Uniform are as aware as the rest of us that food theft is more likely to kill their children than a world war is."

"What, Uniform?" said Catherine, in her best Gerard Cochrane imitation. "Nah, you was right the first time, guv. Load of idle bastards!"

At Beech Lane, Doctor Minto and her team were still at work. "Any more bodies?" asked Greg.

"No, it's been quite boring this last hour or so. Let me introduce you to our gun-bloke."

"Is that his official title?"

Minto shrugged. "If it isn't, he's never said."

Zac Day was very short and mind-bogglingly scruffy. He looked as if surplus bits of him might fall off at any moment. His entire head, face and neck appeared to be covered in the pubic hair of a black poodle. Or several poodles. Greg reckoned he was the last bloke you'd want anywhere near a live crime scene; where would you find a hairnet that shape, for a start? But Minto introduced him to them with evident pride, so presumably he was one of her proteges. Well, that was good enough for Greg. The day he couldn't trust the Doctor's judgement was the day he applied to retrain as a citrus grafter.

From the cafe, Catherine had phoned Nesta Popperwell, secretary of the street committee, and asked her to round up the local armoury deputies and meet the police at her house. Number four, Beech Lane was, as far as Greg could see, exactly the same as number nineteen, except that it was on the other side of the road and, of course, fully equipped with furniture and fittings. It was also, judging by the noise coming from upstairs, home to a few dozen children.

"Sorry about the racket," said Nesta, showing them through to the larger of the two living-rooms. "Bit of a houseful - we've got two of our own, and my sister's and my sister-in-law's makes five altogether."

She didn't say why she'd got three young lodgers, and nobody asked; people tended not to, these days, having learned that explanations could so easily lead to tears, or the even worse embarrassment of witnessing what was meant to be a private row.

Greg introduced the gun-bloke, and Nesta introduced the two armoury deputies. One of them was a rather old woman, who had her hands firmly shoved in her cardigan pockets, and who hastened to explain that she wasn't the real deputy. "It's my son, really, but he's on holiday, so I'm his officially registered deputy-deputy."

Greg smiled reassuringly. "As long as you can open the door, that's fine, Mrs King."

"Well, let's hope I can - I've never tried before, not for real."

"It'll be fine," said Nesta, patting her guest's arm. "Everything always is."

The other deputy looked more the part, Greg thought. Will Brewin was in his forties, stocky, bespectacled, bearded. He gave the impression of a man who was very calm but quietly tough; the sort of person you'd instinctively have faith in during an emergency. It occurred to Greg that every armoury deputy he'd ever met - male or female, and not counting Mrs King - had been middle-aged; never young or old. Instinctively, it seemed to be a job people elected the middle-aged to. Unless it was simply that young people and retired people had better things to do. Playing bowls and having sex, perhaps, or vice versa.

"Right," he said. "Shall we go?"

It was a short walk, during which Greg asked the gun-bloke a question which had been puzzling him: why wasn't the shot from the Spitfire heard by the Nottles' neighbours?

"Very quiet weapon," the expert explained. "Deliberately made that way - so as not to terrify the amateurs who use it, every time it goes bang. Besides, your neighbour might hear one shot, listen for the next one ... "

"And when it doesn't come, assume they were mistaken. Yes, that sounds right."

The armoury for this neighbourhood had been built on what had clearly once been the car park of what was still a pub. This juxtaposition made the copper in Greg shudder, though he knew that the chances of drunken revellers nipping in through a window at the back of the armoury and settling a darts dispute with a couple of rounds from a Spitfire rifle were not merely remote, but simply unimaginable. For a start, the armoury had no windows. It didn't have a visible door. It was a squat, square block of bomb-proof, ram-proof, quarried stone, the size of a suburban stable. In fact, armoury buildings were supposed to be just about everything proof; the co-op that had won the contract to design them had famously said at their launch that they intended them to be hindsight-proof.

The only clues to the entrance were two signs, one large and one discreet. The large one said *No Smoking*. "Takes you back," said Mrs King. "Old Uncle Nosmo doesn't get much work these days."

"Well, these days he's very selective about which gigs he'll take on," said Will Brewin. "Not so many engagements, but much higher quality. He'll only appear where he's truly appreciated." They all hurried to comply with the no smoking rule, except the old woman who made a fine mocking show of taking out her snuff tin and smugly enjoying a pinch up each nostril.

The smaller sign, above a computer screen, said *Deputies sign in here*. Zac the gun-bloke had already made contact with the MoD, and was now on the mobile phone to them. The ministry operated its remote key, and the screen asked Deputy One to approach. They were called "spit keys," but more accurately, Greg thought, they were "lick keys." First Mrs King, and then Will Brewin, licked their right index fingers and placed them on the screen. The computer read their DNA - Mrs King audibly phewing her relief as hers was accepted - and the door slid back.

They all stepped through it, into a tiny lobby which contained a couple of desks and chairs, one computer terminal, a communications set, and of course a kettle and large military-issue teapot, next to a large box of long-life Garibaldi biscuits. In case of invasion, the two deputies having opened the armoury would take up their positions in this vestibule, issuing weapons and ammunition, doing the paperwork, liasing with other bodies, and taking charge of defending the armoury itself.

Straight ahead there was an inner door, leading to the armoury proper.

"This one only requires the two spit keys," Will explained. "So does the main door, from this side."

"You need MoD approval to get in, but not out?" said Catherine.

Will laughed. "Don't worry, Sergeant - I've already signed the petition."

Greg found himself wondering what happened if one of the deputies dropped dead while they were all inside, but he was fairly sure there'd be a contingency for that. There was for everything. Must be. Probably. Anyway, the deputies both looked quite healthy. Although, as his mum used to say, it's always the healthy ones go first.

There was only really space in the inner room for two people; Will and Zac went through, while the other four waited in the lobby. The inspection didn't take long; it was, after all, only a matter of counting the number of Spitfires. The deputy and the gun-bloke emerged to report that there were no rifles missing.

Nesta and the two deputies were clearly relieved by this news, but Greg and Catherine exchanged puzzled and frustrated looks: they were no further forward.

"Is it possible," Catherine asked Zac, "not now, I mean, but with the right equipment, to tell whether any of the rifles have been - "

"Already thought of that." Zac fished a small, grey box out of his jacket pocket. "None of the Spitfires in there have been fired within the last three weeks. If they had, and were then stored in that enclosed space without cleaning, the residue in the air would show up on this."

"And if any of them had been cleaned," Will added, "someone would have wanted to know why. We haven't had a live-ammo exercise here since April."

Greg frowned. That was it, then: the gun didn't come from here, so it could presumably have come from any one of the thousands of armouries around the country.

CHAPTER FOUR

When Ginger Thom had told Gerard Cochrane, a while back, that Uniform reckoned they'd spotted a pattern to a spate of thefts from rooftop gardens - and therefore would Ginger like to take over the investigations? - Gerard had laughed an old copper's laugh. *Yeah, I bet they have. Some things never change!* Ginger had smiled along, but that phrase was one he hated: "Some things never change." People meant it as a cynical joke, nothing more, but the way Ginger saw it, if there were too many things that never changed, then the whole world was doomed. Especially if they were the sort of things that people meant when they said "Some things never change."

As it turned out, and as he'd told the briefing, Ginger suspected that there was no pattern, and that it was quite possible that Uniform were, indeed, merely engaged in shedding some caseload. Some things, to coin a phrase, never changed. *Must write that down,* thought Ginger.

There was nothing to suggest that the spate of raids had, or had not, been carried out by the same person or gang. There was similarly no evidence either way to suggest that the thefts were, or were not, part of an organised racket. There was nothing - nothing that Ginger had found, anyway - to say that the spate was a series.

He thought, perhaps, that there was just rather a lot of rooftop theft around at the moment. This sort of crime could easily go in cycles; there was a run of thefts, so people beefed up security measures; the crime rate thus fell, so security measures fell into disuse and weren't replaced or updated; thus the crime rate rose, opportunistically; thus people beefed up security and ...

Still, he didn't mind giving up an hour or so of what remained of his evening to look into one more rooftop raid. You never knew - and where food security was concerned, you didn't take chances. The Serious Crime Squad had actually been set up in the first place to deal with black market food racketeering, in the early days of rationing, and food security remained at the heart of its officers' priorities, officially and by instinct.

Overtime was illegal, of course, so he wouldn't be earning extra money for this off-duty call-out. It had been known since the 1990s that shift-work was a main cause of heart attacks amongst working-class men, but for political reasons it had been necessary to place the blame instead on what were then called 'lifestyle choices.' Today, in a more determinedly rational era, all such 'knowns' were looked on with suspicion, even when they conveniently supported current policies or prejudices, being based largely on now abandoned pseudo-sciences, and on methodologies which were these days handled only with long tongs, such as statistical epidemiology.

Overtime was illegal, and shift-working severely restricted to cases of absolute necessity, not primarily for supposed health reasons, but because it was considered self-evidently Contrary to Unity in numerous ways. It was unfair - to those who had to do the overtime, and to those who didn't. Shift-working was unfair to those who had to do it, as well as to their families. Both shift-working and overtime lead to divorce, and to social isolation. And overtime could distort labour statistics, thus leading to inefficient application of labour resources. In a system in which every atom of efficiency counted, that was a grave charge, indeed.

But various categories of 'urgency and emergency' trades - including detectives - would always, unavoidably, have to work extra hours, or even days, here and there. This time was very carefully accounted, and paid back as time off in lieu. Ginger generally got at least one extra holiday a year - by the sea, or walking in the Lake District, or visiting old Home Front sites of interest - from adding up his in-lieus.

When he arrived at the address he'd been given - a requisitioned turn-of-the-century building in the City, which had once housed a leading firm of stockbrokers - he was moderately amused to discover that he was at the head office of the Potato Research

Council. The secretary of that body, wearing one of the most popular slogan t-shirts of the moment - 'This is the Morning of our Lives' - met him at the main door.

"We're jointly funded," Professor Hale explained, as they climbed the external staircase, "by the various potato growing and distributing co-ops, by the National Union of Allotment Societies, and by central government. We research every aspect of potato growing - on a commercial and domestic scale - at various sites around the country. This building houses mainly those of us involved in admin and publications. But of course," he said, as they stepped onto the roof garden, "we're all potato people, and we can't resist growing a few spuds!"

Professor Hale didn't, Ginger thought, look like a potato person - he looked more like a radish person. He was almost round in body, the top part of his bald head bright white, when he took off his hat to wipe his pate with a handkerchief, and his face quite red. His busy and enthusiastic manner also struck Ginger as somewhat radishy. His accent, however, was more fitting to his calling: the professor came, Ginger was sure, from the east coast of Scotland, long home to Britain's seed potato industry.

"Do you know much about spuds?" he asked the DC.

"A bit, as it happens," Ginger admitted, trying to keep his tone the right side of boastful. His Home Front interest had led to a natural spur into spudology. "I know, for instance, that the potato made the industrial revolution possible."

Hale beamed. "Ah - excellent! Quite right, of course. Because the potato is so comparatively effortlessly productive, and so nutritious, its adoption in these islands liberated large amounts of human labour from food growing, which could then be employed elsewhere. You can't build railways if all your work-time is of necessity devoted to mere sustenance. There are statues of great industrialists and inventors," the professor added, "but I have long felt there ought to be one of the spud."

For the next several minutes, DC Thom busied himself with a

coughing fit, as he tried to avoid corpsing. It would be impolite to laugh: the potato man was clearly sincere. Ginger ordered himself not to imagine what a statue of a potato might look like. How would you know which way up it went?

"That advance," the professor continued, "has inevitably been partly reversed by the events of the last few years."

"The industrial revolution?"

"The diversion of labour from staying alive towards *living*. The drive to achieve national food security, the reduction in imports, and the need to expend resources on things other than food processing - which perforce means that much more of the food we consume has to be eaten fresh - all this in turn means that we, collectively and individually, are spending more of our time and energy simply on feeding ourselves than has been the case for many generations."

"Returning to the caves, you mean." Ginger had, indeed, heard such talk. Some people - and not only those diehards who their opponents labelled 'beefeaters,' but even the occasional thinker who was broadly supportive of the Process - warned of the danger of entering a post-industrial age; a new medievalism, where all anyone did was farm, eat, and die.

"It's mostly alarmism and exaggeration, of course," said Hale. "We have, after all, the advantage of forewarning, and this is still a highly technological society. But it is worth a thought, occasionally. We are building a better life than our parents' - we want our children to have better lives than our grandparents, too."

"But surely vast amounts of labour - of resources generally - have also been released by the Process. Think of all the unproductive effort and expenditure that used to go into ... " He waved an arm at their surroundings. " ... well, stockbroking, for instance. Or manufacturing nuclear weapons. Or - "

"Oh, quite so, quite so. We have far more leisure time than we did twenty years ago, precisely because of the huge saving in not playing at empires any more. Even so. During Cuba's transformation at the turn of the century, from importer to self-feeder - from which this country has drawn many of its models - agronomists calculated that twenty per cent of all labour time was devoted to food. In Britain, in the early days, it was even higher."

"Higher?"

"Oh, yes. In the thirties for a short while, until the informal sector - I refer to rooftops, allotments, front gardens, and so on - began to take up some of the strain."

Those had been exciting days, Ginger remembered - which was all very well, if you thought excitement invariably a desirable thing. Changing the national mind of a country which had for centuries believed that food was grown 'in the countryside,' and doing so in a hurry, had been quite a task. Today, it was understood that whenever possible, food should be produced as close as possible to where it was consumed; and that all and any space which could grow food should do so, if that was its most efficient use.

"This organisation," the professor explained, "amongst other things, studies methods of growing potatoes to maximise output per unit of space, for patio farmers and urban gardeners. But we also study diseases."

"Ah, yes," said Ginger. "Comrade Spud's Achilles heel."

Hale smiled. "Indeed. The potato is a wonderful beast, but its great weakness is, and always has been, that once removed from its natural home in the Andes, and grown in mild and wet climates like our own, it immediately becomes susceptible to an almost comical number and range of diseases. Now, for most of its recent history, that has been merely a nuisance. But in certain situations - "

"Like Ireland in the 1840s."

"Yes - but also Britain, and much of the world, in our own time; today potato disease is potentially disastrous. Fatal, even! More of us are more dependent on spuds than ever before. And the potato is the most chemical-dependent major crop ever grown. Of course, the European Union thought they'd solved that problem with genetic engineering. Unfortunately they took their advice from seed salesmen not from scientists."

Ginger couldn't resist. "Or rather, from scientists who were working for the seed salesmen?"

The potato man looked even more radishy of face as he conceded that point with an uncomfortable grunt. "I suppose the politicians thought they were getting plants that were genetically resistant to potato diseases. They weren't, of course - they were getting plants genetically designed to be able to survive much higher concentrations of fungicides, herbicides and pesticides. Short term solution, medium term profits. Whereas if it were genuinely possible to genetically engineer potatoes with immunity to blight, for instance - which is itself debatable - there would be only a very modest, short-term profit in it."

"So perhaps it wasn't science they were ignorant of, but basic economics?"

"Perhaps, Constable. At any event, the Euros have ended up importing most of their potatoes, and eating a lot more parsnips than any man should be expected to stomach." His shudder of distaste was unmistakeably involuntary; the authentic reaction of a potato man to the thought of lesser roots. "Here at the Potato Research Council, we do our research the old-fashioned way: sex and housework."

He paused for Ginger to express appreciation of what was, no doubt, a traditional joke amongst plant researchers, and Ginger obliged. Why not? "Ha!" said Ginger. Why not, yeah, but no sense in overdoing it.

"By which I mean, plant breeding and good husbandry."

Ginger was clocking the security measures: pretty good, he thought, for a rooftop garden. He could see solar-powered twitch lights, plenty of slippery fencing - properly maintained, which was a bloody rarity - a decent array of cameras, and a serious main gate with solid locks on it. True, the best gate in the world became your enemy if you just forgot to lock it, but all the same ...

"I reckon your thieves must have been pretty determined, Professor. Your security's the best I've seen on a rooftop in a while." Ginger smiled as he spoke, and tried to keep the unspoken words *Inside job* from echoing across the canyons of the City.

"I'm rather afraid they were determined," Hale replied. "Over here, this is where they struck." He showed Ginger to a bay of a dozen raised beds, all of which had clearly been emptied of their crops. "I was on the rota for watering this evening, and - "

"Sorry," Ginger interrupted. "The watering's not done automatically?"

"No, you see although this is primarily a food garden, to help feed the staff who work here, many members of that staff are scientists - we're the sort of people who can't help but monitor and record and analyse our crops. All watering is done manually, therefore, for greater control of recordable inputs. So, I came in about an hour ago - and this is what awaited me."

"These are spuds that have been stolen?"

"Actually, no. There's plenty of edibles around, as you can see, and they've all been ignored." The professor looked momentarily, and untypically, grim. "Here we had experimental beds of some other tuberous vegetables - oca, mashua, ulluco."

"I know mashua," said Ginger. "My dad tried growing that on his allotment. It was all right, but you didn't get much yield for the space compared to potatoes, so - "

"So he gave up on them." Hale nodded. "Most people do, I'm afraid, which means that they've never gone through that process of informal selection that potatoes - and other popular vegetables - went through. Structured research is important, but when it comes to turning a novelty crop into a staple food, you can't beat mass democracy."

"How do you mean, democracy?"

"People voting with their taste buds. And their weighing scales. What you want is thousands upon thousands of amateur gardeners all over the country sowing or planting your new vegetable, and then saving the best of their own stock to replant the next year, and then saving the best of next year's stock, and so on. So bit by bit you're developing races of the vegetables that are suited to local growing conditions. The first spuds to arrive in this country, you'd hardly recognise them. The yield was poor, and you couldn't store them."

"It's a wonder people persisted with them," said Ginger.

"They had the motivation, I suppose - they were hungry. The frustrating thing is that if you read books from the 1960s, you'll find mashua talked about as the next big thing, way back then. And oca has been grown in Britain since the seventeenth century. Their great advantage over potatoes is that, in this country at least, they don't suffer much in the way of pests and diseases."

"So you're researching them as alternatives to the potato?"

"Oh, certainly not - there'd be mass resignations if such a thing were even suggested! We are potato people, and we would never engage in such filthy acts of infidelity. No, you see, in their native lands, these plants are grown alongside potatoes - all four species together, in the same field. The idea is that in any one year, no matter what the situation with weather or pests, at least one of the crops is going to do well."

"An insurance scheme - you're always going to have at least some tubers to eat, whatever happens. No more Irish Famine."

"Exactly. An approach we should very much like to adopt over here - if we can get the yields up. Now, the chief *disadvantage* with these three fellows is that they begin to put on growth after mid-summer. In our part of the world, that means that they're liable to be cut down by autumn frosts just as they get going."

"And that's what you're researching?"

"Developing strains that are less fussy about day-length. Precisely."

"And how's it going?"

The professor grimaced. "This is the thing. This is why I'm rather afraid this may be more than simple food theft; we are making remarkable progress." He looked away into the middle distance, and tapped his fingers against his chin. "Yes, I think that's reasonable, I think I can say that: remarkable progress."

"Which means that your specimen tubers, growing in these beds here, have a remarkable value? To thieves, I mean."

"Now, Constable, this I find a little puzzling." He paused to light his pipe. "I'm not entirely clear in my mind what the thieves hope to gain."

"Your remarkable progress, surely? So that they can sell it abroad."

Hale shook his head vigorously. Ginger was quite impressed by the fact that he didn't remove his pipe before doing so. "Without the paperwork to back them up, the samples on their own are of very little value. They're nowhere near marketable, we've got generations to go yet."

"*Generations?*"

The professor put a reassuring hand on the startled detective's arm. "Plant generations, I mean, not human ones. Even so, we're nowhere near seeing these things on sale at your local farmer's market. Besides, if you did try to market our work, we could prove it was ours pretty easily. And there is still *some* international law, if not as much as once there was. It would surely be more trouble than it's worth for any reputable company. But above all, in research the paperwork is everything - without it, even though you've stolen our samples, we're still way ahead of you. Paperwork without samples, fairly useful; samples without paperwork - slightly more useful than a one-legged donkey on a steep hill."

Ginger had a horrible thought. "Professor, have you actually checked the - "

"Second thing I did." Hale smiled. "Between calling the police and going downstairs to wait for you, I checked the paperwork. The safe-room is inviolate, the papers intact. Security in our line of work is tight, though mainly against sabotage rather than actual theft."

"Well, I'm afraid I have to agree with you. Looking at your security systems, I'd say it's likely that this theft was carried out by professionals." He took out his phone. "So the first thing I'm going to do is call in a full-scale evidence team. And meanwhile, I think you and I had better go back downstairs, to avoid contaminating the scene."

"Oh, Christ!" said Professor Hale. He whipped his pipe out of his mouth and began knocking it out against his shoe. Ginger thought that was unlikely to make matters better, but he didn't have the heart to reprimand him. It had occurred to DC Thom, as it clearly hadn't to Professor Hale, that if the thief was someone on the staff, they wouldn't need to steal the paperwork when they could just copy it instead.

Inside job: Ginger feared that the events of the next few weeks might break the potato man's radishy heart.

Catherine hadn't always hated her husband. She could remember, though admittedly she couldn't now recreate an impression of, a time when she ... had she loved him? She must have done. They hadn't married young or pregnant. She must have.

Tonight, late and tired, she arrived home to find that he hadn't watered the veg patch. OK: he was lazy, he was absent-minded, and he'd been engrossed in watching a day-night match between Britain and Afghanistan on the TV. It was an oversight. Even on a hot day in *fucking July*, it wasn't actually a crime.

But when she mentioned it, he didn't really see why it was such a big deal. That was a crime, surely? Or a sin. Or something. Watering the garden these days - it wasn't a hobby, it wasn't a game. It wasn't a chore so trivial that it could legitimately be used as a weapon in a disintegrating marriage. This was about survival. She still remembered, if he chose not to, a government advertising campaign from the time of the shortages, the early days of rationing: "We need the food!" Did he think that wasn't true any more, just because there weren't any shortages now? Did he think, perhaps, that it was a coincidence that there was enough to eat nowadays, and that people remembered to water their veg patches? Two discrete facts, entirely unconnected?

She didn't bother arguing with him. She took off her hat, had a drink of water, put her work bag down, and went out and watered the vegetables, remembering happier days when she'd wondered what they'd do with their unused ration points. If you didn't claim any part of your entitlement of rationed goods - because you didn't need to, because you were growing some of your own produce - the unused ration points were translated into time credits, towards either extra annual leave, or earlier retirement, or a mixture of the two.

"If we could squeeze in a couple of chickens," she'd said to him (back when they were still saying things to each other, other than things like *No idea; you had it last*, or *Don't bother, I'll eat out, expect me when you see me*), "and went without our entire egg ration, I reckon in three years we could have enough time credits to ... "

She'd used a pocket calculator and a couple of wall charts, and each time she came in from the garden with a basket of strawberries or a bag of potatoes, she'd work it out and tell him how much closer they were to retirement, or a week in an ancient inn by a Scottish loch.

As she drenched the salad patch - which was where the bee hive had been going to go, once upon a time - she shook her head. The last thing she wanted now was days off to spend with her husband, and the idea of early retirement - *any* retirement - was a dread to be pushed to the back of her mind. Her job was the best bit of her life at the moment, and when that happened to you, you knew something was wrong.

Later, in bed, she was just dropping off when she suddenly heard herself - in that cafe, eating his chips - calling the DI 'dear.' The fires of embarrassment kept her awake for another hour and a half.

CHAPTER FIVE

"You'd better go and get it then, hadn't you?" said one of the Loftys.

"*I'd* better go and get it?" said the other one. "You're the senior man by age and experience. You go and get it."

"It's because I'm the senior man that I'm ordering you to go and get it."

"Being old doesn't give you rank. You can't order me to do anything."

"There's a boat over there," said the older Lofty.

"What does that prove? You're still not the - "

"There's a *boat*," Lofty repeated, pointing with his finger, "over there. Tethered there, at the edge of the pond. With a big, long boathook laid across it. It's entirely possible, I should imagine, that this boat and that hook are retained for the express purpose of hoicking debris out of the pond."

The young one looked where his colleague was pointing. "Right. Yeah. I was wondering how long it'd take you to spot that. OK - you row and I'll operate the hook."

Lofty shook his head. "Rowing's a young man's game," he said. "I haven't got the joints for it. Whereas hoicking things out of ponds with a hook - that is skilled work, and therefore, by definition, my province."

They capsized twice, but neither of them drowned much.

Embarrassed by their performance at the previous evening's all-staff, the Loftys had agreed that they needed a common approach to the pond problem. The first thing to do was to reappraise the scene, so, early and shiny on the Wednesday morning, they returned to Wood Green and the polluted pond.

It had been dug on the site of a former supermarket, in a place where a number of roads rolled down into something approaching a convergence, and was intended to collect run-off during periods of heavy or prolonged wet weather, providing the rain with a home of its own so that it didn't need to borrow anyone else's. There had never been much doubt that the position chosen for the pond was the right one: the supermarket, during its nine year existence, had flooded fourteen times.

Full, according to season, of frogs and birds, dragonflies and children, it was a pleasant scene; a community treasure which earned its keep in all weathers. But at the moment, its prettiness was fouled by a sizeable island of rubbish which had appeared - overnight, according to local dog-walkers interviewed by Uniform - in one part of the pond, just a few wades in from the water's edge.

There was "about a van's worth," according to the wheezy old sergeant who'd made the call to Serious Crimes, suggesting that the squad might like to have a look "just to be on the safe side," before the local police did the routine thing, which would be to get the council, or British Waterways, in to clear the debris, get the pond back in order, and then identity the owners or origins of the individual items of waste wherever possible. Identified dumpers would be prosecuted; unidentified dumpings would ultimately go to the Re.

The van's-worth turned out to consist of various types of rubbish, such as rusty machinery, old lengths of timber, discarded household items, and sundry broken bits of this and that. The local police were a bit puzzled by it all, hence the referral to Serious Crimes. Most of this stuff looked as if it came from, as the wheezy sergeant put it, "The National Museum of Crap." It belonged to a previous age - or ages. "When was the last time," the sergeant had asked the Loftys, "you saw a jumbo-size supermarket trolley, complete with twin baby seats?"

So-called 'total recycling' - the closed-loop system under which (in theory, or rather in target) nothing was ever wasted or ultimately discarded, everything was endlessly reused and recycled - had been in place for some years now. So, even supposing you wanted to befoul a flood pond with junk, where would you lay your hands on a van's-worth of bits of old fridges and staved-in tumble driers, all of which should have been recycled long ago?

A few sample pieces retrieved by Uniform had so far given no clues as to provenance. That in itself was not especially surprising; the technology which enabled universal, mandatory property-marking was relatively recent.

But then there was the bicycle, its rear wheel poking out above the water. It looked from the shore - and on retrieval, proved to be - brand new. From its position, entangled amid the rest, it had at first appeared to be part of the same lot, but it differed in one obvious and surely significant respect: it wasn't junk.

Back at the office, the Loftys handed the bicycle in to Evidence, having first taken a note of its serial number. From this, they were swiftly able to establish the retail co-op from which it had been bought on the previous Saturday, and the name and contact details of the buyer: a Mr Kieran Rider, who lived in Tottenham. There was no report of the item as lost or stolen.

"I don't get that," said the younger Lofty. "I mean, OK, he buys a smart new bike, some kids nick it, ride it around a bit and then chuck it in a pond. But why hasn't he reported it missing?"

Some shared instinct made them want to know more about Mr Rider before they called him to tell him his property had been recovered. They asked Jade if she could look him up on the computer for them.

"As I have reason to believe you might possibly be aware," she told them, "under the privacy laws you can only check a citizen out on the computer, without a Chief Inspector's permission, if you suspect him of a crime. Do you suspect him of a crime?"

"Well, we ... " said the younger Lofty.

"Not suspect, as such," said the older Lofty.

"Not as such. Which means 'not'. Thank you, gentlemen. To continue. The only other exemption from the privacy rules is if you consider him to be in danger." She looked up at them and smiled. "Do you consider him to be in danger?"

"Well, actually - " the younger Lofty began.

"No," Jade interrupted, "when you begin a sentence with 'Well, actually,' what you actually mean is 'No,' isn't it?"

The Loftys exercised their right to remain silent.

"Well ... ?" Jade asked.

"Well ... yes, actually," said the older Lofty.

"Thank you. In conclusion, you have no reason, within the parameters of the privacy laws, to look him up."

The Loftys thanked her, and walked away from her desk. "We could always go and have a look at him in the flesh," suggested the younger Lofty to the older, in a whisper.

"No, you couldn't," Jade called out. "When you are a police detective, 'having a look at someone' is known as 'putting them under surveillance,' and is covered by the privacy laws."

Dispirited, they returned to their own desks.

"What's up boys?" asked Gerard Cochrane. "Found out you've drawn me and Bob Lemon in the departmental tennis doubles?"

The Loftys explained their dead end.

"What is it you want to know about this bloke?" asked Gerard.

One of the Loftys shrugged. "Well, what he does for a living would be a start."

Gerard rolled his eyes. "I sometimes fear, colleagues, that in our rush to embrace the future we are in danger of losing many of the traditional folk skills upon which our forefathers depended for their livelihoods. You got his mobile number there?" The Loftys handed it over, and Gerard dialled it. "Yes, hello - is that Kieran Rider the solar heating engineer? Sorry? Hospital accountant, you say? Oh, right - well, no, I haven't got any hospitals that need accounting just now. Sorry to trouble you, pal, obviously got the wrong bloke. Cheers, then." He hung up and turned to the Loftys with a pitying smile. "He's a hospital accountant. Says so himself."

The Loftys reckoned they deserved a cup of tea and a bun after that, so they repaired to the canteen. "How much does a hospital accountant earn?" said the younger Lofty.

His partner nodded; the same thought had occurred to him. "That's not a cheap bike."

By luck, the next table to theirs was occupied by a custody officer, named Tony, who was an acknowledged expert on such matters.

"Hospital accountant?" Tony thought about it for a moment. "I reckon that's Band C, isn't it?"

"My God," said the younger Lofty, with a sneer. "You'd have to pay me a hell of a lot more than Band C to spend all day adding up bills for bandages."

Tony shrugged. "It's all done on supply and demand, though, isn't it? The less popular the job, the higher the wages. So obviously, there's plenty of people who are quite happy to count bandages on Band C."

"Yeah, I reckon they fiddle the figures," said the young Lofty.

"Who does?" said the older one. "What are you nuttering on about now?"

"Think about it, right? Suppose you're a hospital accountant, and you've got to advertise for another hospital accountant, to keep you company. Right, what you do is, if you get a hundred applicants for the job, you fill in the form saying there's only been ten - that way, hospital accounting gets re-graded, and your wages go up to Band B."

Tony smiled round his pipe. "I think it's a *bit* more complicated than that, mate. There are checks, you know, security procedures. They take into account national and regional averages, skill shortages, all sorts. They don't just take your word for it."

"Anyway," said Lofty, changing tack as subtly as a cargo ship in a swimming pool, "using supply and demand to fix wages - that is pure capitalism!"

Tony took his pipe out of his mouth and put it on the table next to his custard slice. "It's not pure *anything*-ism - it's just pure logic. Otherwise, you'll end up with a TV comedian earning more than a hospital matron."

"Couldn't have that," the other Lofty agreed, smiling to himself. "That'd be unthinkable."

"And what would you do," Tony continued, "about really dirty, dangerous, smelly jobs that no one wants, if they didn't come with top wages? You'd have every public toilet in the country ankle-deep in piss, and a 'Staff Wanted' sign in the window."

"But people still used to do those jobs in the old days, didn't they?"

"True," the older Lofty admitted, "but every public toilet in the country was, in fact, ankle-deep in piss."

"Anyway, it's fascinating," said Tony, who was known to follow the regularly published wages tables with the same interest that some of his colleagues expended on county cricket scores, "seeing which jobs people *really* want to do, and which ones they only ever did for the money, whatever they said."

"All right, but why should teachers, for instance, be punished just because a lot of people want to teach? They get low wages, but it's a socially useful job."

"What you're forgetting," said Tony, "is the National Minimum Income, the - "

"The Bland Tax," said the young Lofty. "Designed to make us all the same."

Instead of the myriad benefits which had existed back when old Lofty was young Lofty - old age pensions, family benefits, student grants, disability allowances, and scores of others - today there was simply the NMI; or, slightly less simply, the adjusted NMI. Everyone in the country, from their fifteenth birthday until the day they died, had the weekly NMI paid directly into their bank account. The amount was essentially index-linked, subject to overview by a standing committee of trade unionists, co-operative business leaders and MPs. Any surplus was simply reclaimed in the normal run of things through graduated income tax, all indirect taxes having been abolished at the time of the shortages. Thus, you could be the highest paid person in the country, and you would still automatically receive your NMI every week - but you would also automatically lose it in taxation every month.

A plurality of benefits and taxes, let alone means testing, was clearly contrary to efficiency: the present, entirely automated system required almost no bureaucracy to run it, which freed considerable labour and other resources for more productive areas. To those who hated the Process deep in their marrow, however - and even to aspiring beefeaters, like the younger Lofty - the NMI was the symbol of everything that had gone wrong.

"You're forgetting," Tony carried on, "a hugely enlarged social wage compared to the old days - "

Seeing his colleague's puzzled frown, the older Lofty explained. "Lots of things are free or subsidised, these days. Like, we used to have to pay for our prescriptions when we were ill."

"No you didn't!" Lofty treated his partner to a look of triumphant disgust. "If you people really believed in your precious 'Revo,' you wouldn't need to make up scare stories like that."

"Also," said Tony, who'd worked in Custody a long time, and was used to ignoring interruptions, "the rationing, to make sure we all get out fair share, and the fact that the difference between the top band of pay and the lowest is much less than in the old days. In other words, everyone's reasonably well off. You're not being penalised by being on a low band, you're being rewarded by being on a high band."

"Tell you what, though," said the older Lofty, "it's a bloody insult that they pay uniformed cops more than they do detectives."

"I know," Tony agreed. "I'm so offended I'm thinking of giving some of it back."

The Loftys just had time to check the system again before the all-staff briefing began. There was still no report of the bicycle being lost or stolen.

"So," said the younger one, "a hospital accountant, whose income is nothing special, buys a very smart new bike, a few days later it ends up in a pond a few miles away from his home, and he isn't in any hurry to report it missing. What does that mean?"

"Perhaps," said the other one, "it means he was drunk when he lost it and now he can't figure out where he's left it."

They had gone off duty at eleven last night, there being nothing much else they could usefully do. Now it was breakfast time, and Phil and Dahlia were back at work, following up on interviews with neighbours who'd already been spoken to by the local police. The door-knocking teams had flagged for Serious Crime's attention any interviewees who they thought might be worth a second look.

Still no news of the missing girl, but Phil was pretty bubbly all the same. Even Dahlia had to admit it was intriguing news: the first witness, other than the mother, who claimed to have heard the mysterious Americans.

The witness lived ten minutes' brisk walk from Sarla Brown's house, but that did nothing to dampen Phil's spirits. "Two different lots of Yanks? What are the odds? I don't think so, Dahlia."

Austin Molloy had been canvassed, as part of a programme of increasing concentric circles based on the Browns' home, right at the end of the previous evening's work - and the PC who spoke to him reported him as "very insistent" about what he'd heard.

DC Kotane enjoyed a laugh as much as the next copper, and she was looking forward to having one as soon as she was alone. It would be undiplomatic, she fancied, to let the laugh go here and now. But honestly ... Phil Kale's face, when the middle-aged man who opened the door, and confirmed that he was Austin Molloy, spoke to them in a charmingly soft US accent.

It *was* funny. And when she told a few, carefully selected friends about it later on, she might add the punch line: "And you didn't even need to be there." But it was also annoying. Dahlia found anti-Americanism embarrassing, as many people did, but she also found it stupid. It frustrated her that people only ever talked about the *Yanks* invading, as if everybody had forgotten about, or didn't take seriously, Europa. The Europeans were just as likely to invade, she thought, as the Yanks were. More likely, you could argue: the Yanks would say they were here to rescue Britain from communism and/or atheism. World opinion would be unimpressed. But Europe could say it was defending Britain pre-emptively against the Yanks - and much of the world would swallow that. Much of Britain, she feared, would swallow that. And who could deny that European capitalism had just as many reasons to hate the Process as US capitalism had.

And Europa was much closer - it was simply more practical for them to invade, apart from anything else. Never underestimate the effect of geography on history, she reckoned.

Or, OK - leave ideology out of it. The Yanks (she never knew what to call them, really; 'Yanks' sounded derogatory, 'Americans' was just plain wrong, because Venezuelans and Mexicans were Americans, and 'the US' didn't really work because parts of it claimed not to be in the US any more; but whatever you called them) the Yanks might invade Britain to "close down the terrible threat of a good example," as someone had once said in another context. But if anyone was to follow the current imperial fashion - of invading countries to steal their topsoil, and then shipping it back home - surely that made more sense for Europa, being that much closer? Soil was the fourth most sought after resource on the planet, after water, petroleum and calories. Even at the start of the century, it was calculated that twenty-four billion tons were lost every year, globally, through erosion, building and pollution; several tons per person on earth.

Geology, too; she had geology, geography and history on her side of the argument, and still people banged on and on about the Yanks.

All the same: Phil's face. That *was* funny.

The witness was in his fifties, with a grey ponytail and white spectacles. Over a t-shirt commemorating a US college that she'd never heard of, he wore braces holding up what looked like decorator's trousers. Taking her cue from the DS's stupefied, uncomfortable, palpably suspicious silence, Dahlia began the questioning.

Austin Molloy didn't take much persuasion to talk. Describing himself as a refugee from the former US, he was loudly and enthusiastically pro-Process and pro-Britain. Just out of curiosity, mostly, she tried to get him to say something mildly critical of his new homeland, but relented when his hopeless floundering became too much for her heart to bear. He was a born-again patriot, and that was that.

"What's your trade, Mr Molloy?"

"Back in the States I was a college professor - English and Drama. Over here, I've been lucky enough to find a very fulfilling position as a senior editor with a publisher of textbooks. Best job I ever had, believe me. Plus, I don't have to keep looking over my shoulder all the time. Living under authorities that obey the rule of law, Detective - that's worth quite a lot, when you've experienced the opposite."

Phil spoke at last, though what he said didn't strike Dahlia as massively helpful, or minutely relevant. "Funny, isn't it - all the US refugees seem to be college lecturers or something of that status. Never seem to be factory workers or cleaners."

Molloy gave Phil a pacifying smile; Dahlia got the clear impression that he was used to hostility, to some people listening to his accent rather than his words. "Nothing odd about it, friend - we're the only ones who could afford to get out."

Neat, thought Dahlia. Deal with innuendo by openly stating the thing that your attacker has hinted at. She made a mental note of that, sure that it would come in handy one day. "You were working in your front garden yesterday morning ... ?"

"That's right. This would have been round about quarter to ten in the morning. I had a day off, made an early start. I only moved in here a few weeks ago, so I'm a bit behind with the ol' veg patch, you know? But I'm hoping to get some collard greens in there, if I can get the ground ready in time."

"And you heard something unusual?"

He nodded. "Couldn't see anything, as such, because of that hedge. But what I heard, or overheard I should say, I have no doubts about. A conversation between a man and a woman with American accents." He stopped speaking and beamed proudly at his guests.

The two detectives exchanged a glance: a *man* and a woman? But they didn't ask anything further about that. Deluded, false or mistaken witnesses could usually be relied upon to talk their own way into disqualification.

"Which direction were they walking in, could you tell?" Dahlia asked.

"Oh, yes. For sure. They were walking roughly to the west - towards the street where that poor little girl was taken, as I now know. No news about that, I guess?"

"Sorry." Dahlia shook her head. "Are you certain they were US or former US accents?"

"Absolutely. No doubt at all."

"Couldn't have been Canadian, or - "

He laughed. "I'm sorry, detective, but that's like me asking you if you can tell the difference between an Irish accent and a French one. These people were Yanks."

"OK. That's great. From whereabouts in the States, could you tell?"

His confidence ebbed a little, for the first time. "Well, that's trickier. It's a big place, you know, and I'm not that well-travelled a man. If I had to guess I'd say these two were New Englanders. Boston, maybe? But that *is* a guess."

"Did you overhear what they were saying?"

Austin looked regretful. "Nothing that aroused my suspicion, I have to say - it was only when the officer knocked on the door and told me about the little girl that I kind of wondered, you know? I mean, we've all heard the stories. But they were just talking about the weather, I guess - it was hotter than they expected."

"You weren't inclined to speak to them," Phil demanded, "being fellow-countrymen? Hearing a familiar accent far from home?"

"Not that familiar, Sergeant. I'm from Kansas. I've visited New England maybe three times in my life."

"Still ... " Phil wasn't letting it go. "Same country. Sort of. You didn't say 'Howdy! Where you folks from?'"

And this time, Dahlia noted with some satisfaction, Austin Molloy wasn't letting it go, either. "Detective Sergeant," he said, quietly and firmly, "I am a refugee. One thing you learn quite quickly, when you find yourself in that station in life, is to keep yourself to yourself, especially where people from the old country are concerned."

"But a couple from the US, walking down a suburban street in London - the chances are they're refugees too, surely?" Phil said. "Who else would they be - diplomats, businessmen? People like that aren't going to be strolling round the suburbs, chatting about the weather, are they? And we don't exactly get a lot of US tourists these days."

"I don't know who they were," the witness replied, " but I don't think they were refugees."

"Why not?" asked Dahlia.

"What can I say - you get to know your own. The walk, the tone of voice ... " He ran his hands through his hair, and down his ponytail. "Officers, you see me living in a nice enough house in a nice enough neighbourhood, doing a nice enough job, and you don't see it. But the fact is, once you're a refugee, you're always on the defensive for the rest of your life. You understand that?"

"I can believe that," said Dahlia.

"OK. Now, those two? They were walking down this road like they owned the fucking place."

CHAPTER SIX

The DI had called the all-staff for noon, to allow people who'd been working late a chance to sleep, and so as to catch some of those who hadn't been at the previous evening's briefing. While he was leaning against a wall, checking his notes, it suddenly occurred to him that he hadn't yet had a chance to speak properly to Erin, the work-sampling girl. No doubt Gerard and Jade between them would be taking good care of her, and she'd certainly never have eaten as much cake in her life. But he was the boss; he made a note to speak to her right after this.

"I'll start with an update on the Beech Lane killings - I'm sure you'll all have heard that there are now two bodies."

"They're breeding," someone called out.

Greg noticed Phil Kale and Dahlia Kotane slide in at the back of the room. Dahlia gave him an apologetic grimace for their lateness, but Phil didn't look apologetic at all. Phil was bouncing up and down on his heels, and grinning. *Oh God*, thought Greg, *he looks excited - what fresh bollocks is this?*

"The first body - the one under the paving - is as yet still unidentified. However, we do now have the post mortem results on him, and some preliminary forensics. I'll summarise: damage to back of skull, suggestive of some force; could be accident, quite possibly violence, the best guess being a blow with a heavy object yielded by a second party. Scientific are able to say for certain that he wasn't killed in situ, but I think we'd probably worked that out for ourselves. The nature of the burial means that it is hard to be precise on when he was killed and when he was buried. But when we told Scientific that we think the drive was last paved in the mid-to-late 1990s, they say they're perfectly happy with that as a date. They couldn't swear to it, but it fits well enough. One thing they are firm on: the paving over the grave site went down at the same time as the rest. In other words, he was definitely buried when the drive was done. That's not necessarily when he was killed, of course."

"So the summary is - we think he died a long time ago?"

"That's about right, Nasser, yes. However, with the second body, which was buried in the back garden, we've had better luck. This man has been positively identified overnight from dental records as the householder, Bradley Nottle."

Gerard Cochrane interrupted. "Just on that point, sir - him being the householder, I mean. We've only just got confirmation of this, a few minutes ago. He was indeed - *him*, not *them*, by the way - the owner of the house. But Erin and I have been digging into these old town hall records. They're incomplete, and pretty difficult to access, because, incredible though it will seem to our younger colleagues, back then an awful lot of things were done on computer only, with no paper back-up, which means of course that every time the technology changed whole generations of records became permanently inaccessible. However, in this particular case, we're lucky, and we've managed to piece together a brief history of number nineteen. We now know that Bradley Nottle's *granny* lived there and left the house to Bradley when she died - that is, 1996. Bradley Nottle has owned the house ever since."

This news caused a general widening of eyes and pursing of lips around the room. It knocked out one of the assumptions on which they'd been operating: that the Nottles weren't suspects in the case of the body under the drive, because they hadn't owned the house when the drive was laid.

"Right." Greg rubbed his brow with his knuckles. "Thanks, Gerard. And Erin. We're going to need the implications of that sorted out - apart from anything, what does it do to our timelines? However, we still need to trace former occupants, that hasn't changed. But our absolute priority now, for this investigation and for this squad as a whole, is tracing Mrs Kim Nottle - she is obviously a suspect in the death of her husband, but she's also a potential victim. Either way, we need to find her without delay. We were told that the Nottles were going on holiday to stay with relatives, probably in Cornwall. As soon as we can find confirmatory details of that, assuming we do, DS Blake and I will be going down there - "

Traditional briefing-room cries of *Separate rooms!* and *Junket!* and *Have you packed your bucket and spade?* rang out.

"Thank you, colleagues, for your good wishes. The second priority, clearly, is finding out where the Spitfire rifle came from that was used to kill Bradley Nottle. The only thing we know at the moment, as explained in your briefing sheet, is that it didn't come from the armoury which covers Beech Lane. What that means is that it could come from absolutely anywhere in Britain. Any theories on that, from anyone - on where it came from, or how we find it - will no doubt be welcomed by DC Cochrane who will be co-ordinating that aspect of the investigation. Work out how many people you need for that, please Gerard, and then ask Catherine to assign them. Or, if she's not here - "

"*Junket!*"

" - DS Dale Emmett, who we welcome back from sick leave. How's the foot, Dale?"

"I fear my career in top-flight football is over, boss," replied the big-bellied, fifty-year-old sergeant, "but the surgeon specifically confirmed that I can still boot the arses of lazy DCs without feeling excessive pain."

"Excellent. Now, as briefly as possible, please, further reports. Ginger, there's been a development in the rooftop garden thefts?"

DC Thom detailed his meeting the previous evening with the potato man. He left out the bit about radishes, which he thought was probably of lesser importance. "It looks very much like stealing-to-order," he concluded. "Only the tubers from test beds were taken, while plenty of edible stuff was left behind."

"You mean ... " Greg searched his mind for the correct phrase. "Like, industrial espionage?"

"Agricultural espionage," Dale corrected him.

"That's how it looks, boss. Which," Ginger added ruefully, "definitely makes it one for us, doesn't it?"

Greg had to agree: this was pretty much a living definition of Serious Crime. "Any connection with the other rooftop thefts?"

"I don't see how," said Ginger.

"OK, Ginger, you're full-time on that for as long as you think it's necessary or useful. But I'm afraid you'll have to carry it on your own, for now. At least until we've found Kim Nottle."

"You'll probably find she's hiding in one of those lovely little smugglers' pubs down in Cornwall, boss," DC Nasser Agarkar suggested. "I'd look there first if I were you."

"I'll make a note of that, Nasser, thank you. Right, Lofty?"

"Yes, sir," said both Loftys.

"How are you getting on with your pond?"

The Loftys looked at each other, and had a quick bicker amongst themselves with their eyebrows and frowns. Eventually, the older one said: "We'd like to stay on that just for a few more hours if possible, chief. There is one aspect of it that's very slightly odd." He explained about the hospital accountant's brand new, unreported, missing bike.

"How do you know he's a hospital accountant?" Greg asked.

The Loftys were uncomfortably silent for a moment, before Gerard spoke. "They just do," he explained.

"I see," said Greg. "Fine. Well, I agree with you, that is slightly odd, and it's the sort of loose end I would sooner not leave dangling." *What a stupid thing to say*, he thought: makes it sound like there are some types of loose end I actually want to leave dangling. "So tidy it up, but I will need both of you on the murder as soon as possible, so bear that in mind."

"Sir."

"And Phil - Jade tells me there's still no sign of the missing girl?"

Phil Kale's excitement was palpable to all in the room - and embarrassing to some - as he told them of the new witness who had placed a pair of Yank accents in the vicinity of Sarla Brown's disappearance. He kept the best bit for last.

"And I should add that this witness who has come forward is, himself, a citizen of the former US."

"Probably an ex-citizen," said Dahlia. "I think they're automatically stripped of citizenship if they live overseas."

"He is, at any rate," Phil insisted, "an American."

Greg thought Phil could probably do with a little deflating at this point. "But there's nothing whatsoever to actually link these American passers-by with the missing girl?" He didn't wait for Phil's reply, adding: "Right, that case is certainly looking unlikely to have a happy ending, so you and Dahlia must obviously stay on it. Do you need anyone else, Phil?"

"Not really," said Phil, a little grudgingly. "The locals are doing all the routine, DC Kotane and I can handle the Squad side of it."

"OK, thanks for that, but let us know if the situation changes." As Greg spoke, he made sure he was looking at Dahlia, letting her know that he expected her, not the DS, to give him the honest word on whether or not they needed more or less manpower.

Greg didn't need to seek Erin out after the briefing, because she sought him out.

"Sir? I've noticed, and I wondered - why doesn't Serious Crimes have any mounted officers? Most police units do, don't they?"

Greg was careful not to smile. Teenage girls and horses: he'd never understood it. Actually, he thought he probably had understood it once, and it was so embarrassing he'd deliberately forgotten it. "Ah, now, Erin - there's a very important and technical operational reason for that."

"Sir?"

"We haven't got anybody who can ride."

She grinned enormously. "You have now."

"Oh, really?"

"Yes, sir. My mum's a district nurse."

"I thought district nurses had motor cars?"

Erin nodded. "She has got a car, yes, but she uses the horse more. When the weather's nice, she prefers it, and also you can get a horse through a flooded road easier than you can a car. Besides, she always says, you can't put car-droppings on your veg patch."

Greg thought about it, but not for long. He liked officers who came up with ideas - and actually came *out* with ideas, instead of just pondering about them privately for years until it was too late - and he liked it when things changed. New stuff is good stuff, he'd always thought. Except when it wasn't, obviously, but then you just went back to the old. You rarely lost by giving something a go, he reckoned.

"Right, Erin. Come with me."

The nearest police stables was a short-ish walk - there was one in every policing area - and before long, Erin had chosen, and Greg had requisitioned, a horse. It was a grey one, it hadn't bitten him yet, and that was as much as Greg knew about it.

"There we are," he said. "You are now North London Serious Crime Squad's first mounted officer."

"Except I'm not really an officer."

"Mounted person, then. Let's not quibble."

They walked the horse back to the station. Greg was finding the double journey a bit noticeable, but Erin didn't seem to mind: she'd grown up in walking times, he supposed, it was perfectly natural to her to cover miles a day on foot.

"This is brilliant, sir. I'll be able to run messages between officers out on assignment, and carry samples to and from the labs, and collect - "

"I'll have to speak to Gerard to make sure this doesn't interfere with your work-sampling, but I think it should work out well. As you say, you can run errands, and then perhaps spend an hour or two with whichever officers you end up with, observing what they do. Does that sound all right?"

"Sounds great, sir."

"Good. I'm making it up on the - on the hoof. But I don't see why it shouldn't work. If it doesn't, tell Gerard or Jade and they'll sort you out." Suddenly he stopped walking and slapped his forehead. "Hell, I'm an idiot! Where are we going to put Rover when we get him back to the station?"

"Rover?"

"Horses make me a bit nervous," said Greg. "I've decided to just pretend he's a large dog."

She laughed. "Don't worry - there's a small stable at the station, room enough for two horses. So if Tiddles turns up ... "

"Is there? A stable? How come I've never seen it?"

"You know that shed behind the lock-up? Where you store all the recycling awaiting collection?"

"That's a stable? I had no idea. You sure?"

"I looked it up on the computer. Our place is a fairly new building, but it has several out-buildings, and semi-detached areas, which are much older. Including what was quite obviously a stable originally, and is in fact still officially designated by the police estates office as a stable."

"Is it, indeed?"

"Sir. It's just that you've never had a horse before."

"Well, I never. So what are we going to with all the recycling awaiting collection?"

Erin patted the horse. "We put a covered cart in the courtyard, and whenever it's full me and Rover will trot it over to the recycling centre."

"Yeah, that makes sense. So, you're still enjoying Serious Crime?"

She nodded vigorously, and rubbed the horse's side. "Oh yeah. Very much. It's fascinating. I've always been interested in crime - you know, how it changes. What is a crime, what people think about it, the relationship between people and the law - it's all dependent on which era you're talking about, isn't it?"

"You studied this at school?"

"Yes, a bit, but also I just got it from listening to people talk - my Nan, especially. In her day, she reckons crime was all anyone talked

about in London, or thought about. Everyone was obsessed with it."
She looked at him sideways, rather shyly. Trying to guess his age, he
assumed from context. "You were a policeman in the old days, yeah?
Are the crimes different? Are the criminals different, or the victims?"

Greg strolled on in thoughtful silence for a moment, simply
taking the time to enjoy his own delight. He hadn't been sure about
this work-sampling business, but if this girl was typical, then it was
a terrific idea. She was being stimulated to ask stimulating questions.
That had to be worthwhile. And that fact that her source
information came from listening to her nan, rather than from
lessons at school, strongly suggested to Greg that she had some
copper in her own DNA.

"If you decide to do the formal training course," he said, "they'll
tell you there's five types of crime. First, crimes of madness -
Napoleon comes to me in a dream and tells me to cut your head off
and I do. All right. But of course, while crimes of madness are
crimes in practical effect - they create crime scenes, victims, and so
on - they're not crimes in a philosophical or legal sense. You see?"

"Sure."

"All right. Related to them - but legally very distinct from them
- are crimes of emotion: I come home from work and find you in
bed with my brother - "

"So you cut my head off, OK."

"Actually, I think I'll cut *his* head off, instead. I haven't got a
brother, so I'd probably get a lighter sentence."

"I'd probably be quite glad to have my head chopped off," said
Erin, shuddering theatrically, "when I realised I'd slept with my own
uncle."

There was a short - but, for Greg, moderately epiphanic - pause,
while he dealt with the realisation that he was significantly older than
he felt. Probably best to press on, he decided, without giving Erin
too much time to figure out that he'd meant that she was sleeping
with her brother-in-law, not her uncle. Just in case he could tell from
her face that she thought that was even worse.

"OK, so then you have the three categories of practical crime, unchanged from the old days, or from thousands of years ago. Crimes of need, crimes of - "

"Need?"

He hadn't expected her to interrupt at that point. Surely that was an obvious one. "Man's starving, so he nicks a loaf of bread."

"Well, right, but surely we couldn't have that sort of crime these days, because nobody's starving?"

Fair point. It was a while since he'd done the course. "Well, I don't know - a teenager could run away from home, couldn't he? Can't get a job or use his ration card, because as soon as he pops his head above the wall he'll be sent home to his parents. He might need to steal to eat."

Erin shook her head. "He'd just go to a displacement centre, wouldn't he? They'll give him a meal, no questions asked."

Good. No, no, this was good. She had a good detective's mind - flexible, but tidy. "You're making a natural error, a common one: you're universalising behaviour. If *you* ran away from home, *you'd* get your grub from the DP centre. But someone else, for whatever reason - upbringing, personality, prior experience, could be anything - might not. Understand?"

He watched her thinking about it. "OK," she said, and he was impressed that she said nothing more. *OK* covered it.

"All right: crimes of need, then comes crimes of alienation - vandalism, for instance. Crimes which don't have a motivation of personal gain, or anger specifically directed, but arise from an individual feeling that he is not part of society. The theory is you get fewer of those in a more collective society - it's harder to feel the community is nothing to do with you, when in point of practical, objective fact it has a lot to do with you in almost every aspect of your daily life. And certainly we see less of that than we did when I first joined - in those days, half our time was spent on what they called 'anti-social behaviour,' mostly by people your age."

"That does still go on," she said, as if she were telling him a secret that she feared might shock him.

"It does, but believe me - nothing like the old days. Ask Gerard, he'll tell you some stories that'll make your hair drop out. Finally, the big one: crimes of greed. Now, those you're always going to get. It's possible that you get fewer when things are more equally shared out, and when greed itself is socially unacceptable, but you'll still always get them."

"And that's what we mostly deal with?"

He nodded. "More than anything else, yes. We live a life now where everything is valuable - everything is precious, much more so than in the old days. Nobody goes short, because of the way things are organised, but there's no plenty, as there used to be. There are no cheap imports any more, because of actual world shortages, of food and fuel and so on, and because of wars and invasions and everything else. Our priorities, as a society, are conserving resources and reducing pollution - this is a necessity of survival that's been turned into half an ideology. And of course, in those circumstances there's plenty of people who want more."

"And are willing to take it," said Erin.

"That's it."

Again, she rubbed the horse and grinned. "And then we nick 'em, guv, and bang 'em up, quick as you like, 'cos we ain't havin' no toerags on our manor!"

He looked over at her in astonishment. "Good God, Erin! You sound like you've already *been* on the training course."

" ... which is contrary to the Agreement of the People," Bob Lemon concluded, before asking the arrestee if he understood the grounds for his arrest. Bob tried never to gabble the caution; it was, he thought, a vital element of the Commonwealth's constitutional settlement, not a piece of bureaucratic necessity to be rushed through with elision. Trouble was, it was almost impossible not to gabble something - anything - that you said over and over, day after day and year after year.

The elderly man he'd arrested knew fine why he'd been arrested: promoting religion in public, in a manner likely to be injurious to unity. Which was, as the caution pointed out, contrary to the Agreement of the People.

Bob had been on his way to the school where Bradley Nottle had been employed, when he turned a corner and happened upon this little fellow, all on his own, standing literally on a soap box, literally on a street corner, literally talking to himself. Declaiming to himself, if you preferred - preaching, loudly and eloquently, fluently and unafraid, in a voice much stronger than the stringy body that housed it.

Rather impressive. Completely mad, of course, as rather impressive things and people so often were. Bob wondered if anyone had ever stopped to listen to the poor old nut. *Ever.*

The poor old nut was obviously delighted to be arrested. Bob didn't blame him - standing there on a hot day all on your lonesome, preaching to an absent audience. He imagined that the only attention Mr X was ever likely to receive would come from angry secularists, or hilarious schoolchildren. Or yobs. Having said all that, a few years ago Bob had been involved in the aftermath of a riot triggered by a lone street preacher which had left twenty-seven people in hospital, and a public library in flames. Never for a moment had he considered not arresting Mr X, no matter the preacher's impressiveness.

He rang the school to tell them he'd be late, then turned to his prisoner. "Now then, Mr X, are you all right to walk? The nearest police station is only about ten minutes up that way."

"I'm perfectly happy to walk, thank you, Detective Constable. It's a lovely day that God has sent us." The preacher twinkled his eyes at the detective. "*If* I'm allowed to say that, am I?"

Bob always found this bit of the process very boring, because you weren't supposed to talk to a prisoner who'd been cautioned until he was back at the station and had been given a chance to consult a lawyer. That was bad enough in a two minute cart ride, but for Bob, during a ten minute walk, it was positively painful.

He'd have been happy to call for transport to take them to the nick. If the prisoner had been big and young, obviously, he couldn't have, because it would have looked as if Bob thought he couldn't walk him back on his own. But since this prisoner was small and old, and therefore didn't need a lift for security reasons, it would have been perfectly acceptable to call for a lift for time and bother reasons.

Mr X's somewhat unexpected reply put the kibosh on that. So they set off walking.

At the front desk, Bob blipped his identity to the duty sergeant, and explained that he'd arrested this man, who gave his name as Mr X, for street preaching.

The sergeant started filling in the forms.

"Right. What was he preaching?"

"The Word of God," said Mr X.

The sergeant didn't look up. "Not you, sir, I was talking to my colleague."

"I do beg your pardon."

"DC Lemon: what was the accused preaching?"

"Word of God, Sarge," said Bob, and received a friendly nod of approval from his prisoner.

"Which god?" said the sergeant.

"Technically," said Mr X, in a voice full of apology for the interruption, "there is only one God."

"You'd be surprised, sir," said the sergeant. "From this side of the desk, there seem to be hundreds of the bastards. DC Lemon, can you tell me which religion the accused was preaching?"

Bob felt the beginnings of a stomach ache. "Not as such, Sarge, no." Christianity, he'd assumed - though he knew better than to offer assumptions to the sergeant - but he couldn't have said which flavour. The prisoner was white, so he'd guess Protestantism, but he knew better than to offer guesses to the sergeant, and besides - which *flavour* of Protestantism? He'd never actually nicked anyone for street preaching before, now he came to think of it.

"Can you, in that case, verbally reproduce for the record a sample of same, such as a passage, or form of words, used by the accused during the commission of the offence?"

Bob couldn't. He hadn't really been listening. It was all such bollocks - just streams of archaisms and non sequiturs and funny noises. Could *anybody* make head or tail of any of it? Surely the fact that none of it made sense - well, wasn't that rather the point?

"Not really, Sarge, no."

The sergeant sighed and set aside his pen. "You can't charge a man for his words, DC Lemon, if you can't say what those words were. For all the record shows, he might have been singing old disco hits in Portuguese."

"I wasn't, though," said Mr X. "I was preaching Christianity, in English." He turned to Bob, and patted him on the arm. "Bad luck, DC Lemon. Not your fault - the whole law is absurdly complicated, in my view."

"Thank you," mumbled Bob. "Sorry for all the bother."

"Mr X," said the sergeant, "as your arrest has ended without a charge being laid I am legally obliged to offer you a lift back to the place at which you were arrested, or to your home or other reasonable destination, such as workplace or the nearby home of a friend or relative."

"You're very kind, Sergeant, but no thank you - here will do just fine." With a cheery wave, Mr X toddled off.

"Don't worry yourself, mate," said the sergeant, seeing Bob's embarrassment. Bob didn't doubt that this generosity stemmed largely from the fact that seeing a Serious Crimes veteran make a fool of himself in a way which few freshly-minted street bobbies would be likely to, out-counted any annoyance the sergeant might feel at the waste of his time, or at the preacher getting away with it. "You know why he didn't want a lift anywhere?"

"No, Sarge?"

The sergeant nodded towards the door through which Mr X had recently departed. "Give him ten minutes to get his breath back, and he'll be right outside this nick, preaching again. They want to be arrested you see, it's the only point of the thing."

"Makes them martyrs, I suppose."

"Besides which," said the sergeant, "it's the only attention the poor mad bastards ever get. Tell you what - have a cup of tea, and then you can pop out and nick him again. You'll know how to do it, this time."

Bob thanked him for the kind offer, but explained that he was late for an appointment. The sergeant arranged a lift for him, and while they were waiting for it he said: "There's been a hell of a lot of street preaching arrests this summer, more than I can ever remember."

"Really?"

"Almost all of them white Protestants, as you'd expect. We also get black Catholics, and the odd Buddhist and Hindu. Very rarely Jews or Muslims for some reason. They don't seem to go in for it." Bob thought he sounded almost disapproving, as if these people were being selfish, not seeking to share their mad message with the rest of us.

"Same bodies all the time, is it?"

"You do get mostly repeat offenders, as a rule - though currently we're seeing quite a lot of new faces."

"How do the regulars pay their fines, over and over?"

"Well, that's the big question, isn't it?" said the sergeant. "It's assumed, though rarely proven, that the Protestants are financed by the Yanks, and the Catholics by the Euros. But you know what the even bigger question is?"

"No?" said Bob.

The sergeant smiled at him, like a man relishing a battle to come. "What happens when they *stop* paying their fines ... ?"

CHAPTER SEVEN

During the afternoon, confirmation finally arrived that Kim Nottle, missing wife of the recently deceased Bradley Nottle, did indeed have relatives in Cornwall.

"See if you can get us two train tickets to St. Ives, please Jade," said Greg. "Catherine and I will go down as soon as possible."

Although, naturally, all public transport was free - it would be contrary to efficiency to waste resources on collecting, processing and enforcing fares, a totally illogical system - nonetheless, you still needed a ticket; the rail authority still needed to know how many people there were going to be on each train.

"We're not going to let the relatives know we're coming?" asked Catherine, as they settled into a smoking carriage and the train began to pull out of Paddington. Jade was sorting out accommodation for them in St. Ives, and would send them the details later.

"They might be hiding Kim," said Greg. "Best if we turn up unannounced, I think."

Catherine felt quite excited, and she suspected Greg did, too. Despite the circumstances, there was inescapably something of a going-away-on-holiday feeling about any long train journey, especially one to the South West, with all its connotations of beaches and bed and breakfast, cockles and cream teas. Once the rhythm of the wheels had settled, Greg fetched beer and sandwiches from the buffct. For the first time in a long time, Catherine felt her toes relax; as if they were wriggling in sand, she thought. With relaxation - and, indeed, with beer - came conversation.

"Do you ever miss your old life?" Greg asked her. "Working in sales?"

"I do, of course, but then - am I missing my old life, or just the fact that back then I was young and ... "

Greg filled the gap left by her hesitation. "Young and in love."

That had been what she was going to say, but what she said now was: "Actually, I was going to say 'young and fit,' but then I realised I'm probably fitter now than I ever was."

Greg chuckled. "I was thinking the same earlier today. All that walking. You'd have had a car laid on as part of the job, I suppose?"

"New one each year!" Now they both chuckled, and shook their heads. "I'd hardly go to the corner shop without it. I used to drive to the gym in it, then spend an hour walking on a moving pavement, then drive home again! Honestly, the shock when the day came that we couldn't afford to fill it up any more ... "

"Were you resentful, when it all came to an end? I mean, I've always been a humble copper, more or less since school, but your old life sounds pretty privileged."

She nodded, staring out of the window. "It was. The car, big salary, expenses - 'great package,' as they used to call it. But it was also hell on earth, really; the hours were unbelievable. Some weeks, I'd spend thirty hours just driving, never mind the time I spent actually working."

"No regrets about joining the police?"

"None at all." She was firm on that, at least. "When the emergency employment regulations came in - I just didn't know what to do. The entire world that I'd grown up in had effectively disappeared over night. Either abolished by government diktat, or swept away by the hurricane of history - depending on which side you listened to. It wasn't just the practicalities. To be told, effectively, that the career you'd worked hard in - perfectly legal, decent, honest toil that you'd dedicated your waking life to since leaving college - that this was now viewed in retrospect as parasitism, that was quite hard to take." She hoped she didn't sound like her husband: resentful, still refusing to accept what had happened.

"Was that how it seemed?"

She considered. "How it *felt*, more than seemed, I suppose. Felt inside. Once you began to look at it from the outside - well, let's face it, if all those non-productive jobs still existed, we'd be starving, wouldn't we? Or if not actually starving, at least living like savages."

"Like Euros," Greg joked.

"Well, quite. You look back on it ... it all seemed so normal at the time. Millions and millions of people, buildings, land, electricity, water - everything, all spent on doing business that didn't contribute. Didn't generate energy, produce food, provide medicine, education, transport, entertainment. Just basically doing nothing but moving money from place to place. You couldn't argue with the logic of the Process - I couldn't, anyway. Not honestly. We - the world, this country - were on the verge of being desperately short of the things we needed to get by. If we were going to survive as a civilization, we had to start working collectively, efficiently. In the rich times, maybe, we could afford to have half the labour force of the nation working as lifestyle coaches and stockbrokers. In the times when food was imported for next to nothing, and there was a petrol station every hundred yards. But even then, the rich times were only rich for some, weren't they?"

"I suppose that's true."

"And these days we know - we've accepted at last - that we can't waste anything; labour, energy, raw materials, anything. No need for sales teams when goods are distributed primarily according to need, not desire." She smiled, again looking out of the window. "I was bloody good at it, though. And I did love being good at it."

"So, why the police?"

Catherine rolled her eyes. "My mum wanted me to retrain as a nurse. 'Always going to need nurses, with all the riots coming.'"

Greg laughed. "Cheerful woman, your mother?"

"Irish, rather religious - rather conservative. I've always held on to the fact that things never got anywhere near as bad as my mum kept predicting they would. It gives me a hopeful feeling about humanity, that does."

"You didn't fancy nursing?"

"God, no." She held a hand to her face; looked at him around it. "This is embarrassing but - well, I was very senior in my job, you know? In sales." She snorted. "Sounds ridiculous now. *Senior in sales.* I was once someone quite important in something that no longer exists and which didn't matter a toss when it did exist, but there you are. I was. And the idea of wearing a piss-proof tunic and trailing after doctors carrying rolls of bandages around - my ego couldn't face it."

"Ah," said Greg, and she could see that he knew where she was heading. He was an intuitive bloke - as a man as well as a copper - and that was one reason why she liked him so much, felt so relaxed in his company.

"The thing about the police," she confirmed, "is that it has a structure, a hierarchy. You start at the bottom, true, but then whatever I did next I was going to be starting at the bottom, despite my age and experience, because my experience was all in a now defunct trade. In theory, having started at the bottom, I could rise to the top. That was something to cling on to. Not something I'm very proud of."

"Nothing to be ashamed of - you wanted to make the best of your talents, nothing wrong with that. And the promotion boards have obviously agreed with you, Detective Sergeant."

"Right after I was made redundant, I went on one of those Defunct Professions Conversion courses that the government was running back then. It culminated in a jobs fair run by the Useful Occupations Board."

"Both of which organisations, presumably, are now themselves redundant."

"History takes no prisoners, true. Anyway, they asked what I was good at and I shrugged and said 'Selling.' And they said, no, that was your job, what you were good at, surely, was getting people to do what you want them to do."

Good job the carriage wasn't full, they had a fair bit of privacy, because the DI was starting a laugh which he really didn't look capable of containing. "And so they suggested you - "

"They suggested I call in at the police recruiting stand."

Laughter felled them both for a few minutes. Eventually, Greg said, "I'm not sure that's exactly the idea of the police service that we're trying to get across to the public - 'We persuade you to do things.'"

"It's not quite as snappy as Protect and Serve, is it?" Catherine agreed.

Still no report on the bike, lost or stolen. The Loftys were in rare unison: something interesting was going on here. Unless the bloke was just on holiday.

On the tram-ride over to the hospital, their conversation turned again to the original puzzle; not the new bicycle, but the old junk.

'Junk' was, of course, a word out of its time; a relict. Every scrap of everything was precious nowadays: national survival depended on not wasting anything. Most things could no longer be replaced easily or cheaply - some things couldn't be replaced at all, such as anything which required imported materials that were no longer easily obtained, or which involved prohibitively expensive expenditures of energy in its manufacture.

In the old days, total recycling itself would have been prohibitively expensive, in terms of labour-intensiveness; and reusing consumer goods has an inevitable deflationary effect in a profit-based system, as it leads to lower consumption, lower profits, lower employment, lower consumption, in a self-reinforcing cycle. If recycling had ever really caught on under the old system, as the old Lofty was fond of pointing out, the result would have been the deepest and most fundamental recession the planet had ever seen. But now, things were run according to a different accounting, and anything which conserved scarce resources was worth doing.

Point being: there was no such thing as junk. There wasn't a National Museum of Crap, because nothing was crap any more. So where did all that stuff in the pond come from?

One Lofty suggested that the debris had fallen through a time loop. The other one appeared not to hear this theory, instead offering his own: that some old hoarder had just died, and the relatives who cleared out his basement, loft and garage couldn't be bothered to go through the proper channels.

"Seems fantastically unlikely though, surely?" said the young one. "In those circumstances, all you've got to do is call up the Re, and they come and collect everything you don't want. You don't even have to sort it - they do that for you. It's what people in your day used to call the granny state."

"Nanny state."

The young one frowned. "What's the difference? A nan's the same as a gran, surely?"

The old one searched inside himself to discover if he had, firstly, the energy to frame an explanation of the meaning of the old cliche - and then, secondly, the energy to deliver it in such a way that it could be understood by someone as young and impatient as Lofty. It was when he heard himself say "Yeah, you're right: granny state. Carry on," that he realised the answer must be No.

"Thank you. Thing is, the dumping-it-in-a-pond option is actually more trouble than calling the Re. You've got to pack it all up in a donkey cart or whatever, take it to the pond, unload it and heave it into the water."

"All without being seen."

"Well, that's the other bit, isn't it? You're running the risk of getting arrested, plus you're throwing away the money that you would have been paid for the stuff if you'd recycled it. There's just no possible way that makes sense."

"And that's before we get to the hospital accountant's brand new bike," the other one agreed.

Kieran Rider was a large man, tall and well-built, and the fact that his office at the hospital was rather small made him seem even larger. He became a nervous big man when the Loftys introduced themselves as detectives from the Serious Crimes Squad.

"What is this all about? Has something happened?"

"Don't worry, sir," the older Lofty assured him. "It's good news, not bad news."

Still nervous, but now puzzled as well, the accountant said: "Good news?"

"That's right, sir - we've found your bicycle."

Was Rider acting now, Lofty wondered; he seemed entirely baffled. But bafflement was one of the easier states to fake. "I don't use a bicycle, officer. I only live a few minutes away from work."

"You don't ever use a bicycle for leisure, for visiting friends or family, doing the shopping ... ?"

"I'm not much of a cyclist, I'm afraid. I prefer public transport, it's so reliable these days."

"Well, this is a bit worrying," said the older Lofty, faking the facial symptoms of mild worry with practised ease. "You see, the bicycle we're recovered was bought on a debit card registered to you, and your details were given, by the purchaser, for the guarantee registration."

"It looks," said the other Lofty, "as if you may have been the victim of identity theft."

There was a pause before Rider answered. Not a long pause by any means, but long enough to confirm the Loftys' belief that they were onto something here. "Oh!" The accountant raised his hands to shoulder level, faking the signs of suddenly catching on to what someone was talking about, and not faking them terribly well. "Oh, *that* bike. Oh dear, oh no, that was stolen? How awful. I bought it as a birthday present for my girlfriend. I had no idea it had been stolen - that's terrible. But you say you got it back anyway? Well, that's great news."

"Oddly," said a Lofty, "your girlfriend has yet to report the bicycle as missing."

"Really? That's ... actually, I think she might have been away for a couple of days. Probably doesn't even know. Is it much damaged?"

"Damaged? Not really - I expect it'll brush up OK."

"Great." He clapped his hands together. "Well, if you'd like to leave it here, I'll make sure it gets back to her."

"Ah," said Lofty, faking the expression which conveyed regret.

"Can't do that, I'm afraid," said the other Lofty. "Since by your own account it no longer belongs to you - it belongs to your girlfriend."

"But I paid for it. As you know."

"Yes, sir, but you see a gift given is title transferred. It now belongs to her, so we'll have to return it to her. We'll need her details."

This time the pause was longer, and correspondingly less convincing. "I'm not sure I'd like to give you her details - she's a bit of a privacy nut. I don't means she's a beefeater or anything, but she's rather a civil liberties type."

"I see, sir."

"Yes, yes ... that's ... well, perhaps if I take your details instead, and ring her and get her to come in and pick it up. Would that be all right?"

The Loftys looked at each other and nodded. That would be better than all right; that would be perfect. "That should be OK, sir," said the older one, sounding a little doubtful.

"But you'll have to come with her," said the younger one, "so as to give a statement saying that the bike is hers. Seeing as it's still in your name."

Kieran Rider sat down. He stood up. He half sat down again, but aborted the procedure at a late stage and instead scratched his left knee with his right hand. The Loftys got the impression that the big man was not used to thinking quickly under pressure, otherwise he would probably have been able to do it with greater economy of movement.

"Right," he said. He sat down. "Right - yes, right, we'll arrange that, then. I'll arrange that. Thank you. Is that all?"

"We'll leave you in peace, sir. Thanks for your help."

Once they were outside Rider's office, the older Lofty paused, signalled *Sssh* with his finger, and put his ear against the door. After a second or two he shook his head. "No good. Soundproofed. Pity - I'd have liked to hear the phone call I strongly suspect Mr Rider is making at the moment."

"To his girlfriend?"

"Could be, could be."

"How about this," said the younger one. "The bike was a gift for his girlfriend, and she's chucked it in the pond in a fit of temper because they've broken up. Simple as that. That's why he's being so shifty - he's embarrassed. Maybe the girlfriend's married. Or the accountant is."

"Who knows everything that goes on in a hospital?" the older one said, before answering his own question. "The gardener, that's who. Everyone chats to the gardener, don't they? You can't chat to the ear specialist unless you know something about ears, but everyone has an opinion on gardening - even if it's only that the weather's no good. Let's go and have a chat with the gardener."

"About the weather?"

"Certainly, my young colleague. About the weather. No law against that."

In point of fact, Greg wasn't all that keen on mottos. This train, for instance; he'd noticed the wording on its nose when they'd boarded it. Because British Railways was owned by the nation as a whole, and managed on behalf of parliament by an elected board of passengers and workers, its trains carried the seal of the Co-operative Commonwealth of Great Britain, complete with its borrowed motto:

IN THINGS ESSENTIAL, UNITY
IN THINGS DOUBTFUL, LIBERTY
IN ALL THINGS, FRATERNITY

- borrowed, as Greg had always understood it, from the co-operative movement in the old USA, of the beginning of the twentieth century. But a DCI he knew in South London Serious Crime swore that it was in fact an even older Protestant slogan. And Greg had never cared enough either way to look it up.

And he couldn't argue with the sentiments, it wasn't that - it was as neat a summary of how most harmoniously to run a co-op, a state, a police squad, a family, as he had ever heard. He just didn't like mottos. Perhaps partly because he had entered the police at a time when the service had been so busily engaged in what was then called rebranding - new logos, new liveries, new typefaces, and, yes, new mottos - that it had spent millions of pounds from its already reddened budget on public relations consultants, whereas at his first nick no-one had ever managed to get the showers to produce hot water. The language of priorities, an old sergeant had once told him, is certainly not the religion of public relations. He'd cared enough to look that one up, and it had stuck.

Somewhere around Exeter, after another beer and as she leant across to take a light from his match, Catherine asked him: "What do you make of it all, then, Greg? I've never really heard you say."

The question surprised him. He'd always thought of her as not really interested in politics; just interested in practicalities. She was a very practical person, he thought - one of the best sergeants he'd ever worked with. Not dull or cold - not excessively practical in any pejorative sense - but one of those lucky people whose minds always automatically sought to grind rocks into flour; situations into solutions. Actually, *rocks into flour* - that wouldn't be much use, would it? Rocks into mineral dust fertiliser, that'd be better.

He had rarely, if ever, heard her express a political opinion, he thought. Except on that armoury business, the petition thing, that was the one big exception, and even then he thought her strong feelings came more from a sort of rugged pedantry: if the armoury belongs to the people's militia, then it ought to belong to them properly.

She was a supporter of the Process, he thought, simply because it offered, as far as her practical mind could see, the only immediately available means by which her civilization might survive. In fact, now that he came to think of it, sometime last year they'd been interviewing some bloke who'd evidently fancied himself as something of a bar-room lawyer, but of a specialist stripe: a self-taught and self-appointed constitutional expert. And that guy had quoted something at them. Greg had looked that one up, as well, he'd thought it was worth noting, and he could pretty much remember it now: "There is no everlasting principle in government, as to any one particular form. For, the rules and reasons of government cannot be always the same, it depending upon future contingents; and therefore must be alterable according to the variety of emergent circumstances and accidents; so that no certain form can be prescribed at all times, seeing that which may be most commendable at one time, may be most condemnable at another."

The suspect - who really did fancy himself, Greg recalled - had sat back smugly and said "You know who wrote that? Marchamont Nedham, in 1657."

To which Catherine had replied. "I take his point, but he was a long-winded old bugger, wasn't he? I prefer Alexander Pope. We did him at school: 'For forms of Government let fools contest; What e're is best administered is best.'"

It had been a Pyrrhic victory. They'd been working on opening up this bloke for two days, but he was so disgusted at being out-quoted by a middle-aged copper that from that moment on he'd never said another word.

But Catherine's pragmatism had impressed itself on Greg; that she was so wedded to pragmatism that she even wanted it expressed in as boiled-down, unfancy a form as possible. And now here she was, sitting on a train, asking him his political views?

The irony was, when Greg was a youth talking politics was taboo. Or perhaps not even taboo, just something no-one had any interest in. Today, it was more or less considered impolite - *Injurious to Practicality*, perhaps - not to talk about politics, in its practical and philosophical, timely and timeless aspects. Ginger assured him it had been much the same in the 1940s: people talk about what matters to them. At times that might be what's on TV, and at times it might be the constitution. No subject is inherently interesting or dull; it largely depends on how much you've got to eat. Context is everything, always.

On the whole, as it happened, Greg's view was not too distant from Catherine's. It went something like this:

The beginning of this century had provided Britain - and the world, probably, but it was the British bit of the world that was Greg's concern - with both a necessity and an opportunity. We had a necessity to fundamentally change the way we organised our lives; and we had an opportunity to fundamentally change the way we organised our lives. The latter having been enabled by the existence of the former. In other words, if you've got to do something, you might as well do it. Now, that was a decent enough motto.

Or: if we need to change everything in order to ensure our survival, then while we're at it, let's see if we can't find a way of ending up - against all odds and predictions - actually *better* off than we were before the emergency arose.

And all in all, as Greg looked around the country today, and looked around, in his memory, the country of his childhood and young manhood, he was cautiously pleased with the modern version.

One example: he'd been trying to explain to Hugo, his eleven-year-old son, what unemployment was. It had come up at school, in an economics project. Hugo was a bright enough kid, but Greg just hadn't been able to get the concept over to him, any more than his teachers had. Hugo couldn't imagine a situation where there wasn't any more work that needed doing - and if there was work that needed doing, then surely they'd get the unemployed people doing that and ... well, they wouldn't be unemployed any more, would they? He couldn't really get past that unassailable logic.

Greg himself struggled a bit, to be honest. He'd never studied economics, but he just about knew enough to know that under a profit-led system it was necessary, in certain periods of the economic cycle, to keep a reservoir of unemployed workers so as to regulate labour costs. But he was buggered if he could express that to himself, let alone to an eleven-year-old, in a way that didn't make the old world sound completely insane. And it hadn't been, that was the point: it was a world that had served its purpose more or less adequately for hundreds of years, before running out of history.

It had been a frustrating conversation - but also an inspiring one. If Hugo's generation found the very concept of unemployment inexplicably crazy - not just morally wrong, or socially undesirable, but absolutely mad beyond words - then surely they'd never let it happen again?

What Greg actually said to Catherine in reply to her question was: "Oh, you know, I'm just a copper. I just get on with it."

He could have kicked himself - kicked and punched and gouged himself - when he saw the hurt disappointment in her eyes.

CHAPTER EIGHT

Not all that keen on schools, really, Bob Lemon; not all that comfortable in them, even now.

It wasn't that his own schooldays had left him scarred with awful memories. It was just that his main memory was of spending more than a dozen years being constantly told to stop talking at the back. Talking at the back, of course, was the one thing at school he did really well. He'd have talked at the front if they'd let him, quite happily, he wasn't fixated on the back. But schools, in his day and in his memory at least, were places where silence was the goal, if not the norm, and *Shut up* was the answer to almost every question.

It was some satisfaction to him, in adult life, that he had been proved right and the school ethos had been proved wrong. Talking - at the back, or anywhere else - had proven to be his vocation, his source of bread and purpose. Why was he here today, in this school, but to chat? He was getting paid for it, and he had never yet in his adult life had occasion to speak German or operate a Bunsen burner. Vindication.

He'd heard that school had changed a lot since his day, to be fair. And some of the curriculum did seem a bit more interesting, at least.

Bradley Nottle's head of department was a friendly-looking Welshman in his thirties, who introduced himself as "Yeatman, Head of Food." It was years since Bob had met someone who only gave their surname by way of introduction, and he was a bit taken aback. Perhaps Mr Yeatman thought that using two names would be contrary to efficiency? Or perhaps it was vanity: I'm so good they named me once.

"Sounds a fine job title, Mr Yeatman," he said.

"Grand enough, isn't it?" Yeatman agreed. "In line with the modern philosophy of schools being part of the community, sown into the fabric of life in all directions rather than, as you might recall from your own schooldays, mere isolation units for unproductive young humans, the Head of Food is in ultimate charge of all aspects of edible matter at the school. The head gardener reports to me, as does the cook, and the provisioner, as well as all those teaching staff whose subjects are food related - cooking, preserving, growing, and the more academic food-related subjects. My own speciality is plain fruit storage."

"Plain?"

"Ah! In our jargon that means not pickled, frozen, dried, and so on."

Bob wondered about that. To preserve fruit 'plain,' didn't one just stick it on a shelf in the garage, wrapped in newspaper? It didn't seem polite to say so, though, and, of course, there must be much more to it than that, he didn't doubt - just as there were so many fruits around these days that he'd never heard of in his youth. And some imported ones that were common when he was a kid and rare these days. Mind, when Bob was young you didn't need to store fruit through the winter. You could buy it from the supermarket all year round. His granny, who had memories of the shortages of World War Two, used to make a point in her latter years of going out on Christmas morning to buy a punnet of strawberries at the convenience store - just because she could. To her, it was a matter of pride - it was a symbol of survival and victory; they'd won the war, they'd lived through the austerity that followed, and here they were, able to buy any fruit known to man on any day of the year, all from the one shop which was just a short car journey away. He was glad she hadn't lived into the new times; what his generation saw as a symbol of survival - seasonal and local eating - hers would have seen simply as a surrender, a step backward, a delayed defeat.

"Fancy that," he said. "The subjects studied by school kids have certainly changed. I myself did a year of Sociology A Level, before I chucked it in and went to work. My secondary school did offer Latin, in which it was quite unusual, but it didn't offer Fruit Storing."

"Ah yes," said Yeatman, "but what did your grandparents think of you studying sociology? They'd barely heard of it, had they? Every generation's the same, since I suppose the beginning of industrialisation - new subjects to suit the times, which the oldies think are a lot of nonsense, and 'Why don't they go back to teaching what they taught when I were a nipper, it never did me any harm.' The only difference is that in the past, subjects were tailored to the needs of employers - of profit in other words, if not always very successfully. Now they're tailored to the needs of the nation."

"Successfully?"

Yeatman gave this question serious consideration. "There is still a time lag, inevitably. Needs rise faster than the education system could possibly respond, even if it had infinite resources and zero bureaucratic obstacles. But it's not bad, and it's getting better - as in so many areas, massively increased devolution of powers, the huge national emphasis on democratisation of every aspect of life, makes things much more accurately responsive to what people actually need."

"I suppose so."

"They're the ones doing the choosing, so they're more likely to choose what they really want. On the other hand, endless consultation takes time. Though not, I suspect, any longer than it did when we lived in a purely representative democracy, and only the politically elect did the pondering. Consultation expands to fill the time available for it, I suspect, under whatever system."

Yeatman led him through a series of corridors. Bob assumed they had some destination in view. "This wasn't built as a school?"

Yeatman laughed. "Spotted that, did you? No, it was requisitioned. Used to be a call centre, I believe, for a bank or an insurance company. Like almost all such buildings, it became redundant as the casino economy was steadily rationalised."

"I gather you're a supporter of the Process," said Bob.

"Well, good God, aren't you? How, in a country struggling to survive and become secure, could you justify having more than one bank or insurance company - how could you justify building new houses on green or brown sites, when some high streets had three or four buildings, all offering the same services? Madness."

Now, there was just the one, national, state-owned banking and insurance company. More sensible, obviously, though Bob had heard arguments against this from radical co-operators, who supported what they called non-excessive competition, arguing that even patriotic monopolies must be subject to institutional sclerosis - bureaucracy, empire building, complacency, even corruption. And it was a debate that continued. He mentioned some of this to the Head of Food.

"True, that's fair, they may have a point. But who but the most extreme beefeater would want to return to the old days, with premises and functions endlessly duplicated? Remember how the shortage of buildings, commercial and residential, disappeared almost overnight? I don't see how any sane person could argue against that."

There spoke a teacher, thought Bob; as far as he could recall, he never had met one who thought that 'any sane person' could disagree with them on anything. As a police officer, Bob acknowledged that so many things about the new ways, great and small, made his job easier than it had been before. People tended to live and work and go to school locally, and so spent their lives in genuine communities. Neighbours knew each other, which meant that, for coppers, door-to-door enquiries were more rewarding than they had been for many decades. And, of course, crime itself was reduced by the fact that people knew each other, and where each other lived: robbing strangers had always been easier to get away with than robbing acquaintances.

The mass requisitioning of redundant buildings, like this one, for useful social amenities had led to one of the minor, but significant, ways in which pressure had been taken off the police. For some reason, former estate agent's shops seemed to have been mostly turned into public lavatories. There were now, in contrast to Bob's earliest days on the beat, such conveniences plentifully provided in every town and suburb, fully staffed, properly maintained, always open night and day. To the ordinary citizen, this was either a pleasant improvement or a scandalous waste of resources, depending on point of view - and perhaps state of bladder. But to a policeman, it was a blessed relief, given the effect that public pissing, and worse, used to have on public order and confidence, and on police time, especially on Friday nights and in the vicinity of pubs.

"That's why it takes bloody ages to get anywhere," Yeatman explained. "The building not being designed as a school, I mean. You never seem to be able to go in the direction you want to go, and nobody ever knows where anything is. Bloody irritating. But we are hoping to move into a purpose-refurbed new school down the road within a couple of years."

At length, they emerged from the maze. Bob was disappointed to find that the shelves in Yeatman's office held only books and papers, and no pears wrapped in newsprint.

"I'm assuming," said Yeatman, having cleared a seat for the DC, "that this is about poor Brad Nottle. I heard on the news that you'd identified his body."

"I'm afraid so. At the moment, we have very little idea how he might have ended up dead in his garden - "

"Didn't bury himself, though, did he?"

"Probably not. So, we need to know something about his background, what sort of person he was, whether he seemed to have any worries in recent weeks, and generally - "

"And about the state of his marriage," said Yeatman. "There was no mention of Mrs Nottle on the news. I imagine her relationship with Brad will be of especial interest?"

"Anything along those lines," said Bob, his voice as neutral as he could make it, "would be most helpful."

"And confidential, as to source?"

"Certainly."

The teacher stretched his lips across his teeth, in a grimace which suggested one about to perform an unpleasant duty. "You'd better get your notebook out, Mr Lemon."

The guv'nor had made an error with this horse business, Gerard had reckoned. Potentially. He was a good DI, one of the best Gerard had worked with in a long career, but when you came down to it - good bosses? That just meant they made good mistakes.

Gerard's worry was this: how could young Erin be taught to appreciate the importance, and perhaps even the esoteric joys, of the really boring bits of police work - such as this lot, today - when all she can think of is getting on her bloody horse and trotting off on some glamorous errand?

But as the shift went on, he began to think he'd maybe underestimated the kid. She wasn't casting longing looks towards the stable; instead, she seemed absolutely riveted by the task of sitting in the squad office, phoning up armouries all round London, in an ever-spreading radius of Beech Lane, asking if they've mislaid a rifle.

That warmed Gerard's old cockles. Face it, if she was riveted by a task as fucking dull and fruitless as this one, then she was a detective. Not potentially, not perhaps: no escape, she was a detective and she'd better get used to the idea.

During a break in the tedious phone calls, to compare lack of progress, she asked him what happened if they got negative replies from every armoury in London. He gave her a look which he hoped said *You can work that out for yourself.* "If we get no joy from London, then we tackle the south east. And then the south ... "

"Or maybe the east?" Erin suggested.

"Then the midlands, the north, south Wales, north Wales, southern Scotland ... "

There was, of course, a centralised procedure for reporting armoury losses. It was possible for a gun to become *actually* lost during exercises; fallen in a deep river, perhaps. Gerard had never heard of one being stolen, as such, because it would be too bloody obvious who had stolen it: the citizen who had signed his name in the book as taking out spitfire number 1917/1959 would need a pretty good story if he came back without it. In theory, he supposed a gang could steal a rifle from someone on exercises; but again, in practice this was unlikely - they didn't exactly allow militia members to wander around on their own clutching their rifles in their little pink hands.

Anyway, they'd checked with the MoD, and no - no rifle had been reported missing anywhere in the country. So, Erin had asked, why were they still checking?

"Because all systems are run by humans, or computers, or a mixture of the two," Gerard explained. "All humans make mistakes, and all computers are heaps of crap."

"Oh, is that a technical term? I was never much good at computer science at school."

"You'd have liked it when I started in CID," he told her. "There was one computer, and they kept it in a special room of its own at HQ. It had its own staff to run it - all women, I remember. I think they reckoned men were too rough."

"Delicate machinery, was it? All glass valves and wires made out of cats' whiskers?"

"Couldn't tell you. I never saw it. You had to be Inspector rank or above to get out of the lift on the same floor as the computer room."

"You've sort of seen the rise and fall, then," she said.

He smiled wickedly in agreement. "We beat the little buggers."

"What they said at school was the main motive during the era of mass computerisation was reducing labour costs, not increasing efficiency. So a company would replace its workers with computers, even if it made their service less efficient - because it increased profit. But since, now, we're interested in efficiency, not profit, that's why computers are only used where they're needed."

He nodded. "You can believe that if you choose, Erin. The truth is, the little buggers tried to take over, and we beat them."

She smiled. "I thought it must be something like that. Our computer teacher wasn't much good."

"The point being," Gerard said, "a Spitfire rifle *has* been used in a murder, even though the system says there isn't one missing. Accounting systems can be wrong - bullets can't. If your dog gets killed by a bear it's no good saying 'But there aren't bears around here.' You've still got to bury your dog."

"Unless the bear eats it."

He shook his head. "Bears are fussy," he said. "You'd still have to bury its bum."

"If it turns out that the gun didn't come from any armoury, could it have come direct from the factory - a crooked worker smuggling it out and selling it perhaps?"

"Great minds think alike," he said, which he thought was a good way of not saying to a keen young student "Believe it or not we did think of that." So much of success in detective work depended precisely on people stating the obvious over and over, and always assuming that everyone else had not thought of it. Nine hundred and ninety-nine times they had, of course, but on the thousandth occasion everyone else in the room went "Shit, of course, that's it!" and they all rushed off to make the arrests. Stating the obvious without shyness or apology was a hard, counterintuitive habit to acquire, and he had often seen it tragically beaten out of promising youngsters over the years by sarky veterans. "Great minds think alike - DI Wallace had the very same idea. But the factory also says they have no missing guns, and as you might expect they are confident of their security procedures."

She opened her mouth and frowned, as if about to come up with something else. Then the phones started ringing, two at once - armoury deputies from the suburbs returning their calls - and Erin and Gerard got back to work.

Having booked into the bed and breakfast in St. Ives, Greg and Catherine walked to the local police station and introduced themselves to the officer with whom they'd liased on the phone, DC Vaughan.

She assured them that Kim Nottle's relatives - a retired couple, named McFarlane - having been identified through records, had been located and placed under discreet surveillance.

"No sign so far," she added, "of anyone matching Mrs Nottle's description has been seen. You said you've no photograph of the missing woman?"

"We haven't yet," said Greg, remembering the near-empty house in Beech Lane, "and the reason we haven't is a bit of tale in itself."

"Good - then why don't you both join me for a traditional, Cornish fish and chip supper, courtesy of our hospitality budget? Unless you want to go straight over to the McFarlanes' house?"

"No, we'll leave that until it's dark, I think. Fish and chips would be just the job - many thanks."

"How does a traditional, Cornish fish and chips differ from a non-Cornish fish and chips?" asked Catherine.

"Comes with clotted cream," said DC Vaughan. "How could you not guess that?"

"This, you understand, is not the sort of thing one would normally talk about behind a colleague's back," said Mr Yeatman.

"Naturally," Bob Lemon agreed. "But when the colleague has been murdered ... "

"Well, quite. Quite so."

Yeatman exhaled noisily, looked at the floor and then at the ceiling, and interlaced his fingers. You'd be able to pick out his professional calling from fifty yards away, in a blizzard, Bob thought.

"I got the impression," said Yeatman, "and the on-dit here in school was certainly supportive of this impression, that the Nottle marriage was far from happy."

"Do you have any ideas about the source of the unhappiness?"

"Yes. Yes, I believe I have. Quite simply, she wanted to move, and he didn't."

"Move house?"

"Move house. They'd lived in that house since, if I remember correctly, 1998."

"Long time."

"Long time. Yet I understand, you see, that this had been meant to be a temporary arrangement - "

"Understand from ...?"

"Well, from Mrs Nottle - from Kim. I only met her once or twice. They didn't come to many school functions as a couple."

"Is that unusual?"

"Not unknown. Not everyone's marriage is an idyll. But, obviously, if you're a teacher you are expected to play a pretty full part in the life of the school and the community, and in general the spouse does too. Sometimes he or she has a job, or other commitments, that make that less possible, of course - but, well, every now and then you get one who just doesn't *want* to."

"And that was Kim?"

Yeatman smiled. Teachers always smiled, Bob remembered, when they had tricked you into giving the expected wrong answer. "No - no, I don't think so. I got the impression - " The teacher interrupted himself. "All this, I must caution you, is from one night at a Christmas party, two years ago, when she got rather drunk and did a bit of unburdening to whoever happened to be standing nearest, which happened to be me."

"So this is first-hand information? That's very valuable."

"Well, it's mostly first-hand, with a bit of my impressions and a sprinkling of the aforementioned on-dit. But even where it is first-hand, it is, let us bear in mind, the first-hand testimony of a drunk, unhappy woman, talking to someone she hardly knew."

Fair enough, thought Bob. This bloke would make a good witness. If a slightly tiring one. "Understood. Invaluable to us all the same, especially until we are able to talk to Kim herself."

"Good. Now, I was saying: I don't think it was her that didn't want to take part in school life - I think it was him. Brad. He didn't want *her* taking part, you understand? He didn't want them taking part as a couple. She seemed quite devoted to him, but he was somewhat cold and almost contemptuous to her. He brought her along to the absolute minimum of functions he could without it turning into a staff-room talking-point."

"And on this particular drunken night - "

Yeatman held up his hands, and chuckled. "Not an orgy, Detective Constable, I assure you! A very seemly, rather dull, staff do. Kim, Mrs Nottle, told me how she hated that house, had always hated that house, how it held only bad memories for her - "

"What did she mean, could you tell?"

Yeatman stroked his chin, and pondered a moment. "I suppose I just guessed that she hadn't got on with the granny, perhaps? You know that it was Brad's grandmother who - "

"Left him the house, yes."

"Or that the old woman had died hard - a long illness, perhaps - and maybe Kim had found that difficult to expunge from the house. Or it might simply have been that it just wasn't the sort of place - a boring, suburban street, in those days, mostly full of old people - where a relatively young couple, as they would have been then, would have found much fun."

Bob read over his notes. "So, she gave the impression she'd never wanted to live there, had always wanted to get out?"

"Absolutely."

"And that Brad was against moving?"

"Absolutely *refused* to move - wouldn't talk about it. And that his refusal to do so poisoned their marriage. It was, I felt, a trapped, unhappy union. They had no children, you know. No particular friends, as far as I could see, not much social or civic life."

Well, thought Bob: was Kim desperate to move because she knew there was a body under the drive? Or did Brad refuse to move because he knew there was a body under the drive? And the other thing he thought, was - we've been talking for half an hour, you'd think it wouldn't kill a man, even a teacher, to offer me a biscuit.

*

"Hope you don't mind me asking," said the older Lofty.

"Not at all," said the hospital gardener, a middle-aged Yorkshireman, who had random tufts of grey hair bouncing out from beneath his camouflage cap. "Not at all, mate - I'm very glad. People should do a lot more asking if you ask me. People don't ask enough. In general, I mean, as a rule. How do you learn except by asking? That's how I learned all this lot." He gestured around him at the neat and bounteous beds of produce. "I didn't learn it by keeping my mouth shut, did I?"

"I'm willing to believe that," said Lofty.

"That young'un of yours." The gardener squinted at the other Lofty. "I'll bet he never asks you anything, does he?"

"Never asks me a thing," Lofty agreed. "Tells me plenty, mind."

"Exactly. How do they think they're going to learn? They don't want to learn, the youngsters. You and me, we went through the hard times, we know the value of knowledge. You ask me anything you like, mate. If I know it, you're welcome to it."

"Urine," said Lofty.

The Yorkshireman nodded. "Now, you've asked the right bloke," he said.

The younger Lofty excused himself, and went a few yards away to blow his nose.

"The thing is," said the older Lofty, "my neighbour says he uses all the urine from his urine trap on his compost heaps - to heat them up, like."

"Fair enough. No better compost activator than urine." The gardener scowled. "It used to break my heart, knowing all the millions of gallons of perfectly good piss that were flushed away every day in the old times."

"Ah," said Lofty, "yes, but - what about during the winter? When the heap's quiet? Surely there's no point in pouring pint after pint onto a cold heap?"

"No, you don't want to overdo it, that's true enough."

"So what do you do with the contents of your urine trap? In the cold weather?"

The gardener looked at him as if he were mad. "Sell it, of course. Sell it to the Re. They use it in the textile industry, I believe, like they did in the nineteenth century."

"Sure, but I've got another friend - he has the plot next to mine on the allotments - who says he uses it as a liquid fertiliser. He stores it up in a big drum, and then in the summer, he feeds all his nitrogen-hungry crops with it."

"Not bad. It'll do quite nicely." The gardener shrugged. "Mind, I'd rather sell mine, and make a tea out of horse dung for a fertiliser. There's no shortage of horse dung in this city. Donkeys, too."

"Well, what I wanted to ask you was - if I did want to try it out as a feed, what's the rate of dilution? My mate says half and half, but it stinks."

"Half and half? Half water and half urine? It will stink! No, one part urine to twenty parts rainwater, that's your recipe."

"Brilliant," said Lofty. "That's marvellous. Many thanks. I'll tell him. His wife might even let him back in the house." He rolled two cigarettes, one for himself and one for the gardener. "I bet you know everything that goes on around here don't you? I'll bet you know everyone, in your job."

The gardener took a long drag, then patted Lofty on the shoulder. "Right then. That's good advice I've given you about the urine trap, and if you've any sense you'll write it down in your notebook. But now we'll get down to the real business, shall we? Who is it you're investigating?"

Lofty didn't bother looking abashed. He'd got bored with that decades ago. "We're not actually investigating anyone," he began.

"Not much use as detectives then, are you?"

This bit was legally tricky, Lofty reflected. The accountant was not a suspect; was not considered in danger. But Lofty reckoned he'd worked out a form of words that should cover them. "No, in fact we've just been talking to a colleague of yours, about returning some lost property."

"That's nice."

"Yes, guy called Kieran Rider, hospital accountant. I expect you know him?"

"Go on, then."

Oh well, thought Lofty: in for a penny. Pun intended. "Keen cyclist, is he?"

The Yorkshireman shook his head. "Nope. Never seen him on a bike. Too big and clumsy, I shouldn't wonder - he'd come straight off at the first corner."

"I dare say you're right," said Lofty. "What about his girlfriend? She a cyclist?"

"He's single."

"Completely single?"

"Very single. Never seen him with a woman. Or a man. Not in that way. Never heard him mention a girlfriend."

"How confident of that are you?" Lofty asked.

"Oh, you can take my word for it," the gardener promised him. "If I say I know something about somebody, I know it. I have a very good memory." He picked up the handles of his wheelbarrow, and turned to leave, adding: "Plus, I am the nosiest old bastard you've met this year."

Surveillance of the McFarlanes' house in St. Ives was being carried out by a specialist team from County - necessarily, since these days local officers tended to be known faces to the residents of their areas. It was for this reason also that DC Vaughan didn't accompany Catherine and Greg all the way; she walked them to the end of the McFarlanes' street and left them to it.

A few doors down, on the other side of the road, from the house where Kim Nottle's relatives lived - and where, perhaps, Kim herself might currently be residing - two council workmen were doing something methodical to a storm drain. Catherine and Greg, themselves dressed in waterproof overalls, stopped for a chat.

"Morning, sir," said one of the drain men.

"How's it going?" Greg asked.

"I have a horrible feeling we're going to leave this worse than what we found it. If they get flooded in this street come August, I'm going to ask for a transfer."

"You're not actually *doing* anything to the drain, surely?" asked Catherine.

"Nothing useful," the officer assured her. "But it's near impossible to do absolutely nothing and make it look convincing. So we just keep undoing things and doing them up again, over and over. From a distance, looks like we know what we're doing."

"Which we don't," said the other half of the surveillance team.

"No sign of your target, by the way. Just the ordinary comings and goings of a retired couple."

"No?" said Greg. "Pity. Could she have arrived here before we asked for surveillance, and stayed in there all the time, out of sight?"

"Heat sensors suggest there's only two people in there - but we haven't been able to get round the rear side without attracting attention, the gardens here are back to back. So, yeah, it's possible she could be in a room at the back of the house. But if she is, she's literally never leaving it. I mean, literally: not to go to the loo, have a wash, go to the kitchen, walk round the garden. That would mean, presumably, that the occupiers know she's hiding, rather than just visiting. In which case, they are very good indeed at acting calm."

"You don't think she's there?"

Both surveillance men shook their heads. "Not yet," said one of them.

Greg thought about it. "OK, thanks. I reckon if there's still no sign in the morning, we'll go in anyway."

"Excellent. By then, we should have arsed up this storm drain good and proper."

CHAPTER NINE

Yesterday had been another long day, rushing around for the most part doing nothing. But in police work, she knew, doing nothing wasn't always the same as achieving nothing. It just felt like it. Come to that, even doing nothing wasn't the same as doing nothing - they'd been busy all day, there'd hardly been a moment when they hadn't been doing something, somewhere, or been on the way to do it somewhere else. It was just that all the busyness they were doing was essentially nothing.

A hurried Chinese meal - Phil had insisted on paying for them both, a curious traditional penalty of rank Dahlia had always struggled to understand; it wasn't as if she'd stayed late as a favour to him, it was her job - and then they'd set off to their respective beds, Phil on his speedy bike, her in a covered tricycle taxi with deep, padded seats and a perfectly-angled neck rest.

And now, not nearly enough hours later, here she was again. The great thing about cases where the victim was known to be already dead was that you didn't really have to rush around and clock up enough in-lieus to take you through to the next century; you didn't have to feel guilty about every minute spent eating breakfast or cleaning your teeth, as if it were stolen from a terrified little girl. Dahlia would rather be on the murder, and she tried not to blame Phil for the fact that she wasn't.

This morning, he wasn't talking about Americans. It had been a strange episode, that whole business with the ponytailed witness. Phil had seemed so discomfited in his presence, as if meeting an anti-Yank Yank upset his entire view of the universe. But as soon as they'd left Austin Molloy's place, the DS had lit up with enthusiasm. They had a witness to back up the rescue theory; the fact that Phil couldn't bear to be in the same room as the witness was evidently irrelevant.

Dahlia, however thought - and said - that Molloy's account still looked like a coincidence to her. All right, it was *quite* a coincidence, but that didn't stop it being a coincidence. The course she'd done on patterning had been quite insistent on that point.

Dahlia also thought - and this she didn't say - that the US refugee seemed just about as blinded by anti-Americanism as was the DS. That, surely, undermined the value of his evidence. It was ironic, but just because something was ironic didn't mean it wasn't true. She hadn't learned that from a course; she'd learned that from reading books and watching TV, and from following the same non-league football club since her fourth birthday.

As the previous day had worn on, without any further sightings or soundings of mysterious Americans, Phil's excitement had ebbed. Dahlia was glad about that. As far as she could tell, he was a very good detective when he wasn't excited.

This morning, Phil kept coming back to this: how did they get the girl away? Of the options they had so far discussed, they had pretty much ruled out just two.

First, that Sarla had gone of her own accord. Still possible, of course, but if so how come nothing had been heard of her since? She would either have come home, been found wandering the streets or hiding, or have turned up dead or injured. No, she'd been taken. Everyone involved in the investigation accepted that now.

Secondly, that she was taken by motor vehicle. There were no reports from witnesses of any motor vehicle in the area anywhere near the kidnap time, and traffic police had no tracking of any MVs, legitimate or otherwise, in the area at the time.

So, how *did* they get her away? One thing seemed obvious: it must have been quick. Two adults could use shock and awe to overwhelm a child of her age - she would take a while to think of disobeying them against her natural instincts, especially if they were women, or if even one of them was - but fear would take over pretty quickly, and she would start crying or screaming or struggling. So they - the ones that took her - had to have her and be off in next to no time; get her almost instantly to somewhere where she could scream all she liked, or where they could take their time to subdue or sedate her.

She was dead, of course. They both thought that, but neither of them said it.

Phil had decided that they should walk the scene. He'd heard about how Greg had worked out how the furniture vanished from Beech Lane. Dahlia knew - everyone in the Squad knew, it wasn't a secret or anything - how much Phil admired DI Wallace's detective skills. He was hoping for some similar revelation in this case.

They started at Sarla's bedroom at home, because that was where she'd started from, according to her mother's statement, moments before her disappearance. Phil touched the door handle of the girl's room, as if this were a technicality he was obliged to observe, a rule in an arcane sporting event, which naturally you obeyed even if there was no umpire around to check.

From the landing, they walked downstairs and straight out of the front door. There was a moment when Dahlia felt herself go cold, fearful that the rules, *his* rules, might require Phil to call out "Bye, Mum, I'm going to Jodie's," but he didn't say anything until they were outside.

"Definitely the front door? You believe that?"

Dahlia shrugged. Sarla's disappearance - the how of it, anyway, if not the why - would have been a lot less puzzling if she'd gone out through the back door. She might have wriggled off through a gap in a hedge, and been gone in seconds into a world barred to adults by their ungainly size. "I must've asked the mum ten times, Sarge. Her story's consistent - she's certain she heard the front door go, not the back door. Plus, several people have confirmed that Sarla always went to Jodie's house via both their front doors."

So, into the front garden, full of cabbages and nasturtiums. Down the path, through the gate, turn left, a few paces down the pavement, in at the gate of the friend's house.

"Nowhere for her to be taken in that journey," said Phil.

"Nowhere convenient."

Dahlia agreed. "Not by a stranger, or someone she was afraid of."

But supposing Sarla had been taken during that short walk between front doors; assuming that she had, indeed, walked directly from her house to Jodie's house, had not wandered on a little further, following an interesting beetle or a roaming puppy or simply her own, inscrutable, infant thoughts ...

"No-one saw her," said Phil. "No-one looking out of the window, or weeding the garden, or heading off to the shops. So, let's say she was taken between hers and Jodie's. They're able somehow to overwhelm or reassure her for as long as it takes to get her to - where?"

Phil and Dahlia walked on, past the friend's front door, away from the Browns' house.

"How about," said Dahlia, "they bundled her, or tricked her, into the passenger seat of a covered trike - in there, someone is waiting to give her, I don't know, chloroform or something. All right, they can't zoom away as they would in a motor vehicle, all other forms of transport take time to accelerate, no matter what their eventual top speed. But at least they would be hidden from gaze, with a now acquiescent child."

Phil scowled. He wasn't convinced, and neither was Dahlia, really. She was just saying it out loud for the sake of thoroughness. "All that risks being overseen," said Phil. "Or going wrong - she might slip free, plus now she's screaming her head off in terror."

"I know."

"And in either case, the big disadvantage is the lack of acceleration you just mentioned. You can't get away quickly enough, with or without your prey - if you're seen, chances are you'll be caught."

They walked a while, but this part of the street offered no more helpful kidnapping spots than the stretch between Sarla's and Jodie's: no turn-offs, no sheds or handy buildings or hiding places.

"No," said Phil, as they retraced their steps. "If she went away by foot or in a non-motor vehicle then I think she has to have gone quietly. At least until they were a few streets away. That leaves two possibilities, in my mind. One is that she wandered much further, maybe right to the end of the road, without being seen by anyone. And I just don't think that's even vaguely likely."

"Me neither. And besides, it only postpones the question - where did she go after that? Why didn't someone see her?"

"Which lead to a surely inescapable conclusion," said Phil, and he looked at Dahlia, inviting her to finish his thought.

She nodded. "I don't think there's any doubt. She was taken by someone she knew and trusted."

When Greg, Catherine, and four local uniformed officers arrived to serve their search warrant, they found the McFarlanes watching TV coverage of the opening minutes of the final ODI between Afghanistan and Britain, live from Edinburgh.

The McFarlanes looked horrified, but not shocked; shaken, but not surprised. The search didn't take long; Kim Nottle was not on the premises, and the search team found nothing to suggest that she ever had been.

"We were expecting a visit from the police," Alicia McFarlane told Greg, "but we weren't expecting a search warrant."

"I'm sorry about that, but it was a necessary precaution. I'm sure the officers will be careful to return everything to its proper place."

"They'd better be," said Andrew McFarlane, with what Catherine took to be an attempt at a brave smile for his wife. "I know most of their parents."

The McFarlanes - second cousins of Kim Nottle, or once-removeds, or something; DC Vaughan had explained, but Catherine hadn't bother to retain the information - looked very much like what she knew them to be: a couple of retired professionals, in their seventies now, living out a no doubt hectic retirement by the sea.

"I'm not sure how much you know about what's been going on in Beech Lane?" said Greg.

"We heard on the news," Alicia replied, "that you had identified the second body, and that you were eager to speak to the wife. We took that to mean that the body was Brad's?"

"I'm afraid so."

"But no sign of Kim? No sign at all?"

Greg was quick to assure her. "Nothing at all to suggest she has come to any harm."

Andrew kissed his wife on the temple. "Well, that's good news, anyway, my love."

"It means she's a suspect, though, doesn't it?" said Alicia.

"Honestly, we just don't know. The only thing I can say for certain is that we desperately need to find her - whatever she's done, or had done to her."

"And the other body?" Alicia persisted. "You don't know who that is?"

"Still unidentified, I'm afraid."

Catherine could almost see the next question written on Alicia's forehead: *Did she kill them both?* But Andrew rubbed his wife's upper arm, with small, firm strokes, until, it seemed, the moment had passed.

Mr McFarlane turned his attention to Greg. "We've no idea where she is. I'm sorry - we'd tell you if we had, I can promise you that."

"I understand. Of course. Do you mind if we sit down?"

That simple, mechanical phrase broke the spell, as Catherine had seen it do so many times in her police career, in so many kitchens. Both McFarlanes started apologising for their manners, and Andrew moved off to see to the kettle.

"We understood," Greg continued, once tea had been served, and toast declined, "that the Nottles were due on holiday here last weekend."

"Yes, they were," said Alicia, "but Kim messaged us to cancel."

"When was that? The message?"

The McFarlanes conferred by glance. "Saturday," said Andrew. "They were due here on Sunday."

"Were you surprised?"

"I suppose we were, a little," said Alicia. "She and Brad have been staying here with us just about every year for ever such a long time."

"Almost since we moved down here," her husband agreed. "And that's ages, now."

"They always came down here in the summer, did they?" Catherine asked.

"For a week or so, yes," said Alicia. "In the early days, it wasn't their main holiday, you understand. They'd go abroad a couple of times a year, too. But for some time now, I think this was probably the only holiday they took."

"And that," said Andrew, with an apologetic glance at his wife, "was perhaps more habit than anything."

"What would they do here?" Catherine asked. "How would they spend their days?"

"Well, we wouldn't see much of Brad. He'd be off shell-collecting. That was what he did his original degree in, you know, and I think it was always his first love. He'd mostly base himself in our caravan down by the beach. Rickety old thing, we've had it thirty years, but I suppose it was convenient for his shells."

"Did Kim stay in the caravan with him?"

The McFarlanes looked uncomfortable. "No, no - she'd stop here. Sit in the garden, if it was nice, you know - read a book. Relax. That's what you want on holiday, isn't it?"

"We've heard," said Greg, "that theirs was not perhaps an ideal marriage."

Catherine thought she could hear the relief steaming out of the McFarlanes, like a whistling kettle: relief that they didn't have to be discreet on someone else's behalf.

"Well, it's that bloody house, isn't it?" said Alicia, and her husband nodded firmly. "That's what came between them. They were so happy, so *perfect* together when they were young."

Catherine wrote it all down. This was only the version of the

Nottles' story that Kim's cousin and cousin-in-law happened to know, of course - and only the version that they chose to tell - so not to be treated as gospel. But it was the fullest narrative they'd had yet, so she wrote it all down.

Kim and Brad had met at university, and married immediately on graduation. That was in 1992. They were happy, interesting youngsters, living in what Mrs McFarlane called a "funky" little rented flat near Brixton, and working at whatever jobs they could find while they waited for their careers to find them.

In 1996, Brad's grandmother had died, and left number nineteen, Beech Lane to her only grandson.

"Being young folk," Alicia explained, "living in a flat in a more exciting area, he and Kim certainly didn't want to live there in the dull suburbs, but rather than sell it they decided to let it for easy income. Very sensible, we thought, didn't we?"

Her husband nodded. "Brad was very practical - physically, I mean, you know. Terrific at DIY, he could do the lot. Just a natural talent for it - give him a library book on electrics, and he could re-wire your house a week later. Do a safer, neater job than the professionals."

The Nottles' first experiences as landlords went smoothly enough, and two or three short-stay tenants came and went. But in, the McFarlanes thought, late 1997 or early 1998, they rented number nineteen to a man in his thirties, who worked in public relations as a self-employed freelance.

"Well," said Alicia, "he was there for, it must've been, a few months - and then he disappeared."

"Disappeared?" said both police officers at once.

Andrew nodded. "Did a runner. Owed them rent, just buggered off. Brad was furious, of course, and I think Kim was more sad than anything."

"Disappointed," Alicia agreed. "That they'd been betrayed in that way by someone they'd trusted."

"They never caught up with the tenant?" Greg asked.

"Brad tried to trace him, apparently," Andrew explained, "but he seemed to have no family or anything. He'd given references, but, foolishly as it transpired, they'd never taken them up - he was just a con man, presumably."

"That put them right off," said Alicia. "The whole idea of renting the place out, I mean. They'd thought it was free money, but now they realised being a landlord wasn't as easy as it sounded."

"But they didn't sell up?"

Alicia looked sad. "I wish they had. Brad persuaded Kim that having tenants was more trouble than it was worth, and that with property prices constantly going up - in those days, you'll remember, house prices were fixed by the market - if they sold the house and then bought another they'd be throwing money down the drain. Moving house, you know - it was an expensive business in those days. Solicitors and what not."

"So Brad says to Kim, let's just move in for now - no rent, no mortgage, we'll be quids in, we don't have to stay here forever. That made sense to her - "

"Though I'm not sure being sensible was what attracted her to him in the first place," said Alicia, with a sigh. "Still, that was what they did. But the trouble was, he would never move. He'd said it was just temporary, Kim wouldn't have agreed otherwise, but he would just never move. We never knew why. Inertia, we thought, maybe, simple as that."

I think we all know why now, thought Catherine.

"And it came between them badly. They stayed together, but... " Alicia shook her head. "They weren't together, not really."

"One other thing," said Greg. "Do you have a recent photograph of Kim we could borrow?"

Andrew looked puzzled. "There wasn't one in their house?"

"We haven't found one," said Greg, carefully.

The McFarlanes looked at each other. "I don't think we have," said Alicia. "Not one from recent years. They weren't ... well, they weren't those sort of stays, I suppose. Not ... *jolly*."

"What we mean," said Andrew, "is that we felt Kim came down here mainly to get away from Beech Lane."

"And Brad? Why did he come?"

Alicia steeled herself for one more betrayal of a confidence. "Because he didn't like her going places where he couldn't keep an eye on her. That was how we saw it."

John Brown, Sarla's dad, had gone back to work that morning, which DS Kale and DC Kotane found interesting, but not necessarily significant. Cliches are not cliches in police work, they are invaluable tools of analysis and mnemonic, and it was a well known fact that different people reacted differently to grief and fear.

In any case, Dahlia was rather excited about visiting the dad at work.

"It's just a recycling works, isn't it?" said Phil, as they got off the bus and settled themselves into a ride-and-return, two-seater pedal car.

"Just a recycling ... ?" Dahlia was almost speechless. "No, Sarge, these places aren't *just* anything. This is the cream at the top of the recycling world."

She explained. John Brown worked as a 'last-sort spotter' at a large warehouse near Alexandra Park. Most non-organic waste - whether it originated in private homes or factories or institutions or wherever - was sorted at point of disposal; you put your beer bottles in this bin, your newspapers in that one. But inevitably, a lot of small stuff - unidentified bits and bobs of often uncertain origin - still ended up gathering in shoals of miscellany, unused and essentially unsorted.

Places like this - and men and women like John Brown - were miscellanea's final chance. If it didn't get picked out this time, the society it had once served would at last, however reluctantly, classify it as rubbish and send it for destruction. No-one was under any illusions: in the world they lived in now, to class something as rubbish because you couldn't find any further use for it, and because it was not practicably recyclable, was a defeat. And they all knew what lots of small defeats could add up to, given time.

"So they send for a superhero, do they?" said Phil.

"They have special skills, that's for certain. Or talents, perhaps."

"They're obsessive bores, you mean?" said Phil, and Dahlia was very nearly astonished to see what she thought was a glimpse of humour on the earnest DS's thin face. Perhaps he was just one of those people who found it difficult to relax with new acquaintances. Great career choice, if so.

As a spectacle, the last-sort facility itself was a little disappointing. It looked like a big barn, in the centre of which was an immense, circular conveyor belt system. Around the belt, a couple of dozen men and women sat or stood, staring intently at the parade of junk as it slowly turned in front of them, and periodically leaping forward to grab a prize.

It took a certain amount of pressured persuasion to drag John Brown from his post, for a talk in an empty office. Dahlia could quite understand how the work of a spotter might become hypnotic.

"My brother works for the Re," she told him. "You've got his dream job. This is what he hopes to end up doing."

"He probably won't make it," said John.

Dahlia blinked. That was fairly blunt. She'd already got the impression that Sarla's dad wasn't rich in social skills. Perhaps it was part of the personality package that made him suitable for this work. "Why's that, John?"

"Very few people are suitable for spotting. That's just a fact. You need a good memory. Good eyes."

"Good instincts, I suppose?"

"You could call it that. Remember, all this stuff has already been through various sorting processes. The spotter's got to be able to see things that loads of other people have already missed. They haven't identified an item, or they've missed its potential value. We see that."

"Could you give us an example?"

His face went blank for a long minute; that was how he looked when he was thinking, Dahlia supposed. "OK. Say there's a small piece of plastic. It's old, it's grubby, it won't recycle well because it's the wrong material. It doesn't look like anything in particular. It's been passed on, from one part of the recycling process to the next, and it's ended up on our belt, out there."

"Right."

"We'll see it, and we'll recognise it for what it is. Like, it's an outlet pipe washer for a specific model of washing machine."

"Right," said Dahlia. "So, you - "

"And we know," John went on, apparently unaware that he'd been interrupted, "that this washing machine is still in use in, let's say, a group of hospitals in Fife. So, we've matched it - that's what it's called, 'matching' - and we'll retrieve it, and it'll be sent to the redistribution centre that deals with that particular type of item in that particular area."

Dahlia couldn't believe it; he'd almost managed to make her brother's dream job sound dull. It wasn't, she was sure of that; she shared her brother's enthusiasm. It must be, she fancied, mentally exhausting work, and highly skilled - though of course, not as well paid as ordinary, entry-level recycling, because so many more people wanted to do it.

"Tell me what you think has happened to Sarla," said Phil.

John Brown looked at him, without apparent concern. "Just some loony's got her, must be."

"That would be very bad news, if that's true. That would probably be the worst news possible."

Dahlia watched carefully to see if Phil's calculatedly cruel remark would have any effect on the missing girl's father. She could detect nothing. Instead, the man looked away, as if distracted, before saying: "She'll come back. She'll be fine."

"We're certainly doing our best to find her," said Phil.

"Well, there you are, then. They've got every police in London looking for her, it said so on the news."

They'd come here to ask just one question, and Dahlia now

asked it. Not that they expected a useful reply to it, but the manner of the answer might be helpful, even if the words weren't. "How's your family life, John? Before this happened, how was everything going?"

John frowned. "Be more specific."

"All right. How's your marriage? Are you and Chloe as close as ever? You getting on well with each other?"

"Close as ever," said John. "Two people couldn't be closer. Nothing could get between us."

"What about Sarla?"

John looked baffled. "Why would Sarla want to get between me and her mum?"

"I'm sorry," said Dahlia, "I expressed that badly. I meant, how's your relationship with Sarla?"

"She adores me and I adore her," he replied, without much emotion in his voice.

"It's a happy family?"

"There's just me and Chloe and Sarla. There's nothing else in the world."

Dahlia smiled. "What about spotting?" she asked.

"That's just a job," he said. "That's not like my family."

Back in the pedal car, Dahlia said: "Odd bloke." She hoped it wasn't an expression that Phil Kale found offensive.

"He is a bit," Phil agreed. "I believed him about loving his wife and daughter, though, didn't you? I can't see him hurting either of them."

"Same here. And the interview teams say there's no hint from anyone that the Browns are anything but a devoted couple. It's not like we've got a custody dispute to give us a motive for him."

"Or for Chloe. But we're still saying Sarla was taken by someone she knew? Well then, that puts both parents firmly on the list. And that guy doesn't feel right."

"He is so calm, isn't he?" said Dahlia. "Why is he so calm, when 'every police in London' is out looking for his little girl's dead body?"

CHAPTER TEN

Catherine phoned Gerard back at the office, to let him know the main result of the interview with Kim Nottle's relatives: that they had a possible lead on the identity of the body found under the Nottles' drive.

"We're looking for a white man, in his thirties, worked in PR, rented number nineteen from Brad Nottle for a few months, probably from late '97 or early '98. Some time in 1998, he disappeared." She paused and nodded. "Yep, exactly - we think we know where he disappeared to. Or at least, it's the best lead we've had. So, can you push this up the priority list? There must be some paperwork somewhere relating to this tenancy agreement between the missing man and the Nottles - tax returns, perhaps?" Another pause. "Damn, hadn't thought of that. Good point." She turned to Greg. "Gerard says what if they were doing it all cash in hand, all unofficial, so they didn't have to declare the income for tax? No paperwork."

"Shit," said Greg, with feeling. "I'll bet he's right."

"You've ruined the boss's morning," she told the phone. "He was quite cheerful until then. Anyway, whatever you can dig up, Gerard ...? Sure, will do. Yeah! Talk to you soon." She put the phone away. "He says to remind you to go easy on the cider."

"That's Somerset, isn't it? Mind you, Gerard Cochrane's such a Londoner, he reckons the West Country starts in Hammersmith."

There was no-one at the McFarlanes' static caravan down near the beach; they hadn't thought there would be. As they were leaving, Alicia McFarlane had taken Greg aside and told him that as soon as she heard Kim was missing, she'd checked the caravan - without letting her husband know. "No signs of recent habitation," she'd told Greg, and there were no signs of recent habitation now.

In theory, Greg should probably have organised surveillance on the van before moving on it, as he had done on the McFarlanes' house. But having spoken to Alicia and Andrew, he really didn't fancy the chances of finding Kim bunked up there - and besides, he was anxious to get back to London. The Cornish end of the story, he felt, was finished. Anyway, if they had surprised her in the van, where would she have run to? Into the sea, and swum to America?

Still, best be thorough. DI Wallace was known for his thoroughness. In fact, he had a little phrase on that subject which he liked to trot out every now and then, for the amusement of his troops.

There were five vans in all on this patch of rough ground. There was no reply to their knocks at the second and third, both of which gave a strong impression of emptiness, confirmed by a spot of window-peeping. The fourth knock, however, did produce a response.

"Don't worry, Sanj, I'll get it." The door opened something a little more than a crack, and a middle-aged woman wearing a sun hat and puffing on a large pipe said: "Sorry to appear rude - my husband's got a stinking cold."

Instinctively, after the flu scares of a few years ago, both detectives took a step backwards.

The woman smiled. "Don't worry, it's only a cold, honestly, I'm a doctor's receptionist, I do know the difference! But I won't ask you in. I won't come out either if you don't mind, I think I'm getting it myself."

"No problem," said Greg. He showed her his ID. "Nothing to worry about, we were just wondering if you've seen anyone using the caravan at the end? The McFarlanes' van."

"Haven't seen anyone down here all week. I think we're the first to arrive this year. Hold on - Sanj? Did you hear all that?" She looked over her shoulder, into the darkened depths of the holiday home. "He's shaking his head, poor love, he hasn't seen anyone around either. Is there anything wrong? The McFarlanes haven't been burgled, have they? That happened to us a couple of years ago."

"No, nothing like that - just tidying up a loose end from an unrelated inquiry." He gave her what he hoped was his most reassuring smile. "If we can just take your names, for our report, we'll leave you in peace. Hope you'll soon feel better."

As they walked back towards the bed and breakfast, Catherine said "Did you see us both jump, when she said she'd got a cold? What must we have looked like ... "

Greg laughed. "I know what you mean. It's not even as if pandemics are all that likely these days, are they? When you haven't got millions of people rushing around all over the globe all the time?"

"Oh, well," she said. "I guess every generation has its own peculiar terrors."

Sarla Brown's paternal grandparents lived and worked on a cooperative poppy farm just outside Sevenoaks. It was a good life, they told Phil and Dahlia. Hard work, fresh air, a thriving, profitable business with neighbours and colleagues they liked and trusted.

"Best thing we ever did," said Mr Brown, "moving in here."

Dahlia thought the nine-foot high armoured fences dotted with watchtowers would have put her off the place a bit - but then, she wasn't a countrywoman by inclination. "I don't think I realised we grew opium in this country," she said, by way of a conversational opener.

It worked. Mrs Brown, in particular, was keen to inform her visitors. "Diamorphine," she explained. "It's primarily used, in a routine way, as a painkiller in, especially, terminal cases. But it's also stockpiled for use in pandemics."

"You'll know there was a flu scare around the turn of the century?" said Mr Brown. "Well, there was a great panic in government circles when they realised that there was a shortage of opium - not just in this country, but worldwide."

"Even in normal times," Mrs Brown continued, "hospitals in Britain get through hundreds of kilos of the stuff a year. You can imagine how that would go up during a pandemic. So, even in pre-Process days, there was a big push on to make us self-sufficient. And everything that's happened since has only strengthened that determination, obviously. Hence, farms like this dotted around the country."

"Self-sufficient in heroin," Phil mused. "Who'd have thought it. You must spend a fortune on security?"

"The Ministry of Health pays for all our security," Mrs Brown said. "Which, since they're our only customer - by law, of course - seems fair enough." She smiled. "As you can imagine, we don't get many burglaries round here, to put it mildly."

"It is a bit like living inside a huge cage," her husband acknowledged, "but you soon get used to it."

Inside their modern cottage - delightfully cool despite the afternoon sun - the Browns admitted to being "absolutely frantic" about Sarla.

"We wanted to rush up to London as soon as we heard," said Mr Brown, "but our John said there was nothing we could do that wasn't already being done, and that Chloe didn't really want a house full of people being sympathetic and getting in the way."

"I can understand that," his wife added.

"So we work on, waiting for news. What else can we do? But it shreds the nerves, I don't mind admitting, as well as the heart. Right now, right this minute, our lovely little granddaughter could be on a boat to America, crying her little eyes out."

"You think she was the victim of a rescue, do you?" Phil asked, sipping his tea. Dahlia had abandoned hers; if there was one thing guaranteed to bring her stomach up through her throat it was tea that was made from something other than tea. This stuff had a definite whiff of the herbal about it. She just hoped it wasn't made from poppies. She'd have to watch the DS carefully for signs of incipient euphoria.

"What else could it be?" said Mr Brown. "We both feel that, don't we, love?"

"We do. If it was a pervert, or a crazy mother or something like that, you'd have found a trace by now, you lot." Her voice broke slightly on the word 'trace.' "I mean, the police, you don't mess around in cases like this, do you? We know you'll be pulling out every stop there is, looking for her. But you've found nothing, have you?"

"Conclusion - it has to be those religious bastards."

"We've got nothing against them," Mrs Brown began.

"I bloody have," said her husband.

"Now," she said, putting her hand over his. "We've both known plenty of decent people who happened to believe in their religion. We've nothing against other people having their own beliefs - as long as they keep them to themselves."

"You may well be right," said Phil, "and let me assure you that avenue is being very thoroughly investigated. But while that's going on, we do need to ask you a few questions about the family, which - "

"No, we understand that," said Sarla's grandfather.

"Don't spare our feelings, Detective Sergeant. Only Sarla matters." She was crying now, Dahlia saw, though there was no noise.

"Thank you. How do you think your son's marriage is doing at the moment?"

"It's a very strong marriage," said Mr Brown. "Strong as rocks, you can count on that."

"Yes, you can," said Mrs Brown, "though I think, love, to be a hundred per cent honest, we have detected a little bit of tension in recent weeks. That's right, isn't it?"

Mr Brown's confirmatory nod was a small one. "We don't like to speak ill."

"Of course," said Phil. "But this is purely for background, entirely confidential."

"We think, perhaps, it's because of Felicity."

Dahlia checked her notes. "Sarla's other granny?"

"Our son's mother-in-law, yes. I'm sure she means well, but since she's been back - "

"Back?"

"She was living abroad for a few years - eastern Europe, was it? Came back to Britain two or three months ago, maybe."

"Something like that."

"The trouble is," said Mrs Brown, "she lives very close to them, a couple of streets away, which is nice of course, but ... "

"She interferes," said Mr Brown. "Maybe. A bit, you know. The way some grandparents do."

"From the best of motives, no doubt - but it can be a bit much for a young couple."

"Mind you," said Mr Brown, "this is only speculation on our part, from what little our boy's let drop. We've not actually met Felicity since she came back to the country. To be absolutely frank, I can't say we're bothered - we never did get on, on the few occasions we've met." He glanced at his wife. "Well, it's true, and we said we were to tell the truth. My feeling, for what it's worth, is that Chloe and John both resent her meddling, as they see it, but naturally John more so, because she's not his flesh and blood."

"But there's no question of the marriage breaking up," said Mrs Brown, firmly.

"Oh no, no chance. Those two are devoted, they're just going through a hard patch. That's all it is. She's the best thing that ever happened to our boy."

"He had a few troubles when he was younger," said Mrs Brown.

"Not legal troubles," her husband stressed. "Not even medical, really. No doctor ever said to us there's such-and-such specifically wrong with him, or anything."

"Personality troubles," said Mrs Brown. "That's the best way to put it. He can be a bit impulsive, he's not always aware of consequences."

"But that's all in the past," said her husband, "since he married that lovely girl. What the school psychiatrist couldn't fix, Chloe has. He's much more settled now."

She'd been fine with him, while they were in Cornwall, not cool towards him, or anything. Catherine Blake wasn't one of life's sulkers, Greg knew. But he still felt badly about what had happened on the train down - when she'd opened up to him, and he'd closed up to her. Wasn't sure what to do about it, though. So, instead:

"What do you like best about the new world?" he asked her, on the train back up. "What one thing is much better now than it was, say, twenty years ago?"

Without hesitation, she replied: "Hats."

"Hats?"

"Hats. Everyone wears hats these days. People look good in hats. Heads were made for hats. A head without a hat is like a something-thingy without a details-to-follow."

He laughed. "So, what - decentralised democracy, collectivisation of the economy, the rediscovery of community life, elimination of poverty ... "

"Hats," she said.

"You like hats best."

She crossed her arms. "I just happen to think hats are very civilized. I think we will look back on the hatless years with shame and sadness."

"So why did people stop wearing hats, then? When I was young, it was only very old people, or teenagers, who wore them. Socially, I mean."

"They stopped, I presume, because they were going everywhere by car, and working in offices. Before that you had to have a hat, to keep the environment off your nut."

"Makes sense," Greg agreed. "And now people walk a lot more, travel by public transport, work outside more, so we're back to hats. And you're glad because you like the look."

"For instance, you look good in your hat," she said.

"Thank you," he said, laughing, and it was only twenty miles further east that he realised he'd been meant to say the same back to her. *Sod-bugger-shit!*

"I still say it should have been called the Ministry *of* Bees, not the Ministry *for* Bees," said Ginger, when Gerard tasked him with visiting Kim Nottle's workplace. "You don't have the Ministry *for* Defence do you? It's Ministry *of* Defence. Ministry *of* Health."

"There's a fine balance to be struck, though, isn't there," said Gerard, "between embracing pedantry, and avoiding being a total laughing stock? You can't have Ministry of Bees - you'd get people ringing up all day asking to speak to the queen."

Ginger liked bees. He'd been stung on the knee by a honeybee when he was four years old, and had found the whole process so fascinating that it had left him with a lifelong interest in and affection for all orders of bee. He was delighted that they had their own Ministry now, even if it wasn't properly named.

Kim's closest colleague, he was assured, was an attractive woman with an open smile, introduced to him as Ella. She was about the same age as Kim, he guessed; somewhere in the still-young fifties.

"Anything and everything to do with bees," she explained, in answer to his question. They were sitting in an otherwise empty staff smoking room. "Amateur and commercial; domesticated bees and wild bees; research and practice. Bee-keeping, bee-farming, honey, pollination, habitat, conservation - everything and anything."

"Bees," Ginger summarised.

"Bees," she agreed. "You've really got to be quite interested in bees to work here." Her face clouded. "I know you're here to ask questions, but can you tell me ... all we know is what we've heard on the news. We didn't even realise Kim was missing - if that's what she is - because she's on leave this week, anyway."

"We are anxious to trace her," said Ginger, "both to eliminate her as a suspect in the death of her husband, and in order to satisfy ourselves that she's safe."

"And you've been unable to do so, in three days? Which means she's either dead or hiding." Ella must have spotted Ginger's surprised eyebrows, as she added: "Sorry - I'm a researcher. I tend to work on the basis that if this, then that - and that leads to this - and so on." She put out her cigarette, drained her teacup, and smoothed her skirt. "Please, ask away."

"Tell me about Kim Nottle - she's a researcher, like you?"

"That's right."

"Forgive me - is that a ... senior job? Middling?"

Ella leaned forward. "That's a fascinating question. How do you tell these days? We're not terribly hierarchical here at Bees, ironically enough, and of course pay scales are no longer a useful guide to status. Hmm." She sat back again, thinking hard. "All right; try this. I spent a long period of my life raising children. Kim had no children; she's been here forever. Yet she works at the same level as I do."

"A woman who hasn't had all that time away from the work should've gone further?"

"Might have been expected to go further, I think is a better way of putting it," said Ella. "I think, if you were to ask around, you'd hear one or two of the other old-timers say that Kim's career in science has been a bit of a disappointment. She was reputedly quite brilliant as a young woman, but she's never quite come up with the breakthrough research everyone anticipated from her."

"Is that a surprise, as well as a disappointment?"

"Not necessarily. Science is like that - the big stuff doesn't always come where and when and from whom you expect. And she's not had an entirely easy life, which might explain a lot. An unhappy marriage, is the general view. Still, she keeps going. In marriage, in work, in life."

"What's her particular field?"

"Do you know much about bees?"

Ginger waggled his hands. "Some."

She grinned. "Well, unfortunately, that's all anyone really knows about bees. You probably know that bee numbers and diversity have recovered somewhat in this country, now that we don't use the old-fashioned, artificial pesticides and herbicides, and petroleum-based fertilisers. And there's less pollution, generally. But the loss of all kinds of bees at the end of the last century and the first part of this one was so massive and widespread that they still are far from out of the woods. In many cases, we've had to bring bee populations virtually back from the dead, and they are still very fragile."

"It's that bad?"

She nodded, grimly. "If another catastrophe were to hit us out of the blue - a new bee disease, for instance - the country could be starving within months. Literally. At least a third of all fruit and vegetables consumed in Britain, for instance, is pollinated by the honeybee. If we lost that, there is simply no way we could feed ourselves. The only things on earth left to eat would be corn, wheat and rice - no meat, incidentally, since livestock is fed on pollinated plants."

"There was a bloke gave a talk at our allotment society last year," Ginger recalled, "and he said there was quite a controversy about whether it's better to grow self-pollinating vegetables. If you do, you'll be fed even if there's no pollinators around, but on the other hand - "

"On the other hand, you might be adding to a vicious circle - no plants to pollinate means no pollinators. Yes, I've never quite understood that argument - admittedly, I'm not a horticulturalist, but surely the answer is to grow both? Self-pollinated French beans, for instance, and bee-pollinated runner beans." She shrugged.

Ginger smiled. "I'll mention that at the next meeting."

"Now, Kim and I work on bumblebees, specifically - they're just as important as honeybees. We both work in habitat research. Kim's speciality is artificial nesting sites for bumblebees."

"To replace natural nesting sites that have been lost?"

"That's it. This has been something of a holy grail in bee research for decades now. People were always inventing bee nests, but with one rather crucial snag - the bumblebees were never very interested in them. This is a worldwide problem. There is an urgent need to develop a model of artificial nest that could be placed in gardens, rooftops, allotments, and so on, all over the country and which would actually be used in a big way by the bees. Kim's working life has been dedicated to that search."

"Successfully?"

"She has made some progress, that's for sure - but the big breakthrough has never quite turned up. She seemed to be getting close to it sometimes, but ... never quite."

Ginger found all this fascinating - all this bee stuff. He'd have to think about getting a hive himself. But he reckoned he knew which bit of this interview would be of greatest interest to DI Wallace; Ella's casual remark suggesting it was common knowledge that the Nottles had endured an unhappy marriage, thus further confirming what the investigation had already learned.

It was looking ever more likely that the second body discovered at nineteen Beech Lane was the victim of a domestic.

The Loftys had prepared for this, and cleared it in advance with DI Wallace. When the hospital accountant, Kieran Rider, and his alleged girlfriend - a nervous, resentful woman in her late thirties, who gave her name as Haley French - arrived to collect the bicycle, they were taken to separate interview rooms, with one Lofty each. "Just routine paperwork," they were told, and neither of them looked thrilled at the idea.

Afterwards, the Loftys compared answers.

"How long have they known each other?" said the younger Lofty. "He says two and a half years."

The other Lofty checked his notebook. "She can't remember. Lots of shrugging and looking annoyed. When pressed: she's known him 'a while.'"

"How long have they been boyfriend and girlfriend?"

"Let's see ... oh, there's a surprise."

"She doesn't remember?"

"When pressed: 'Not long.' What does he reckon?"

"Two months yesterday. She's got a terrible memory, hasn't she? I mean, I'm assuming Kieran Rider has coached her on all this, and she still can't get it right."

"Not very romantic, is it?" said the older Lofty. "Or maybe they didn't have much rehearsal time."

"So why didn't she report her new bicycle missing?"

"Oh well, that's perfectly straightforward. She accidentally left it outside a friend's house - "

"Careless."

"From where it was obviously stolen. She didn't know it was stolen, however, because she's been out of town for a few days."

The Loftys rejoined their prey, and informed them that they were perfectly happy to release the bicycle into Mr Rider's hands - but that it would take a few days to sort out the paperwork. They would deliver the bike to him when it was ready. The pair left the police station - in opposite directions, which the younger Lofty thought might be subtle, but the older thought was merely because they had nothing more to say to each other, now or ever.

"He's a liar," Lofty summed up, "and she's a rubbish liar. Let's find out who she is and what she's up to."

When Ginger Thom returned to the office, he found a message waiting for him. "You're keeping rich company, Ginger," said Jade.

He went in search of DS Dale Emmett. "You can scrub the food robbery at the potato research place off the board, Sarge," he told him. "It's no longer an active squad case."

"Solved it already, Ginge? You deserve a day off."

Ginger showed him the message. "Counter Terrorism are taking it over. It must have triggered a flag when I logged it in."

"Counter Terrorism?" said Dale. "Potatoes?"

"Alternative tuberous foods, to be accurate. Apparently, it's not unusual for foreign agents to steal food research, even if they can't use it themselves. They simply destroy it to prevent the enemy having it."

"Makes sense," said Dale. "You know what they say - famine is mightier than the sword. Inside job, is it?"

"Must be," Ginger agreed. "Someone at the Potato Research Council has been making a few quid on the side."

"Good luck trying to spend it," said Dale, "when they're in prison for the rest of their lives. Oh well, Ginge, old son - a dead end. I daresay you've got enough work to be going on with, though."

"She's got a doctor's appointment," Dahlia told Phil, putting the phone down on Sarla Brown's maternal grandmother.

"What, and she can't get out of it?" demanded Phil. "To help find her missing granddaughter?"

"Apparently not." Dahlia raised her eyebrows. "She says it has to be this afternoon, can't be put off until tomorrow, and it'll take the rest of the day. To be fair, she does sound very upset about it."

"All right," said Phil. "We'll do granny tomorrow. Let's see if Sarla's form teacher is a bit more helpful."

She was, and they arranged to meet her without delay, at a leisure centre in Battersea, where she was getting ready for a ten-pin bowling match. One slight delay did, however, prove unavoidable.

"Oh, hell," said Dahlia, as they got off the bus. "Do you mind if we walk the long way round?"

"Why?" said Phil. "There's a bridge there, take us right to the leisure centre."

Dahlia hated this. It didn't come up often, thank God, but she hated it when it did. "I know, but it's a dynamic bridge."

Phil looked at her blankly.

"A wobble-walk," she explained.

"Is it? How do you know?"

She knew because she knew where all the dynamic bridges and walkways in London were; she had a map of them inside her head. She didn't bother answering what seemed a pretty pointless question. Instead, she answered one he hadn't asked. "You know how they move slightly when you walk on them, so as to store the energy of your movement, convert it to electricity, and transmit it to the grid?"

"I suppose so," said Phil.

"Well, I get seasick on them."

"Bloody hell. That's bad luck. I've never heard of that before."

"No, hardly anybody gets it. Most people can't even tell whether they're on a wobble-walk or a normal pavement. But for a very small number of people, it causes a disorientating sensation of imbalance." As an officer with the Serious Crimes Squad, Dahlia Kotane held one of the most prized positions in modern policing. Dahlia Kotane was not the sort of person who liked to made a fuss about things. She *hated* this.

"I'm sorry to hear about that, Dahlia," said Phil, sympathetically. "It must be a drag for you."

Yup - that, specifically, was the bit she hated. "It's no prob, Sarge, really - if we can just go round the long way."

"Of course, of course."

Dahlia was careful to talk about other things during the five minutes it took them to reach the leisure centre. With luck, this business would never come up again. "You ever been here before?" she asked, as they passed through the main doors.

"Don't think so," said Phil. "We've got a good one near where I live. Big place, isn't it?"

"It's amazing," said Dahlia. "They've got just about everything here. My brother used to play five-a-side football here when he was a kid. It's a regional facility, you see, much bigger than the area ones."

They followed the signs for the bowling alleys, and found Yve Simpson just where she'd said she'd be - in the non-smoking bar. She was a skinny, grey-haired woman, with an old-fashioned East End accent, sad eyes and a big smile. Dahlia wondered which the children in her care took more notice of; the eyes or the smile.

"I'm really a skittles player," she told them, over tea and jam tarts, "but we've got a staff ten-pin team, and there's a couple off with summer colds."

"We were saying," said Dahlia, "this is a pretty impressive place."

Yve nodded enthusiastically, and hurried to swallow her mouthful. "You can say what you like about the Process, about the way things have changed, but I'll tell you one thing - my social life's never been busier! Not even when I was a young girl."

"My parents say the same thing," said Dahlia.

Phil Kale coughed, as if asking permission to interrupt a conversation between two women. Yve turned a kind smile on him. "Turning a necessity into an opportunity," he said.

There was a silent pause, until Yve said "How do you mean, dear?" Dahlia shoved a jam tart into her mouth as a battering ram to beat back the laughter caused by hearing a witness address a DS as 'dear.'

"Well," said Phil, "it's an idea that's at the very heart of the Process, isn't it? That we have had to do certain things in order to survive - so while we're doing them, instead of making the best of a bad job, let's see if we can find ways of making the changes work for us."

"Yes, I see what you mean," said the teacher. "Like, we couldn't run millions of cars any more, but rather than allow that to be a disaster, with proper planning it became an opportunity to reclaim the streets, clean the air, and institute better public transport than we'd ever seen before."

"Exactly - that's exactly what I mean!" Phil's hands were making little clutching motions of excitement. "And you see, it's the same with what you were saying about your social life. We want people to do things more communally than they used to - to spend their time communally, as much as possible, rather than as individuals or family units."

"Because it's a more efficient use of light and heat and so on," suggested Dahlia.

"Yes, and also because it fosters a more active, direct democracy - and the Process just couldn't work if we were relying on old-fashioned, representative democracy. We have to have the devolved type we use now, where decisions are taken as close to the ground as possible, by the people who're actually involved."

"Cast a vote," said Yve, "then forget it about it for another four years." She smiled at Dahlia. "That's all democracy meant in my day."

"I can see that wouldn't work today - the way we live now requires too much involvement in the everyday running of things, everyday decisions. It'd all collapse if we just left it to someone else."

"Modern democracy's got to be flexible and responsive - and faster-moving," said Yve; and then smiled at Phil again, as if giving a bright boy permission to continue addressing the class.

"So, how do you get people to live more communally? There are countries where they've done it by cutting the electricity off every evening - you've no choice but to go to the village hall, or whatever, to keep warm. But we've done it by ensuring that every neighbourhood in the country has plenty of pubs, cafes, cinemas, sports places, games arcades, dance halls, and all the rest of it. And all cheap or free, and all fully staffed, and most of them governed by local communities. We've ended up with something better than we had before all the emergencies - better social lives, and we're a step nearer survival."

Dahlia wondered what Phil's better social life consisted of. It was hard to imagine, somehow. Attending lectures on energy-saving? She wasn't even sure if he was married, or had a girlfriend, or boyfriend. Or a cat. "Necessity becomes opportunity," she said. "Very neat." She sometimes thought that all anyone over the age of thirty wanted to do was talk about the pros and cons of the Process. All right, it was all new and amazing to them, but didn't they realise there was a younger generation who were too busy living it to spend every second waffling on about it? Time for business.

"What sort of little girl is Sarla Brown?" she asked.

"Very ordinary," said Yve. "And I mean that in a good way - she's just a normal, happy, six-year-old. Bright enough, but not especially so. Mixes well with other children." She pressed her lips together. "But lately ... "

"Lately?" Phil prompted.

"I don't think this is hindsight speaking," said Yve. "I have been slightly concerned for a month or so, now. Of course, all children go through phases, so if this terrible business hadn't happened, I might have dismissed it all."

"What sort of things?"

"Sarla has been displaying what I could only describe as a tendency towards religiosity."

"How is that displayed?"

"Partly in her arguing with things she's taught. Now, of course, we encourage our children to be questioning, to find things out for themselves, to be suspicious of orthodoxy. But it's the nature of her arguments - well, they're not really arguments. She'll say something like 'Miss, that's wrong, it says so in the Bible.' But when I try to draw her out, to get her to develop her argument, she just looks embarrassed and retreats into herself."

"In other words," said Phil, "these are things she's been told, not things she believes herself."

Yve nodded. "That's how it seems to me, yes."

"And is there anything else?"

Now, the sad eyes were definitely winning out over the smile. "I'm afraid there have been three or four incidents of her behaving very unkindly towards other children. This was entirely out of character, and each of these events involved a child with what we used to call a 'Jewish surname'."

"A Jewish child?" said Dahlia.

Yve looked uncomfortable. "As you may know, we no longer categorise children according to religion - especially by presuming for them a religion which they, and their parents, might or might not profess."

"Let's put it another way," said Phil. "If you were an anti-Semite, you would be able to identify these children as Jews?"

"Oh, yes," she said, with a grateful look at Phil. "No doubt about that."

"And Sarla's 'unkind behaviour' to these children - it too has had religious tones?"

"Certainly. They can't be her friends any more, because it says so in the Bible - that sort of thing." Yve Simpson sighed. "It's all rather odd, because as far as I know there's no-one in Sarla's home life who holds strong religious views."

"No," said Phil, "but as it happens, this does tie in with another aspect of the case that we've been pursuing." Across the table, Dahlia could read the message in his eyes, a mixture of vindication and despair.

CHAPTER ELEVEN

"Oh, nearly forgot," said Ginger, following the DI into his office. "I've got a photo for you, of Kim Nottle."

"Oh great, let's have a look." Greg put down his overnight bag and took off his hat. Good to be home.

"It's only a mug shot, really," said Ginger, handing it over, "done for her work ID card, but better than nothing."

Greg smiled his thanks, glanced at the photograph, and slumped into his chair. "Oh, Jesus Christ!" He raised his voice. "Catherine! Get in here!"

Half in and half out of her jacket, her own travelling bag still in her hand, DS Blake hurried into the room. "What is it?"

He showed her the photo.

"That's the woman in the caravan," she said, puzzled. "In Cornwall."

"That's Kim Nottle," said Greg.

Gerard Cochrane stirred his tea. "One thing you might want to bear in mind," he told the Loftys, "just as a possibility. How do you get rid of dangerous stuff, in a society where nothing's thrown away?"

"Dangerous?" said the younger Lofty.

"You're a criminal - " Gerard began.

"No, he's not," said the other Lofty. "He's actually a police officer. He can't help the way he looks."

"You're a criminal," said Gerard, "and you've just bumped off one of your rivals, using a revolver. Right?"

"OK ... "

"Now, when I was a young copper, if one gangster shot another gangster, and he needed to get rid of the weapon because he knew he'd be a suspect and all his addresses would be searched, he'd drive over the other side of town, bury the gun in a random dustbin, and the refuse lorry would come along and take it away and incinerate it. Or shove it in a landfill."

"Yes ... " said the older Lofty. "Yes, could be onto something, Gerard."

"But nowadays, just about everything's picked over by someone. There isn't much uninspected rubbish. If you've used a gun in a murder, you can't just send it to be recycled, the way in the old days you'd chuck it in a bin. Or, say, you've got a pile of stolen goods that you need rid of ahead of a police raid. What do you do with them? Where do they go?"

"Dump them in a pond," said the younger Lofty. "Watch them sink. That's neat, Gerard. That could explain an awful lot."

"Just a thought," said Gerard.

That evening, Greg took Erin and Catherine, Ginger and Gerard out to dinner at his regular curry house. He needed a mini case conference, and he needed a big curry, so - with the brilliant flair for efficiency that had already taken him to such heights in his career - he combined the two. Well, it was either that or sandwiches in the office. Sod that, after a long day.

"Any rice today, Tarak?" he asked hopefully, as his guests browsed their menus.

The waiter's regretful grimace contained a hint of a telling-off. "Not today, Inspector, no. Plenty of naan, chapati, mixed grains. Lovely red amaranth, really good. It's best to book, you know? You'll be here for your birthday, as usual?"

"I'll remember to book, Tarak, I promise."

"Guaranteed rice if you book a month in advance, Inspector. Money-back guarantee."

"I'll book." A thought struck him. He was, after all, legendary for his powers of efficiency. All right, except when he was allowing murder suspects in caravans to fool him with big sunhats and cheap ventriloquism. "In fact, I'll book now, Tarak. Is that all right? Usual table, usual date, usual time?"

Tarak smiled - a slightly self-satisfied smile, Greg thought, the sort you might smile when things had worked out precisely as you'd anticipated and intended. "I'll put it in the book, Inspector. Now, do you wish to order yet? Or your friends need more time, perhaps?"

Halfway through the meal, Erin asked Greg: "What is 'mixed grains' exactly? I've never really known."

"I suppose it's a generic term," he said, having never really thought about it, "for various grains, various rice substitutes, that can be grown in this country. Unlike rice itself, which can't. So on the menu, they just call it grains, or mixed grains, because they don't know in advance which particular grains they'll be getting that particular day." He ate a forkful of un-sauced grain. "I reckon this is amaranth."

"I think my granny grows that in her garden," said Erin, a touch suspiciously. "Not to eat, though. Love-lies-bleeding?"

"Same family, I believe. But this form is bred for its edible seeds." He smiled. "You know, when I was your age, rice was just about the cheapest thing there was."

"I've heard that," she said.

"It was what you filled up on when you couldn't afford anything else. Or coming home from the pub, you'd stop off and get a takeaway meal, and it'd be all rice, and you'd be complaining. 'Look at this rip-off, it's all bloody rice!'"

Erin loved that. In her version of a young man's gruff voice, she mimicked: "There's *too much* rice! I demand a refund, my dinner's all full of rice!"

"Well, yeah - you would," said Greg. "You'd be tossing through the rice with your fork, going, 'Where's the meat, it's all bloody rice!'" He slowly shook his head. "God, when I think of the amount of rice I must have thrown away in my lifetime ... "

That stopped her laughter. Now she was pure, focused incredulity. "What, you had so much rice you used to *compost* it?"

Greg had to wash his food down with a mouthful of beer before he had sufficient control over his breathing to attempt an answer. Catherine, who'd caught the last exchange, was similarly incapacitated. "No," said the DI, at last, "no, we didn't compost it, as such ... "

It took Erin a few seconds to figure out what he meant. Her face, when she realised that he was talking about a time when rice had been literally thrown away because there was too much of it, formed such a comically complex picture - of shock and horror, of astonishment and envy - that it made even Ginger and Gerard laugh, and they had no idea what they were laughing at, having not heard a word of the preceding conversation.

Over coffee (or something very similar), and cider brandies, and as the restaurant gradually emptied sufficiently for the detectives to have the requisite privacy in which to talk shop, Gerard brought them up to date with news from the West.

"Cornish police have checked the caravan - "

"The Caravan of *Shame*," said Catherine. "I have never felt so stupid in my life."

"Still, bright side," said Ginger. "None of it's your fault, because you were in the company of a senior officer. Automatically, it's his fault."

All eyes turned to DI Wallace, to be sure that the joke had not yet got beyond itself. He was well known for his often-expressed view that everyone made mistakes sometimes, and that to behave as if that wasn't true was a definition of poor management. But even so - on this occasion, the boss really had cocked up.

Greg's decision to deliver a sombre V-sign to each of his colleagues around the table, one-by-one, in silence, suggested that they had not yet run out of leeway. Gerard continued.

"This time, they checked all the vans, breaking in where necessary, but no sign of anything. Cornwall's assumption is that having had a visit from the police once, and got away with it, she's not going to push her luck, and has moved on. They have no idea where to, any more than we have."

"And speaking of assumptions," said Greg, "or working hypotheses, does everyone agree that, until something says otherwise, we go ahead on the assumption that the body under the drive at nineteen Beech Lane is that of the missing tenant?"

There were general murmurs and nods of assent at this.

"Further," Greg continued, "it seems reasonable to assume for now that Brad's refusal to move house means that it was Brad who killed the tenant. He daren't move, because the next inhabitant might uncover the body."

"And Kim was eager to move," put in Erin, "so presumably she didn't know the body was there."

"Good point. I agree," said Greg, careful not to look at Erin so that she wouldn't see him seeing her blush. "Now, the death of Brad, the source of the rifle that killed him, and the house being almost empty of belongings, are mysteries that we can only hope will be explained when we find Kim." He looked around at his colleagues. "Find her again, I mean."

"Caravan of *Shame*," said Catherine.

"Our priorities as far as this investigation goes are therefore: find Kim Nottle, find where the rifle that killed Brad Nottle came from, and identify the missing lodger."

"So far, no luck on the latter," said Ginger. "There are no relevant missing persons reports for the approximate date. The old neighbour Bob Lemon spoke to, Mrs Denmark, remembered that there was a young man living there briefly, round about the right time by the sound of it, but she can't remember much about him. All the other neighbours are much too recent to remember anything from those days. We're trying to trace other ex-neighbours, but it's not proving easy."

"Erin and I will keep after the gun," said Gerard. "We'll track it down eventually."

"You're confident, Gerard," said Catherine.

"Got to have come from somewhere, hasn't it? Someone's messed up the paperwork somewhere, that's all it'll be."

On the way out, Greg asked Erin: "So, how was your amaranth?"

"Very nice, thank you," she said. "I do like rice, though."

"Know what you mean."

"My mum always does rice at Christmas."

Greg was quite proud of the absolute straightness of his face as he answered. "Well, you can't beat a bit of tradition at Christmas, can you?"

The origins of young Sarla Brown's newfound religiosity seemed clear to Phil Kale and Dahlia Kotane first thing in the morning, when they interviewed Sarla's maternal grandmother, Felicity Cook.

Her one-room flat, a few minutes' walk from the Browns' house, was full of what, to Dahlia's admittedly uneducated eye, seemed a somewhat ecumenical collection of Christian symbols. Around the large, almost bloated, middle-aged woman's neck hung an uncomfortable-looking Jesus on a chunky cross.

"I hope you're feeling better, Mrs Cook?" said Dahlia, as she sat them on her small sofa.

"Better?" The question seemed to startle her.

"You were unable to see us yesterday because you had a doctor's appointment," Phil reminded her.

"Oh - yes, of course. How kind of you to ask." She closed and opened her eyes in a slow blink. "God bless you."

Phil ignored the benediction. "Your daughter seems quite certain that Sarla has been kidnapped by religious extremists. Tell us, Mrs Cook, do you share that opinion?"

She waved away the absurdity of the idea with a hand which was much thinner than the rest of her. In fact, thought Dahlia, she did look a bit haggard altogether, despite her weight. The stigmata of grief, perhaps? Or of guilt?

"My daughter is distraught, Officer. That's why she says such things. I'm sure no person of faith would ever dream of putting a family through what we are all suffering now."

"Then, do you have any alternative theory of your own?"

She sniffed, and tears began to leak from her eyes. "I'm afraid

I'm forced to agree with my son-in-law. Only someone completely deranged could do this to an innocent little girl."

"You've only recently returned to the country from abroad, Mrs Cook - is that right?" Dahlia asked.

"Yes, that's correct."

"Whereabouts were you?"

"Poland. Quite near Gdansk."

"What were you doing out there?" said Phil.

She smiled - not at the detectives, Dahlia noticed, but at the air above them. "Well, now. What I thought I was doing was simply living out my retirement in a culture which I found more to my taste, at the time, than Britain's. But it turned out that what I was actually doing was looking for Jesus - without even knowing I missed him."

"And you found him, did you?" asked Phil, in the sort of voice in which he might inquire after a lost pet.

"I did, Officer."

"So, why did you come back? I gather you don't find life in this country congenial. Why not stay in Poland?"

Interesting, thought Dahlia; that was the first question that had annoyed Mrs Cook. With a visible effort, the woman pulled herself together and answered in an even quieter, humbler tone than before.

"I live in Jesus, Officer. Which country I happen to be in is entirely immaterial."

"But you came back here," Phil persisted.

"I wanted to spend some time with my granddaughter, while she was still - " She stopped, as if choked with tears. *Or quite possibly*, Dahlia reminded herself, *because she actually was choked with tears.* "Still young," Mrs Cook concluded. "If you miss those early years, you can never get them back."

Dahlia could sense Phil thinking the same as her: Felicity Cook hadn't seemed to mind missing the child's *earlier* years.

"Would you say," Phil continued, "that your daughter's marriage is a strong one?"

"I wouldn't dream of holding an opinion on such a private

matter," came the pious reply, "let alone expressing one. And after all, poor John can't help being the way he is. We none of us made ourselves."

And that, Dahlia noted, was surely the fullest answer she had given them so far.

Later - but not much later; the second they were out of her earshot, in fact - Phil said to Dahlia: "Suspect number one. Top of the list."

"It would certainly explain a few things," Dahlia admitted.

"The child goes with Granny, quite happily - and Granny later hands her over to her co-religionists, who spirit her away. She's got no alibi for the time of the disappearance, other than that she was at home."

"So," Dahlia asked , cautiously, "are you saying we're back to the Americans? To a rescue?"

Phil was unusually nonchalant. "Could be. Could easily be. But in fact, this story doesn't even need any Yanks, does it? Granny finds God in Poland, comes home to save her granddaughter's soul from a godless mother and a worthless father - all she's got to do to is hand her over to a group, or just a normal family, who share her beliefs. Job done; heaven achieved."

Dahlia thought about that for a while, then said: "No, I'm not sure about that. It's pretty obvious she has a low opinion of this country - "

"Now," put in Phil. "This country as it is now, you mean."

"Well, exactly - would she go to the risk and trouble of rescuing Sarla from her parents, only to leave her to grow up in this godless nation?" While Phil was digesting that, she added: "Besides, Sarla's not an infant, she's nearly seven. Sooner or later, if she's still in this country, she's going to get to a phone and call home."

"That makes sense," Phil said, making a heroic effort not to sound as if his agreement was reluctant. And not quite succeeding. "You're saying, if it was the gran, Sarla's left the country?"

"Left," said Dahlia, "or yet to leave."

*

Eight members of the squad altogether were involved in trying to identify the lodger that morning. It wasn't very exciting work. Concentrating on the period between the death of Bradley Nottle's grandmother, as discovered from her death certificate, and an estimated date, with generous margins of error, for when the Bradleys themselves had moved in to nineteen Beech Lane, the officers sat at computer screens, asking various repositories of old data if anyone at all had given that as their address.

It was the younger Lofty who had the first and only hit. DS Emmett's delight at finding a match so early in the process was depressed somewhat by the details of the person Lofty had uncovered. One detail in particular.

"This is a woman, Lofty. You've brought me a woman. I thought I told you never to do that, except during the night shift."

"Wrong sex, right address," said Lofty. "I can't help the fact that she wasn't a man. I wasn't even born."

"Rosie Liddle," Dale Emmett read. "Applied for an American Express credit card in February 1998."

"Better than nothing, Sarge," said Lofty, a hint of pleading beginning to enter his voice. "If you can find her, she might be able to tell you the name of the dead lodger."

"'You'? Is that Lofty-talk for 'we'?"

"Oh, Sarge ... "

"I thought you'd be glad to be working on a double murder investigation, instead of some boring, nothing-case about a missing bicycle. Which isn't even missing."

"Well, I would be, Sarge, but the thing is - "

"The thing is, you thought murder investigations would involve more leaping from rooftop to rooftop and shooting at people, and less tapping away at a keyboard."

"It's not that, Sarge, honestly. It's just this bike case, it looks like it's getting to the interesting part."

Dale enjoyed his fun as much as the next sergeant, but he wasn't a cruel man. Not by the standards of the sergeants he'd grown up under, anyway. "Ah, go on," he said, waving Lofty away. "Go and fetch your mate, and tell him I said the pair of you can go out to play."

CHAPTER TWELVE

The mother next. Her GP said that she could talk "for a little while," but warned Phil and Dahlia that he was putting them on their honour: if Chloe Brown started to become upset, or agitated, they were to desist.

"Fair enough," Phil had told the doctor; but what he'd said to Dahlia was "This time, we need answers from her. If she's ever going to see her daughter again, we need answers immediately."

In the event, Chloe seemed strong enough. Her face was red-raw, and looked, from her eyes down to her jawbone, almost as if it was peeling from burns. Her hands shook when she sipped her tea or dragged on her cigarette, and she had developed, since the detectives had last seen her, a presumably unconscious habit of periodically drawing her lips back over her teeth in a chimpanzee-style grimace. But she was awake, and fully present in the room, and ready and eager to answer questions. The more questions the better, Dahlia suspected; answering questions was doing something to help Sarla.

"We've been talking to your mum," Dahlia began.

"She means well."

"I'm sure," said Dahlia, making a written note of Chloe's revealing interjection. "We wanted to ask you - why do you think your mother came back to Britain?"

"Well ... " Chloe swallowed, and stopped speaking.

"We know what she says," Phil put in. "But we need to know what you think."

Chloe tried to roll a cigarette, spilled it halfway through, then remembered she already had one in her mouth, and lit that one instead. She smoked for a moment or two, looking at nothing, very intently, and then she took a deep breath and said: "She's dying."

Dahlia could feel Phil looking at her. She fought not to return the look. Their excitement - the thrill those words had given the detectives - was indecent. It was natural, of course, in their trade, but that didn't stop it being obscene, and she didn't want Chloe seeing it.

"I'm very sorry to hear that," she said. "That's a terrible burden for you, at a time like this."

"Thank you," said Chloe, who suddenly seemed quite washed out.

"Our sympathies," added Phil, a bit stiffly, and with his voice made slightly squeaky by the buzz that Dahlia knew was still rushing through his blood. *Gran was in a race against time: to rescue Sarla's soul before she herself dies. And desperate times call for desperate measures.*

"Thank you," said Chloe.

"May I ask ... ?" said Dahlia.

"It's a type of ovarian cancer. Very advanced. She hasn't got long."

"Chloe," said Phil, "your mother didn't mention any of this to us. Is it a secret?"

"She doesn't like people knowing about it."

"Why do you think that is, Chloe?" asked Dahlia.

Chloe kept staring at one corner of the room and then another. Not as if she was looking for something, Dahlia thought - more as if she was afraid something was looking for her. "She says she doesn't want everybody's sympathy, she doesn't want to be an emotional burden on her family and friends."

"I see," Phil began, but Dahlia, like Chloe, was a daughter, and she had detected underneath Chloe's words the code of a daughter trying not to speak ill of her mother.

"That's what she says," said Dahlia, gently, "but what we need here is your opinion. Why do *you* think your mother keeps her illness a secret?"

"Pride," said Chloe, apparently unable now to look anywhere but at her own knees. "You might have noticed, she's a real old beefeater. She hates everything about the Process, she's always slagging off this country. But you see - where she was living, they haven't got a full national health service. And Mum's never had any money."

"Ah, right," said Dahlia. "So you think she had to come home to take advantage of free medical care?"

"Sure. What else could it be?"

"Perhaps that she wanted to spend some time with Sarla before it was too late?"

"Oh, yeah, I'm sure she's glad to get to know Sarla. She really dotes on her. But the reason I'm not allowed to tell anyone about her being ill is, she's embarrassed. I'm sure that's it."

"Embarrassed," said Phil, "that she's anti-Process, but she still wants the full benefits of a free health service?"

Chloe nodded.

"She is definitely dying?" Dahlia asked.

"Oh yes, there's no doubt about it. She says that prayer will save her - she never used to be religious, that's something that's happened since she got ill, I think. Which is natural enough, I suppose. But the doctors are firm with her. They say she's only months from death. If she had come home earlier ... " Chloe shook her head, and stubbed out another cigarette. "But you see, she always believed in alternative medicine, faith-healing, all that stuff. She left it too late to see a proper doctor."

"Does she get on all right with your husband?" asked Phil.

"No, they never have. To be fair, John used to make an effort, in the early days, but Mum ... he's just not her type. She doesn't see what I see in him."

"Has that put a strain on your marriage? Since your mum came home?"

For the first time, Chloe met Dahlia's eyes. She straightened her back, and said: "It does, of course it does. Lots of couple go through that, don't they? But our marriage will survive, I can promise you that."

Well, yeah, thought Dahlia, but only because your mother won't. "Does John know about your mother's circumstances?"

Chloe Brown chewed her lip, and blinked, in a futile attempt to prevent herself from crying. "That's the hardest thing I've ever had to do, lying to him, but she insisted I mustn't tell him. What could I do? When someone's dying, you have to - you've got to make allowances, haven't you?"

"That's quite understandable," said Dahlia. "So what have you told him?"

"That's she's come here to get to know Sarla. That she'll only be here for a few months, then she's going abroad again, so we only have to stick it out for a while."

"And how about Sarla?" said Phil. "How does she get on with your mother?"

"It's awful, I know, but that just makes it all worse."

"Worse?"

"Between Mum and John. You see, Sarla absolutely worships her granny. Worships the ground she walks on."

Now that the Loftys had formally registered Haley French as a suspect - albeit, they weren't entirely sure what they suspected her of, other than making a false statement to police - they were able to begin investigating her.

The computer had nothing interesting to tell them, about her or about her supposed boyfriend, the hospital account Kieran Rider. Both were single; neither had any criminal convictions. Haley's occupation was given as mobile hairdresser.

"Don't get too close," cautioned the younger Lofty, not for the first time that day.

"Shut up," the older Lofty pointed out. Not for the first time that day.

Physical surveillance of a mobile hairdresser was not especially easy, given that there was only the two of them. She wasn't, after all, suspected of any particularly heinous crime, so they hadn't wasted their time asking for extra bodies. It was just two Loftys, one on a bicycle, and the other on foot, using mobiles to coordinate their efforts or, more frequently, to tell each other to shut up.

Despite the limitations of the operation, one fact had already been established: Haley French went about her business on a bike, with a sidecar for her equipment. It was fairly old, and looked altogether more rugged and businesslike than the one the accountant had bought.

The Loftys didn't follow her for long on her rounds; she'd have spotted them for sure if they'd stuck at it too long. During that time, she appeared to be behaving very much in the manner that the two Loftys would expect a mobile hairdresser to behave - inasmuch as they had any ideas on the subject, that is. She rode from one address to another, rang the doorbells, went inside, came out again half an hour or so later. Rode on to another address.

"Specialises in men's hair," the younger Lofty noted.

"You're not doing that detective stuff again, are you?" said the older one, adding "Over," because he knew it irritated his partner.

"All the people who answer the door to her are men."

"Maybe that's because their wives are busy sitting by the sink with towels round their shoulders. Over."

"All right then," Lofty replied. "She specialises in women's hair. Can't say I care really. Shall we go and get some lunch?"

They did, and afterwards made their way back to Wood Green, to have a look round the police wagon that was briefly being used to house, and would later be used to transport, the debris removed from the pond.

After what Gerard had said, they were half hoping for a gun, or a machete, or at least a dead body. But there was nothing obviously exciting amongst the exhibits. Mysterious, yes - but not exciting.

"Seems to come from different eras," said the older Lofty.

"Does it?"

Lofty pointed at a partially dismembered fridge. "That, for instance, I would say was 1980s. I remember having one like that, same model, in a flat we lived in in the early-mid 80s. Ten years later they looked quite different." He nudged a TV recorder with his foot.

"Whereas that is 2000s, 2010s. Some of the other stuff is in between, I'd reckon."

"Oh, yeah." The younger Lofty didn't sound as if he found that fascinating. "Point is, why dump it? OK, it's not worth a fortune, but there's a few quid's worth there, recycle value."

"Price of a long weekend in the Cotswolds, minimum," agreed the other. "For two, I mean. No point going on your own. Unless you're a rambler, I suppose."

"Suit you, then." Lofty picked up an old electric toaster, which as far as he could see looked unused. "I mean, surely there's no-one these days who simply can't be bothered to cash something in?"

"Can't be many. Even if they're so unpatriotic they can't be bothered for the sake of the recycling, they'd still want the money, wouldn't they? That's why the system works so well. In the old days you had to pay people to take your rubbish away. Now almost everything you don't want is something that you can get paid a few pence for. And it all adds up."

"One of the fading rich?" the younger Lofty suggested.

His colleague shook his head. "OK, they don't care about the money, but even they wouldn't go to the extra trouble of dumping it, would they? There's just nothing to gain."

"'Scuse me," said a woman in coveralls, taking the toaster from Lofty's hands. A scientific unit was still painstakingly sifting through the retrieved dumpings, looking for something that might give them a lead to its origins; a serial number, a retailer's sticker, an owner's security mark.

"How did someone get it here?" one Lofty asked the other.

"All in one go, according to the locals. So it was a decent-sized van or wagon, presumably."

Young Lofty's face screwed up. His frustration seemed to be causing him physical discomfort. "It's a hell of a lot of effort to go to, for no reward."

"And you've got surveillance on the grandmother?" Greg asked.

Phil nodded. "Round-the-clock. Visual, telecommunications,

thermals, everything. Nothing yet, but they've only just started this morning."

"The physical search for the girl is going on?"

"Absolutely," said Phil. "If we're right about the grandmother, then we presume Sarla's still alive. So all the media stuff is stepping up again, we're redoing all the door-to-doors."

"What about search parties?"

"Doesn't seem much point. Let's face it, search parties, whether they know it or not, are looking for dead bodies. They've looked - and there weren't any. If she's alive, and if the grandmother is behind it, then presumably she's going to have her taken out of the country. The cross-agency liaison is trying to make sure we're watertight at ports, rail terminals, and so on. DNA samples are being distributed, so if there's any girl they're suspicious of, they can test to see if it's Sarla."

"Big old coastline, though," said Greg.

"I know. I know. Our best bet is the granny, I think. But to be honest, I'm not optimistic there."

"You think she's being careful? Not contacting her fellow conspirators?"

"She's either very careful," said Phil, "or innocent."

That gave Greg pause. He'd asked Phil for a routine debriefing mainly to monitor his state of mind - was he about to explode into an anti-American episode, or was the other DS Kale, the reliable and assiduous officer, to the fore? What he hadn't expected to uncover was doubt. "You think she might be? I was hoping you and Dahlia might be able to help out with the murder, now you'd identified a suspect for the local shop to deal with."

Phil scratched at his beard, and fiddled with his unlit pipe. "It's the father," he said. "John Brown."

"You're not happy about him?"

"His attitude. He's a bit ... I don't know, a bit calm, perhaps. 'She'll turn up,' that's all he seems to say."

"Bit odd," Greg allowed. "But you said he had some kind of

emotional condition, could that - "

"Maybe," said Phil. "Probably. I suppose what I'm saying is, just because we've got a suspect, doesn't mean we're quite ready to abandon all other avenues."

Greg could hardly deny that this was the correct procedure. "Right. So you want to carry on with this?"

"A little longer. Just a little longer."

The next visitor to the DI's office was also an officer he had been hoping would, from now on, be entirely available to the murder team.

"No more food thefts on our patch, Ginger?"

"Nothing, boss. I reckon it's like I said - you get a rash of thefts, and everyone tightens up security again."

"No pattern to the thefts, then?"

"I don't think so, no."

Greg felt his hopes rising. "So you'll formally hand the outstanding cases back to Uniform, and - "

"There is just one thing, boss."

Oh God, is there? "Go on, Ginger."

"I'm still curious about the quadcycle factory - specifically, why the staff won't set up a rota to protect their own veg. I don't know that there's anything in it, it's just ... well, it's odd, don't you reckon?"

It was, Greg agreed. "It is," he said.

"One more day?" said Ginger.

"Go on, then," said Greg.

Rosie Liddle looked shocked when she opened her front door to the police that afternoon, and even more shocked when they told her what they wanted to talk to her about and how they'd found her. Bob Lemon, Catherine thought, looked almost offended; he was used to people wanting to talk to him. This rather fraught-faced woman in her fifties was a clear exception.

For once, the computer trail had proved not to be a false one, and a mercifully brief series of hops had led from the Rosie Liddle who'd given nineteen Beech Lane as her address on a credit card application form in 1998, to the Rosie Liddle, retired scientific worker, who now lived with her boyfriend in Cricklewood. And, in the first really lifting piece of news Catherine had received since the Caravan of Shame had entered her life, this Rosie Liddle confirmed that she was the same Rosie Liddle.

"His name was Nathan Ackery," she told them, and both Bob and Catherine wrote it down in their notebooks. Catherine underlined it, twice, and Bob ringed it with a celebratory circle. They had a name at last for the missing lodger; there was a good chance they had a name at last for the body under the driveway.

"And he was a friend of yours?"

Rosie kept pressing her palm against the chest, on the left, as if to slow her heartbeat. Catherine hoped the understandable shock of finding two Serious Crimes detectives on your doorstep, wanting to talk about your youth, wasn't going to give her a heart attack. "We went out for a while. It wasn't anything terribly serious, I suppose, although - well, he ended it rather suddenly. Just suddenly seemed to lose interest in me. Hurt my pride a bit, you know."

"He'd got someone else?" Catherine guessed.

"I presume so." She shrugged, to show that it was a long time ago.

"After you'd split up with Nathan," Bob asked, "did you stay in touch?"

"God no! I was quite pissed off at the time, to be honest. I never spoke to him, or heard from him again."

"Or heard of him?" asked Catherine.

"Or that. Honestly, he just vanished from my life. We were in a pizza restaurant when I finally got him to admit that he was seeing another girl. I got up, walked out - that was it. Next time I heard of him was today." She massaged her heart again. "I heard on the news about a body being found in Beech Lane - are you saying ...?"

"In fact, two bodies have been found at that address," said Catherine. "We're still trying to identify one of them."

"And you think it's Nathan?"

"That's one possibility."

"My God."

"I'm not quite clear," said Catherine, "were you actually resident at - "

"Oh, the credit card? No, no - I never lived there. What happened was - well, at that time I didn't really have a proper address of my own. I was not long out of university, moving around a lot - staying with friends for short spells, and so on. In those days, it could be very difficult to get cheap accommodation in London. Nathan allowed me to use his address when I applied for that credit card, because if you didn't have a permanent address, they wouldn't look at you."

"That must have made things tricky when you split up with Nathan?"

Rosie wrinkled her brow, evidently trying to recall events from half a lifetime ago, in a different world. "No, I know what happened. I only had the bloody credit card for a few weeks! I lost my job, you see, and the first thing I did was to cancel the card. So as to avoid the temptation of using it, right?"

"I understand. Do you have any idea what might have become of Nathan, after you broke up with him?"

"It sounds as if *you* might have an idea on that, Sergeant."

"As I said, we're still - "

"No, sure. But I'm afraid I can't help you. I probably only visited that place half a dozen times in my whole life - and never, after that night in the pizza restaurant." She shivered - rather theatrically, Catherine thought. "Still, what a spooky thought - it was such a normal, boring suburban house, and now you've found two bodies there!"

"Did you ever have any contact with the owners of the property, at all?"

"Nathan's landlords? No, I don't think so. Don't even remember their names, if I ever knew them."

"Bradley and Kim Nottle."

Rosie shrugged. "Doesn't ring any."

"Can you tell us anything else," Bob asked, "about Nathan? His home town, any relatives he might have mentioned ... anything?"

"I'm sorry," said Rosie. "He was just Nathan. It's such a long time ago, and such an unimportant episode in my life." She smiled. "It's a miracle I can remember his surname!"

"Nothing to worry about," Ginger reassured the two lads, showing them his police ID. "Just wondered if you could spare me five minutes?"

Pete and Dave - he didn't need surnames, he just needed someone to talk to - were both in their early twenties, and both worked at the quadcycle factory. Ginger had thought they might, since he'd watched them coming out of it at clocking-off time, before waylaying them just round the corner from it. They didn't mind sitting on a park bench with him for five minutes, as he passed round a packet of cigarettes.

"I've been investigating the food theft from the rooftop garden at your factory. I understand you haven't got a nightwatchman, is that right?"

"Yeah, so it seems," said Pete. "So it turns out. Now he tells us!"

"Mr Doyle hadn't told you about it before the theft?"

Dave shook his head. "Apparently he's been trying to find a replacement, but with no luck. Not everyone's idea of a great job, is it?"

"So what are you going to do meantime," Ginger asked. "Set up a rota?"

"Yeah," said Dave, "I think the boss is sorting something out with the shop stewards." He grimaced. "With any luck he'll have found someone before it gets going."

His mate nudged him, hard enough to knock him off the bench. "This one's got a new girlfriend," he explained.

Dave picked himself up, and replaced his cigarette in his mouth. "I just don't want to spend all night on the bloody roof, that's all."

"Don't worry," Pete assured him. "I'll look the other way."

"So, before the theft," said Ginger, "you didn't realise the other bloke had left, the old nightwatchman?"

"You know what it's like with night workers," said Pete. "You hardly ever see them."

"I think I did hear he'd gone," said Dave, "but I just assumed he'd been replaced."

"What was people's reaction when they found out he hadn't?"

Dave rolled his eyes. "Some of the older staff, the ones with families to feed, were furious."

"They were," said Pete.

"Blamed the boss for messing around, putting their food supply at risk. There was talk of a strike - the company had to give us all a bonus as compensation."

"What's it like," asked Ginger, "working for a private company?"

Pete shrugged. "Doesn't make any difference, does it? A boss is a boss."

Dave wasn't so sure. "I don't like it, me. You feel like you've got no say over what happens, no control over your life. I'll get a co-op job as soon as I can. I'm on a waiting list at the job exchange. I mean, this business with the rooftop - that could never happen in a co-op, could it?"

Ginger wondered about that; all system were run by humans, was his experience, so all systems could make mistakes. "I expect you're right," he said.

Centralised dental records were a godsend, not only to holidaymakers with toothache, but to police officers trying to identify corpses. Of course, to have a realistic chance of making a match from millions of records, you still needed a name to begin with. There was considerable relief amongst those taking part in the murder investigation when the name Nathan Ackery proved the key to unlocking the identity of the body found under the drive at nineteen Beech Lane.

"It's not hard to pick a possible motive out of this story," said Greg, late that afternoon, as he and Catherine sat in his office, drinking tea and eating Jade's cake. "I mean, who kills a lodger and buries him under the drive?"

"The husband," Catherine agreed. "He was having an affair with the wife, Brad found out, killed him - "

"Accidentally or deliberately," Greg put in.

"Brad hides the body, and tells everyone - including Kim - that the lodger's cleared off. Sort of thing lodgers do, I daresay. Or did, in those days."

"We're talking about 1998," said Greg. "Is that right? Probably late on in the year."

Catherine checked her notes. "That seems right. Brad's a DIY wizard; he lays his own drive. He and Kim move in to the house."

"And they've lived there ever since, without making any impact on the neighbourhood, keeping themselves to themselves, and perhaps now we know why - guilt, horror, haunting, and a marriage rendered awful by all the above." Greg rubbed at his tired eyes. Long days, these. "That's Brad, anyway. I wonder what explains Kim's reclusiveness? If we're right, she hadn't killed anyone - didn't know that anyone had been killed. Just knew her husband was unwilling to move house."

"Perhaps just the shame of a bad marriage. You don't want people to know how you've failed as a woman." Catherine coughed, and took a mouthful of tea. She smiled. "Oh, don't mind me! I did a course in pop psychology when I was in sales."

"All right," said Greg. "So, many years later, Kim finds out about the dead lodger - "

"Perhaps Brad finally has to tell her, because of the compulsory re-greening? Throws himself on her mercy?"

"And she kills him. In anger or hatred, hot or cold."

"I'm finding it difficult to hold that against her, to be honest," said Catherine.

"I know what you mean. And then, in a panic or perhaps calculatedly, she goes on the run."

"Where currently she remains," said Catherine. "*Bloody* caravan..."

CHAPTER THIRTEEN

Friends, neighbours and relatives of John and Chloe Brown continued to be interviewed - and sometimes re-interviewed - both by local detectives, and by DS Kale and DC Kotane on behalf of the Squad. It was widely agreed that John Brown only had one friend and one relative, and as it happened they were the same man: his cousin, and childhood playmate, Johnny Costas.

"He says can he meet us at work," Dahlia reported, putting her phone away, "because he doesn't want us at home, upsetting his wife. Highly strung, apparently, been seeing the doctor for nerves. She works at home, designing book covers."

"That explains it, maybe." While Dahlia was on the phone, Phil had been checking his notes. "Supposed to be John Brown's closest, or only, friend - but he's not on our list of people who were at the Brown house the day Sarla went missing."

"Didn't rally round, eh? That's not what you'd expect, from what we've heard of their relationship."

"Nervous wife," said Phil. "Decent excuse, I suppose."

"Or the wives don't get on," said Dahlia. "Anyway, he's only working a ten-minute bus ride away from the Browns' house, so I said we'd go straight round."

It was a sweaty, overcast afternoon in London, and Johnny Costas was plainly glad enough to take a break from his labours to sit for a while with the detectives in a nearby greenspot. A little younger than his cousin John, Johnny was a well-covered, strong-looking man, with thick black hair and a full beard. He drank long and lustily from a drinking fountain, then filled and lit his pipe.

"Christ, that's better," he said. "It's got hotter since it clouded over."

"I notice there are no shade trees where you're working," said Phil.

"There can't be - the pipes wouldn't work at optimum in the shade. But we take frequent breaks in the nearest greenspot."

"I'm sorry," said Dahlia, "we don't know exactly what it is you are doing?"

"Ah, right - sorry." He gave her a smile which was easy enough, but she thought she could see the strain behind it. Hardly surprising; if he was that close to John Brown, he must presumably be pretty close to little Sarla, too. "It's experimental - I'm with a road-gang co-operative that's got the contract from the government to install a few miles of it, to see whether it really works."

"A few miles of what?" said Phil.

"Pipes, basically. Tarmac roads get fantastically hot in the summer, right? So - what happens to all that heat?"

"Disappears into the night," suggested Dahlia.

"That's it - it's wasted. What we're doing is burying masses of very small polythene water pipes under the tarmac. On a sunny day, the water in the pipes can double its temperature - more, they reckon. Now, this hot water is pumped to the heavily insulated micro-tanks serving the houses alongside the road, where it's used to heat the water that the residents use, domestically - washing, bathing, whatever."

"But I thought we were getting rid of tarmac?" said Phil. "Because it causes flash floods?"

"Well, there's the maths they need to work out. If you're keeping tarmac roads, you're going to have to install really superb new storm drains. Hence this experiment. They need to know whether the energy gain is sufficient to outweigh the cost of the drains." He took another drink from the fountain. "Hot work. Really hot work. Now - let me say straight away that I'm more than happy to help you any way I can in looking for Sarla, but I really don't think there's anything I can tell you. It's not as if I could have spotted a clue, or anything - I haven't even been near the house for two or three weeks."

"Why is that?" asked Phil. "We understood you and John were good friends."

Johnny waved his hand towards where his colleagues were still drilling into tarmac. "Busy at work, that's all. And since this terrible thing happened - well, you don't want to crowd people too much, you know what I mean?"

"Of course."

"We keep in touch by phone all the time - several times a day. John knows where I am if he needs me."

"Of course," said Phil. "You've known him since childhood?"

"All my life." There seemed to be an element of pride in his voice, Dahlia thought, as if knowing John Brown all your life wasn't merely a fact to be stated, but an achievement to be boasted about. "He's been my best friend since I was younger than Sarla. And when Tressa and I lost our own little one - "

"Lost?" said Phil.

"Died. She died during the hard times."

"I'm very sorry."

"It was a long time ago now," said Johnny, "but what I'm saying is, John was solid for me. You understand? I was boozing and whatever, and he carried me through it. You won't find a better man, Sergeant, not a better man in London."

"Do you agree with him, that Sarla - "

"No question about it." He nodded vigorously, his glistening beard bobbing up and down. "Some nutcase has got her. You can only hope that he'll panic, with all you lot looking for him, and Sarla's face all over the media, and let her go. That could happen, yeah?"

"You don't suspect the involvement of religious fundamentalists, then?" said Phil.

Johnny Costas laughed. "You hardly need Yanks to save her soul, when she's got that poisonous granny hanging around, do you? Sooner that one pops off, the better."

Dahlia felt Phil's knee knock against hers. She pressed back. Thing was, she'd received the coded message, but she wasn't quite sure what it meant: which one of them was supposed to speak next?

The roadman evidently interpreted their silence as disapproval. "Sorry," he said, "that's an awful thing to say about anyone, I know. But, honestly ... well, put it this way - there won't be many tears at her funeral."

Phil recovered his tongue first and managed to ask a few more bland questions, before sending Johnny back to his digging. Phil and Dahlia loitered in the greenspot.

"So much for family secrets," said Phil.

"Amazing," agreed Dahlia. "Did he realise what he'd said, do you reckon?"

Phil fiddled with his pipe. "Don't think so," he said. "But he will, won't he? It'll suddenly come to him, and his stomach will turn to ice."

"So what do we do about John Brown?"

"Front him with it. Straight out, and straight away." Phil took out his phone. "I'll check if he's at home yet."

He was, and when the detectives arrived there, they invited him to step into his garden for a moment, for a little privacy.

"Your cousin Johnny," said Phil, "who we were talking to just now, let slip something about your mother-in-law. You know what we're talking about? About her health."

"Oh," said John. "Yeah, OK."

"And the only place we can think where he might have come by that information, is from you. Except that according to your wife, you don't know about her mum's terminal illness. Could you explain that, please?"

John Brown's face wrinkled in disgust. "She had my Sarla praying with her. Can you imagine that? A little kid? On her knees, *praying* with her granny, asking Jesus to stop her granny dying. So of course when granny dies anyway, Sarla's going to think it's her fault, isn't she? For not praying hard enough. For not being a good little girl." He shook his head. "Sooner the old witch dies, the better. Good riddance. Then we'll be a family again."

"And Sarla told you?"

"Granny had sworn her to secrecy, of course, but you know what they're like at that age. She was bursting with it, poor kid."

"Does your wife know that you know? That Sarla knows?"

"No, and don't you go telling her, either." His face was fierce. "She doesn't need any more pressure on her."

On the bus back to the station, Phil said: "Strengthens the grandmother's motive, doesn't it? John's behaviour towards Felicity will have become even less friendly - "

"He's enraged with jealousy, isn't he?" Dahlia interrupted. "He fears he's losing his family to his own mother-in-law."

"Right - Felicity senses that, senses his increased loathing of her, knows that all her good work indoctrinating the child will be undone as soon as she dies ... "

"Well," said Dahlia. "It doesn't do anything to undermine her status as a suspect, I'll give you that. I'm just not - "

Phil's phone rang. The conversation was brief.

"Muswell Hill?" Dahlia asked.

"They want to stop looking for the Americans - the ones the mother heard, and the ones our friend with the ponytail heard. They say they need the manpower reassigned."

"And you've agreed?"

"I don't think they were really asking my permission, to be honest. More of a courtesy call." He took his pipe out of his pocket, reamed its bowl with his little finger, and put it away again.

"There's never been another report of them," Dahlia pointed out, gently.

"You don't believe in their existence." Phil's tone rejected her gentleness.

"Honestly? No. I think the likeliest explanation is that this is all a case of what folklorists call ostension - an urban myth come to life."

"What do you mean?"

"Rescues are urban myths." She held up a placatory hand. "No, I know, that's just my opinion - I know you don't agree. But I think

Felicity Cook, if it was her who took the girl, has enacted a 'rescue' based on all the stories she's heard."

"She must have had some help," Phil objected, "otherwise how does she get the girl out of the country?"

"I accept that. But these American accents wandering around at the time of the kidnapping - what possible role could they play in any conspiracy, other than to attract attention and ruin the whole thing?"

"You're saying they're irrelevant?"

"Yes. I think so. I don't know who they were - maybe they were diplomats chasing up a genealogy lead, who happened to walk down those streets at that time and never again. Granny could have used anyone as her helpers. English, Polish, anything. And since all her known associates in the country are being checked methodically, there's not much we can do until one of them rings the computer's bells."

Phil still thought the Yanks were involved - she could see that in his eyes, the set of his mouth, the angle of his shoulders. But he agreed with her on the need to keep checking - not only on Felicity Cook's contacts, but also on Sarla's father, mother, neighbours ...

"You know what Greg Wallace always says," said Phil. "Inspiration is excellent, but thoroughness is excellenter."

Ah-ha, thought Ginger Thom: the job exchange. Of course.

There was a branch two streets away from the quadcycle factory. While he was waiting to see the manager, he browsed a few of the vacancies. 'Phenologist.' He wondered if he'd like to be a phenologist. Quite possibly he would, because the money wasn't up to much.

The manager, an attractive young woman of his own age - who actually did have ginger hair, which he thought might give them something in common, albeit something difficult to grasp - was able to tell him that no vacancy for a nightwatchman for any quadcycle factory had been notified either to this branch or, according to the computer, to any other in London.

If there had been such a vacancy, she told him, they'd have filled it without much difficulty. "You're right, it's not the most popular job, but of course the money is good. There's no shortage in London of people who prefer working alone, or working at night, or to whom wages are the only thing that matters."

"How long would it take to find someone, do you suppose?"

She thought about it. "My professional pride would be dented if it took more than two or three days."

"That's very interesting. Thank you." As she showed him out, he said: "Do you think phenology would be a good career choice for a man of my qualities?"

She smiled broadly, while simultaneously trying to keep her face straight, which Ginger had always thought was just about the most erotic expression the female fizzog was capable of. "Do you know much about phenology, Detective Constable?"

"No ... " he admitted. "No, only in the sense of never having heard of it."

If they were right about Brad Nottle killing the lodger - and about his wife, many years later, killing him - then there were really only two mysteries remaining for the murder team to clear up: where did the Spitfire rifle come from, and how did the furniture vanish from nineteen Beech Lane. Neither question was satisfactorily explained by the existing theory. It was possible that Kim Nottle was trying to remove forensic evidence after shooting her husband - but that just raised a new question: how does one middle-aged woman, in a state, on her own, virtually clear a suburban house? Without being noticed?

As for the Spitfire, that was still Gerard and Erin's priority. Erin continued to show absolutely no signs of boredom, which Gerard silently gave her credit for. He himself was utterly bored. He was, to use an expression of his father's, bored-shitless-backwards. But he didn't mind. He hadn't joined the police for excitement, he always said; if he'd wanted excitement, he'd have become a bank robber.

"How often are militia rifles actually fired?" she asked at one point, between phone calls, almost at the very end of the shift.

"Of course, you wouldn't know, would you?" said Gerard. "Militia service doesn't begin until you're twenty-five, is that right?"

"That's why I'm asking you, Detective Constable Cochrane," she said, giving the old man a pitying look.

"Cheeky mare. Well, you got that wrong, then, didn't you? Police officers are exempt from militia duty. Another good reason for you to join us."

"With that and the cakes, I can't really go wrong, can I? So, in the event of invasion, what are all the cops going to do? Hide under tables?"

"We get basic defence training at work instead. There's regular courses, and that. What's on your mind, anyway?"

"Not sure," she replied, "probably nothing. I'd just like to know how often the guns are fired, that's all."

Gerard had to hide a smile at that. If ever he'd heard a true detective's answer to a question ...

"All right, let's ask a civilian."

They did, and Jade was able to tell them that rifle drills were generally "dry" - actual firing practice was carried out twice a year.

"Right," said Erin, "now this might sound a bit mad - "

"The best ideas generally do," Gerard assured her. "Like toasted cheese sandwiches with humus."

"Supposing the rifle that was used in the murder was replaced with a replica? I'm assuming a replica would be easier to make, or get hold of, than a real rifle, because it wouldn't have to have any real workings, would it? It'd just have to fool people from the outside. Just have to look and feel right, to a casual inspection. That way, the armoury wouldn't report being a gun short, and the test to see if any of the guns had been fired would still come back negative."

Gerard sat quite still, working it through in his mind. "It'd be discovered sooner or later, though."

"Yeah," said Erin, "but you're hoping later rather than sooner. By that time, you've done the shooting that you needed the stolen gun for, and you've had time to cover your tracks. If you knew the date of the next live-firing exercise, you could perhaps time it so that there was the maximum gap between you stealing the real rifle, and someone trying to fire the dummy."

"Right," said Gerard. "I like that. Good work, Erin. You know what this means, don't you?"

She cringed, in mock apology. "We've got to start at the top of the list again, haven't we? Phone every armoury in the area, and ask them to check for fakes."

"We'll do that in the morning," said Gerard. "Time you were getting home. For tonight, we'll just send out a mass emailing to every armoury in the country, and hope that when we arrive at work tomorrow, the job will magically have done itself."

As they packed up, Erin asked him: "Do you think it's right that militia service is compulsory? I know a lot of people think it's against the spirit of the Process - a bit, you know, *heavy*."

"I suppose it is," Gerard agreed, "but think about the alternative. If it wasn't compulsory, it'd have to be voluntary."

She frowned. "Yeah ... ?"

"Well, can you imagine the sort of people you'd get volunteering?"

Why hadn't Mr Doyle, the manager of the quadcycle factory, tried to hire a replacement nightwatchman? Was he too mean, Ginger wondered, simply didn't want to pay another wage? Seemed like a big risk to take, just to save a few quid a week.

He went in search of advice, and found DS Blake in the canteen, apparently having a last cup of tea before she headed home. Why she didn't wait until she got home, and drink her tea in comfort, he couldn't imagine. Except, perhaps - why dig into your own rations, when you could use the police service's?

At any rate, Catherine seemed more than happy to hear the

young DC's dilemma, and apply the benefits of her experience to it. One thing struck her immediately. "You haven't mentioned who called in the theft from the rooftop garden? Was it the manager?"

Ginger metaphorically slapped his head. Then, in case she couldn't see that, he did it literally. "God, Sarge, I'm having a caravan moment!"

"Thank you very much, you rotten sod. Someone told me that wasn't my fault, because I was with a senior officer."

"True enough," said Ginger, writing in his notebook: *Who called it in??*

"You said it was a private company? What are the rules for businesses being allowed to stay private?"

"Interesting point," said Ginger, taking out his phone and switching it to search mode. "I don't know. Let's look it up."

While most enterprises in the country - other than those with no employees - were now co-operatives, or were patriotically owned in some form or another, during this period of transition some smaller concerns had been left in private hands. This was mainly to avoid unnecessary upheaval, and partly to maintain the all-important consensus without which the Process would surely fall apart.

For obvious reasons, most people preferred not to work for private companies, and the private sector was fading away fairly rapidly. In the end, most business owners were happy enough to sell out to their employees, who were entitled by law to loans from the Central Transitional Fund to allow them to buy their workplaces as co-ops.

"There can't be many left, can there?" said Catherine, as Ginger pulsed through online menus.

"I think there's still a few. It's not yet compulsory to sell out, and there's some stubborn buggers out there, God knows. Ah, here we are ... " He mumbled to himself as he read from the small screen, then gave Catherine the condensed version. "Seems there's various criteria, based on output, turnover, strategic importance, etcetera, but what it all comes down to in the case of a factory is that if you want to stay private, you can't have more than fifty employees - full-time jobs or equivalent - in total. More than that, and you have to turn yourself into a co-op."

"How many does your quadcycle place employ?"

Ginger shrugged. "Must be about that, I reckon." He remembered something else he'd wanted to ask. "Sarge, what's a phenologist?"

"Phenology? Oh, that's a very important field of science in these difficult days."

"Yeah, but what is it? What does a phenologist actually do?"

"He writes down the date he first sees a butterfly each year," said Catherine.

Ginger was unconvinced. "Yeah ... that can't actually be it though, can it?"

Catherine obviously didn't know. "I don't know," she said. "I think so."

"Yeah, but, that can't actually be the entirety of the trade, profession or calling of phenology, can it? Writing down when you first see a butterfly each year?"

"Basically."

Ginger persisted. "Yes ... it might be *basically*, but I think there must, technically, be more to it than that, even so. What does he do the rest of the year?"

"Waits for the butterfly."

Ginger sighed, and stood up. "Tell you what, Sarge - I'll just look it up, shall I?"

Catherine laughed. "Good night, Ginger." She finished her tea, thought about it, and then went and got another one.

CHAPTER FOURTEEN

Erin was at work the next morning a little before Gerard arrived, and by the time he'd hung his hat up she was close to bursting with excitement. He sent her a cheery wave from the other side of the office and then disappeared into the Gents for ten minutes. Then he went to the canteen to get two cups of tea. You've got to take your fun where you find it; that was something a long career in public service had taught him.

"We've got a reply!"

"Already? That's good going."

"They were doing some sort of stock-take last night, so they read our email straight away and decided - "

"Who did?" Gerard was getting quite excited himself, now.

"Cricklewood Broadway armoury. Anyway, they checked there and then - and they've found one!"

"They've found a replica Spitfire?"

Erin sat on her hands, grinned and bounced up and down.

"That's brilliant. Well done, Erin. The DI owes you a weekend in Paris, or a cheese roll and half a pint, whichever he deems the more appropriate. Where did you say again?"

Erin had already got the map out. "There you go. Not all that near to Beech Lane, I know, but what I'm thinking is, Mrs Nottle might have hired a professional to kill her husband, or it could be - "

"Just a second," said Gerard, looking for his printouts from the last squad briefing. "I thought so. That witness who named the dead lodger for us - Rosie Liddle. That's her neck of the woods." He found the address on the map. "In fact, what's the betting Cricklewood Broadway is the one that covers her home? In actual fact, let's not bet on it, let's look it up." The computer agreed with him: Rosie Liddle was a member of the militia based at Cricklewood Broadway armoury.

"God," said Erin. "Could it be a coincidence?"

"Certainly it could," said Gerard, "but if it is, it's a bloody good one."

A one-purpose intercept was what it sounded as if it was; it was a tap on electronic communications which a magistrate had granted on the basis that it be used for one purpose only. In this case, the two one-purpose intercepts successfully applied for by the Loftys had one purpose between them - to find out whether, and if so how often, the hospital accountant and the mobile hairdresser contacted each other. The answer was, they didn't. Or at least, that they hadn't, so far, during the couple of days the taps had been in place.

"Confirms it," said the younger Lofty. "They're not boyfriend and girlfriend. I mean, even if they're meeting in the flesh, they've got to arrange it, haven't they?"

"Possible, I suppose," said the older Lofty, "that the places and times of their meetings are long-established. No need to phone first."

"Possible," conceded his partner. "But doesn't he ever ring up to say 'Shall I pick up some fish and chips on my way?', or 'I'll be half an hour late, I've just had some truly fascinating spreadsheets delivered'?"

But the other Lofty wasn't really listening any more. Something was occurring to him which really should have occurred to him yesterday. He must have been having what Ginger Thom had taken to referring to as a 'caravan moment.'

With the younger Lofty following impatiently behind him, he hurried over to Jade's desk. "Jade - could you do me a favour? Could you ring this number - it's a mobile hairdresser - and ask for an appointment?"

"Bit late, my love," said Jade, looking at his head appraisingly. "Blob of beeswax and a duster would be more use, surely?"

"Not for me, for you. I want to know whether she takes female clients."

A few minutes later, Jade brought them the answer. Haley French did indeed do women's, but she regretted to say that she was fully booked at the moment; she invited Jade to phone back in a month's time.

"Thanks, Jade."

"My pleasure," said Jade. "I suppose you could always have a curl put into that bit at the back. Might stop it flopping on your collar."

The younger Lofty's impatience was not diminishing. "So, what's all that about? She's a hairdresser who does both sexes - don't most of them?"

"She's a unisex hairdresser who, as far as we've seen, only has male clients." He said nothing more for a while, just looked at his young colleague waiting for the penny to drop. It didn't. Bloody hell, was he really *that* young? "I suspect she might not be working as a mobile hairdresser, after all." Still nothing; just impatience, mixed now with puzzlement. "I suspect, kidda, that she is an unlicensed prostitute."

The older lofty could clearly see the moment when the sheer obviousness of the suggestion hit his colleague. The young DC was not about to give in to exclamation, however; instead, he stood, nodding for a few moments, looking sage and thoughtful, digesting developments and weighing things up. He rather spoiled the effect, Lofty thought, when he finally spoke. "So, what's the advantage of being unlicensed as opposed to licensed?"

"You don't declare the earnings," Lofty explained. "It's money in the hand."

"Right," said the other Lofty, as if this was what he'd thought all along.

Within an hour of Erin and Gerard's report to DI Wallace, full computer checks had been run on Rosie Liddle and the man she lived with, Ed Upsall.

"She's a retired science worker," Bob Lemon reported, "on the citrus research programme."

"This is no time for jokes, Bob," said Greg.

Bob looked up from his screen. He blinked. "Pardon?"

"Doesn't matter." Greg waved a hand in the air. "It was a joke. Move on."

"Right. Well, as I say - "

Erin laughed. "I get it!"

Bob stopped speaking, and looked up.

"Bob, please," said Greg. "My fault. I'll explain later. Carry on."

Bob shrugged. "She worked in citrus research, looking for ways of successfully growing citrus fruits in this country to replace lost sources of imports."

"Like oranges?" said Gerard. "Grapefruits, that sort of thing?" Titters could be heard being repressed.

"Yes, presumably," said Bob. "And limes and fucking lemons as well, I imagine. May I continue?" Amid more general laughter, he did. "She has no criminal convictions, nor does the boyfriend. They've been together for years, joint owners of the flat. He has his own small business - privately-owned, I mean, only two employees - as a furniture man, with premises nearby. And unless anyone wants to squeeze in any more citrus jokes, that's about - "

"Does furniture man mean what I think it means?" said Catherine suddenly.

"I presume it means he runs a removals - *Christ!*" said Bob. "I see what you mean."

"Furniture removals?" said Greg. "So, hold on: the boyfriend of the former girlfriend of the man found dead under the Nottles' drive, removes people's furniture for a living?"

"These coincidences are mucky little buggers," said Gerard. "They're breeding right under our noses."

Greg closed his eyes tight in concentration. "Right. Forget motives, for a moment. For whatever reason, Kim Nottle needed to clear the house after she'd killed Brad, and these two helped her do it. Which makes it all the more probable that they helped her procure the gun." He thought for a moment more, then opened his eyes and clapped his hands together, once. "We've got enough with these two coincidences to consider Rosie Liddle and Ed Upsall as suspects for accessories before and after the fact. But probably not enough for a search warrant. Anyway, we don't want to show our hand just yet. First priority - Gerard, get them put under full surveillance. There must be a good chance they're sheltering Kim."

"The canteen manager, definitely?" said Ginger, who knew Jade didn't commit many inaccuracies, and that she didn't take kindly to being asked things twice, but who wanted to be quite sure on this. "Not the factory manager - the canteen manager?"

Jade gave him a look. Then she gave him the name and home phone number of the canteen manager. Then she gave him a look.

"Right, thanks, Jade. That's very useful. Thanks." He didn't run. He just walked quickly because he was in a hurry to phone the woman who ran the canteen at the quadcycle factory who, according to police records, had been the person who'd reported the theft from the rooftop garden.

"Well, obviously - when I went up to get the veg for lunch, that's when I found it gone!"

"And you reported it to the factory manager, Mr Doyle? How did he react?"

"How would you expect him to react? He was horrified. Feeding fifty hard-working men and women every day takes some planning, I can tell you."

"I'm sure it does."

"Well, it *does*," protested the canteen manager.

I was agreeing with you, you silly cow. "Whose idea was it to call the police?"

"Mine, I suppose. I suggested it, and Doyle could hardly say no, could he? But he didn't look like he was about to do it himself."

"Really?"

"Mind you, I wasn't surprised. He's not up to much in a crisis, poor old Doyle."

"No?"

"Nah - that's the trouble with private firms. The managers aren't elected, so you don't necessarily get the best man for the job."

"Right, I see. And - "

"And sometimes, you get a complete knob, like Doyle."

"Right. Before the thefts, did you know that there was no rooftop nightwatchman?"

"Well of course I bloody didn't! I wouldn't have stood for it, would I? I gave Doyle a word or two about that, you can believe me, and then I got onto the union. Mind you, if they'd been doing their job, they'd have noticed beforehand, wouldn't they?"

"You'd hope so, wouldn't you?"

"But the chairman of the stewards, it's his last couple of months before retirement, so nobody liked to stand against him last time round. He's past it, if you ask me. All right in his time, but he's half asleep these days."

Ginger found Bob Lemon in the kitchen, waiting for a glass of water. It was a hot morning, and there was a queue for the tap: Gerard was waiting for Erin, and Bob was behind Gerard. Ginger joined the line.

"That's your bloody Process for you," said Bob. "Never had to queue for water under free enterprise!"

Ginger laughed. "Get me my passport, mother - I'm off to America." While they waited, and while they drank, he told Bob about the factory manager's apparent reluctance to call the police.

"One obvious thought," Bob suggested. "He was doing something naughty up there. Growing dope without a license, perhaps? If he was up to something, first thing he'd need to do is get rid of the nightwatchman."

"I did wonder," Ginger agreed. "I didn't spot anything suspicious when I was on his roof, but then I wasn't looking for anything. I was investigating a straightforward food theft."

"No point in raiding the place now, anyway," said Bob. "He'll surely have covered his tracks. A raid would just alert him to the fact that we're onto him."

"If, indeed, we are," said Ginger.

The Loftys sat at their desks, trying to work it out logically. If possible, without killing each other.

"Logically," said the older one, "the only reason you dump all that stuff in the pond, instead of recycling it, is because you *can't* recycle it. Either it's stolen - "

"Is it worth stealing?" interrupted the younger. "If we're being logical, I mean. Are you really going to risk prison - never mind all the effort you've got to go to - for a few quid's worth of recyclables? Why not use the same amount of effort, and take the same risks, to steal something that's worth a lot more? Logically, that is."

"All right then. All that leaves us with is, the junk's connected to some other crime, and that's why you have to get rid of it."

"You know what it could be?" said the younger Lofty. "It could be a political protest."

"What - in favour of floods? Against recycling?"

"How about, against micromanagement of people's lives by the state?"

The older Lofty counted to ten. He did it out loud, because he found it worked better that way. "If it was a political protest," he said, "wouldn't there be a slogan, a manifesto, something to let people know?"

"Maybe they're beginners. They forgot that bit."

"Fascinating," said the older one. "But if we put aside your hypothesis concerning L-plated dissidents - "

"Could be sabotage."

"Ten, nine, eight," said the older Lofty, "seven, six, five, bollocks, three, two one. So, never mind the protestors, now we've got a fiendish enemy power which shall remain nameless parachuting in highly-trained undercover agents who are under orders to cause minor and temporary inconvenience to the British authorities by bunging supermarket trolleys into flood ponds?"

"Yeah, but - "

"Where did they get the junk from? Did they bring it with them?"

"Could've stolen it."

"We checked, kidda, remember? Nobody's reported the theft of a load of junk. And you would report it, wouldn't you? Because, as we've established, even if it's not worth stealing, it's still worth recycling."

"Could someone have put the stuff in the pond, in order to bury something more important that's already in there?"

Actually, that wasn't bad. The older Lofty stayed quiet for a moment, thinking that through.

"Stop bloody counting to ten," said his partner.

"I'm not - I'm thinking. No, that doesn't work, does it? Because filling the pond with junk would have - and in fact, has had - the opposite effect. It's caused the pond to be dredged, so you'd be drawing attention to whatever it was you were trying to hide."

They had a cup of tea. The older Lofty had half a small bun, and the younger Lofty had four large ones. The older Lofty thought that, all things considered, that was what he most resented about young people. It wasn't all the sex, or the knees that didn't creak, or that their hangovers only lasted half an hour instead of three days. It was the amount they could eat. Half-grown bastards.

"Forget the junk, then," said the young one. "Let's get back to our hospital accountant. Why did he buy the bike in the first place?"

"How about this. She's a prostitute, he's a client; he falls in love with her, tries to woo her with gifts - "

"Hold on," interrupted the young one. "He's trying to get off with a prostitute? Isn't the whole point of prostitutes that you don't have to - "

"You'll understand when you're older," said his partner. "Or when you're more intelligent, whichever happens first. For now, just accept an old copper's word for it - clients do fall in love with toms. So, she spurns his gift, this splendid bicycle, and in a fit of pique, he chucks the bike in the pond. Then he becomes embarrassed by his childish behaviour - "

"Plus, it's against the law," noted the young one.

"Quite right, so he makes up this story, about how she's his girlfriend, he gave her the bike for her birthday, and she carelessly let it be stolen by joyriders who then dumped it in the pond. She goes along with it because he threatens to report her as an unlicensed prostitute."

"Rotten sod. He's not in love with her any more, then?"

"You're kidding - that's a hell of a nice bike she threw back in his face, the ungrateful hussy!"

The younger Lofty dabbed crumbs off his plate with a wetted finger. After a while, he said: "We haven't given him the bike back yet, have we?"

"Not yet. It's still in Evidence. Why?"

"I was thinking about what Gerard said - how a pond would be one of the few places you could get rid of a gun, or a bloodstained knife, or whatever."

"But Scientific have checked the junk - they can't find anything."

Young Lofty smiled. "They haven't checked the bike, have they? Because it's been - "

"It's been in Evidence all the time," said the other. "And because it wasn't considered part of the main haul. You're right."

"And a bike can be a weapon, can't it? Same as a screwdriver, or a cricket bat?"

The older Lofty picked up his phone. "I'll have them check it straight away."

Straight away took about an hour, but it was worth the wait. The bicycle's rear tyre, which had been clear of the water, carried within its tread traces of a substance which proved, upon analysis, to be human blood.

By lunchtime, those tasked with the surveillance of Rosie Liddle, and her furniture-shifting boyfriend Ed Upsall, had nothing direct to report. Thermal surveillance strongly argued against the presence of a third person in Rosie and Ed's home, or in Ed's business premises.

One thing, though: discreet questioning of neighbours had established that, over the last few days, the pair had been out and about a lot - on one occasion, being gone all day and overnight. Were they visiting Kim, in her hiding place, or were they looking for her? Or, of course - this had to be kept in mind, no matter how unsavoury a thought - were they an innocent couple, simply enjoying days out in the summer sun? At any rate, they were doing nothing of any interest now. No doubt, if they were involved, the earlier visit from the police would have put them on their guard.

Three coincidences linked Rosie to nineteen Beech Lane; if surveillance didn't turn up something soon, it would have to be faced that in this case the coincidences were merely coincidental.

Gerard Cochrane felt somewhat proprietorial over this whole Rosie Liddle business. After all, had it not been his young ward and putative protege - the work-sampler, Erin Smee - who had set this entire train in motion?

And there was something about it that niggled at the back of his mind, but which he couldn't quite put a pin through. This was nothing to do with old age, he knew. He'd been like this all his life, throughout his career. It didn't worry him. He knew how to deal with it.

Gerard did exactly what he had done, so many times over the last thirty years, whenever he'd been faced with this situation: he told work he had a migraine, took the afternoon off, drank three slow pints at the Railway Club in West Hampstead, consumed a late and leisurely lunch at a Thai restaurant in Soho owned by a former colleague, had sex with his brother's ex-wife, and went home for a kip on his sofa, having first set the radio to play a foreign language station, broadcasting in a tongue with which he was entirely unfamiliar and at a volume which he could hardly hear.

Never failed. Never been known to fail. Didn't fail now. It was six forty-five in the evening when he awoke with the answer. They were pleased to see him back at the office.

"Feeling better, Gerard?"

"Much better, thanks, guv. And while I was resting my weary head, a thought came to me. There was something about Rosie Liddle's statement that bothered me, and I've just realised what it is."

"Listening," said Greg.

"She says the lodger, Nathan, let her use the address, nineteen Beech Lane, to apply for a credit card, but that she quickly cancelled the card. And that's the end of the matter. Right?"

"Right," said Catherine.

"But in those days," said Gerard, "that wouldn't have been the end of the matter, would it? Or am I the only one old enough to remember junk mail?"

"Go on ... " said Greg.

"In those days, once your name and address got on the system, it'd be sold onto the people who compiled the junk mail lists, time and time again, endlessly. It was damn near impossible to stop the stuff coming - and any time you moved into a new flat, for years afterwards - "

Catherine was nodding. "Literally, years."

"*Literally* years, you'd continue to get junk mail addressed to the last people who'd lived there. Or the people before that. Just because Rosie cancelled her card, that wouldn't have stopped junk mail addressed to her arriving at Beech Lane. True?"

"Sounds right," said Greg. "Which means ... ?"

"Which means, something doesn't fit with what she told us. Now, we're assuming Brad killed the lodger, Nathan, and got away with it because no-one reported him missing. Our own searches suggest he didn't have much in the way of family, we don't think he had a regular girlfriend, other than Kim, perhaps. We know he was self-employed, so there were no direct colleagues to worry about him when he didn't show up."

"Yes," said Greg, light dawning. "But Brad would have needed to make sure of that."

"Precisely," said Gerard. "So, he's killed the lodger, and then junk mail keeps arriving at number nineteen, addressed to some woman he's never heard of. He has to assume that this woman's connection to his house is via the late lodger."

"And if he does know who she is," said Catherine, "maybe he's heard Nathan mention her as his girlfriend, how does he know for sure that she won't follow up her ex-boyfriend's vanishing?"

"Brad has got to make contact with her," said Gerard. "Surely? I'm not saying he'd have killed her, just to tidy up a loose end, but at the very least, he'd have phoned her and pretended to be searching for Nathan."

"My tenant seems to have done a bunk, he owes me rent, do you have any idea where he is?" said Catherine. "Thus deflecting suspicion from himself. And at the same time, finding out whether the girl is worried about Nathan's disappearance. Got to, I agree."

"But," says Gerard, "you look at Rosie's statement to us: she says she never met or heard from or had any contact with Brad or Kim Nottle."

"Maybe Brad tried to contact her," said Greg, "and failed?"

Gerard shook his head. "I don't think so. Nathan *hasn't* done a runner, remember - Brad has killed him. So Brad must have possession of his mobile phone, his address book, his computer. Somewhere in that lot there's going to be contact details for the ex-girlfriend. And he would have gone to some effort to contact her, wouldn't he?"

"If he does get through to her, how does he explain having her number? Given that Nathan's disappeared with, presumably, all his possessions?"

"Says the number was scribbled on a memo board next to the phone. Or he found a slip of paper down the back of the sofa. The point is, if I'm right, Rosie Liddell lied to us. She can't have forgotten her ex-boyfriend's landlord phoning her to say he'd gone missing. So why did she lie?"

The three of them were quiet for a while. Gerard took a seat. It'd been a busy afternoon, for a man with an imaginary migraine. Catherine and Greg were staring into space, their lips moving silently, their brows wrinkling and clearing, wrinkling and clearing.

"Does this all make more sense," Catherine said at length, "if Rosie was a friend of Brad, or Kim, or both, rather than of Nathan? It was them, not the lodger, who allowed her to use their address for her mail?"

"OK," said Greg. He stuck his head out of the office and shouted. "Bob! Spare us a moment?" When Bob Lemon had joined them, he continued. "Rosie Liddell is already officially a suspect in aiding and abetting a fugitive. Bob, I want you to use the computer to try and link her, at any time in her life, to one or both of the Nottles."

The three of them drank tea and smoked and tried not to be impatient. After forty minutes, Bob returned. "Rosie Liddle and Kim Nottle worked together, briefly, for a multinational drugs company in Hertfordshire - just for a few months in 1995."

"Right," said Greg. "That's great. Now, we've proved an ancient connection between Rosie and Kim. The next challenge is to prove that she's *kept* in touch with the Nottles."

"Request her phone records?" said Catherine.

"I think we'll have to," Greg agreed, but he sounded reluctant.

"It's a risky one," said Gerard. "If we find nothing - no recent calls to the Nottles - we're effectively proving that she has no ongoing connection to Kim, which would make it much harder to make a case for her arrest."

Greg shook his head. "Worse than that. I think we'd have to pull off the surveillance on her. The magistrate's going to say we ourselves have proved that she hasn't been in touch with the fugitive for years. If this goes wrong, it could go very wrong."

"Sorry, guv," said Gerard. "Looks like I've given you a headache."

CHAPTER FIFTEEN

Hospital accountants rarely worked on Saturday evenings, so the Loftys caught a bus to Tottenham, hoping to find Kieran Rider at home, just returned from his allotment.

It was a pleasant, two-roomed flat, in what looked like a lively road. As a matter of public policy, there was scarcely a decent-sized street in the nation that didn't possess a pub, a public hall, a cafe and a co-op general store and post office. But this tree-lined, Victorian street seemed especially *peopled*, if that was a word. Visible in front gardens, and audible from back gardens, glimpsed at open windows upstairs and down, there were people of various ages attending to the sundry matters of their lives.

The older Lofty sniffed a scent of al fresco cooking on the air, and heard the sounds of children nearby playing some ball game or other and adults laughing and pouring drinks - background summer sounds, comforting rather than intrusive - and just for a second, he could imagine himself living here, if things had turned out differently. Of course, things never did turn out differently, and you almost always, in Lofty's experience, ended up living where you lived. But little, fleeting fantasies, when it's hot in July, are no sort of crime and involve no betrayal.

Plenty of foot traffic on the pavements; people coming and going from the pub at one end of the street, perhaps, or the shop in the middle, or the hall at the other end - or just coming and going. Always a good sign. In Lofty's view - as a copper and as a citizen - it was one of the first things you should look for when you were choosing a neighbourhood to live in: were there people walking about? If not, walk on.

Kieran's living-room was tidy, but in a rather savage manner. Lofty wondered whether there was a particular science, or art, which divined people's personalities from the way they maintained order in their surroundings; and if so, what its practitioners might deduce from a room in which every necessary surface was scrupulously clear of muddle, while every shelf and cupboard was violently jammed with seemingly random detritus.

The accountant left them in the room while he went to wash his face and hands, and change his shirt. When he returned, Lofty couldn't help but notice, he looked, if anything, less fresh than he had five minutes earlier.

"We're not here to arrest you today," Lofty told him, because it was often efficacious to introduce the idea of arrest into such a conversation early on. "We just want to tell you what we've got."

"First," said the younger Lofty, "we have human blood on the rear tyre of your new bicycle. Secondly, we think that both you and Ms French have lied to us concerning the true nature of your relationship, and we reckon we can prove that in court, should we need to."

"Oh, God," said Kieran. "I need a glass of water."

They waited for him to fetch one. When he made no move to do so, the older Lofty understood that he had been asking permission. That was a promising sign. "It's your flat, Kieran - help yourself. Have two glasses if you want."

"Thank you."

They followed him into the kitchen. He ran the tap, filled a glass, gulped the water down.

"Third thing," said the younger Lofty.

"Oh God," said Kieran, pouring himself another glass.

"We wanted to make sure you understand the law concerning having sex with an unlicensed prostitute."

"Oh my God," said Kieran.

"It's an element of our job," said the older Lofty, "public education, which we take very seriously."

"You've found the body, haven't you?" Kieran said. "You found it straight away, and you've been keeping quiet about it so as to trap me. I do think that's a bit cruel."

"Right," said Lofty. "Kieran, despite what I said earlier, do we in fact need to arrest you at this point?"

Kieran swished some water around his mouth, and then spat it into the sink. He gave every appearance of devoting serious thought to Lofty's question. Eventually, he said: "That'd probably be best, yes. I'll need to change my shirt."

"You've already done that," the younger Lofty pointed out.

Kieran shook his head. "Different shirt," he explained. "This one's for around the house."

The check on Rosie Liddle's phone and message records was given a high priority, and took very little time to produce a result. DI Greg Wallace and DS Catherine Blake spent that very little time dreading the answer they would receive, and when they did receive an answer found to their horror that they had been right to dread it. Liddle's records showed no electronic communication of any sort between her and either Brad or Kim Nottle.

They'd effectively cleared their own suspect. On the basis of coincidences, they had obtained permission to intrude deeply into the privacy of a citizen - two citizens, in fact, counting the boyfriend. The result was no sign of Kim Nottle, no indication that Rosie knew where Kim was, and a fairly good suggestion that she had not been in touch with her in recent times.

Not only did they have no possible legal basis on which to arrest Rosie Liddle, they likewise had no basis on which to maintain surveillance on her, or to search her boyfriend's furniture store.

"It's back to looking for Kim, I suppose," said Catherine. "She knows the whole story, if anybody does, and she's out there somewhere."

"But where?" said Greg. "We've got no leads whatsoever."

"I think 'client' is the word you're looking for, surely," said the younger Lofty, in the interview room back at the station.

"You might say so," said Kieran Rider.

"More to the point," said the other Lofty, "Haley French might say so. She's a prostitute - albeit an illegal one - and your only relationship with her was that of someone who paid to have sex with her."

Kieran said nothing.

Lofty sighed. "All right," he said. "In your opinion, she was your girlfriend. Fine. So you bought her a flash new bicycle as a present. What next?"

"I was riding it over," said Kieran, swallowing heavily, as his story progressed. "From my place to hers. I'm really not much of a cyclist - I never was, not even as a kid. And I'd ... look, I'd had a couple of drinks. To settle the nerves, you know?"

"How many's a couple?"

"I was a bit ... a bit wobbly."

"I see."

"Coming round by that pond - it's a short cut over the grassy area, cuts off a corner - I lost control. I went straight into this bloke - "

"What was this bloke doing?"

Kieran took a long drink of water. "He was sitting on the ground, leaning up against a van."

"Describe the van?"

"A wagon, I suppose. Two horses. A covered wagon, but the cover had been half stripped off."

"You could see what was in it?"

Kieran looked puzzled, and even annoyed, at having his narrative interrupted by trivialities. "Does this matter?"

"Could you see the wagon's load?" said the older Lofty.

"Yes, I suppose ... just stuff. Junk, I mean. Looked like a load of scrap, on its way to recycling."

"Was it full?"

"Oh, I don't know!" He massaged his forehead roughly with the heels of his hands. "Maybe half full. There was some other stuff - more junk, you know, an old fridge maybe - sitting around the back of the wagon."

"As if they were unloading it when you arrived?"

"I don't know what they were doing, do I? For God's sake. I don't know."

"All right, Kieran. You say you careered into this man who was sitting by the side of the wagon. Can you describe him?"

"Dead," said Kieran.

"Dead?"

"I got off the bike. I looked at the guy on the ground - he was obviously dead. Blood everywhere. He was really - he was bleeding badly."

"Could you see anyone else? Anyone else around the wagon?"

"I thought I heard movement inside the wagon - but I didn't see anyone."

"The man you hit," said the younger Lofty. "He didn't cry out?"

The accountant made a low, awful noise, a growling sound of horror and despair. "I don't think he had time. I think I was into him before he knew it."

"What did you do?"

"You must understand - "

The older Lofty held up a hand. "Don't worry about all that, Kieran. Just tell us what happened."

"All right. I panicked. I wheeled the bike over to the pond edge, and I threw it in as far as it would go."

That would explain the blood on the tyre, thought Lofty; he must have wheeled it through some blood on the ground. "How did you get home?"

"I ran," said Kieran, simply. "I ran and then I walked when I couldn't run any more." He stared at the table in front of him for a while, and then he looked up at the detectives, a frown on his face. "But I don't understand - you must have found the body, surely? Isn't that what all this has been about?"

The Loftys couldn't understand it, either. Having returned Kieran Rider to his cell for the time being, they sat in the canteen, trying to work out what had happened to the body.

"He probably wasn't dead," said the younger one, round a mouthful of bun. "Our guy was in a blind panic, half-drunk - how would he know? So the guy with the wagon just gets up and shuffles off."

The other Lofty finished his phone call. "Don't talk to me while I'm on the bloody phone," he said. "How many times do I have to tell you that?"

"Why not? You got two ears, haven't you?"

"Anyway, there's no hospital reports matching the accountant's story."

"Told you," said the young one. "This is Failure to Report an Accident, that's all." He took another bun. "And Drunk in Charge, I suppose."

"I'm not sure ... all that blood? He was very adamant about that. No matter how many times we took him through the story, little details changed, the way they always do, but the guy on the floor bleeding heavily - he stuck to that. Is that the sort of detail you imagine?"

Dead or not, the man needed to be found - partly so that they knew what to charge Kieran Rider with, and partly so that they could charge the wounded man, and any colleague or colleagues, with illegal dumping.

Ginger Thom, sitting at the next table and happily earwigging, leant over. "You're missing something, boys."

The younger Lofty nodded his agreement. "He's missing a brain," he said, pointing to his partner, "and I'm missing my supper."

"All that blood?" said Ginger. "From being hit by a wobbly cyclist? Doesn't make sense."

One Lofty stopped eating, and the other stopped scratching his head. One of them thanked Ginger, while both of them hurried to retrieve Kieran from his cell.

Ginger had managed to make contact with the quadcycle factory's former nightwatchman, without alerting the factory manager to his interest. He'd contacted the National Union of Mineworkers, and asked them to pass Ginger's number on to their new recruit. Now, at last, his phone rang.

His first question was a slightly delicate one: had the man left his nightwatchman job voluntarily or, as it were, in some otherwise manner?

"No, nothing like that, pal - all perfectly friendly. I left to fulfil a dream, simple as that. To become a coalminer, like my dad."

"And how are you liking it?"

"Bloody hard work!"

"I'll bet."

"You don't get as much quiet time as you do when you're a nightwatchman, if you know what I mean."

"Getting behind with your reading, eh?"

"That sort of thing, yeah. When I want to phone my mates for a chat, now I've got to do it on my own time. I wouldn't have missed it for anything, though, being serious. Beats sitting on that stupid roof, waiting for nothing to happen."

"The factory must have been sorry to lose you, even so - did they beg you to stay on?"

"No, old Doyle - he's the manager - he was perfectly happy to see me go. I was a bit insulted, to be honest."

"Was he, now?" said Ginger. "Was he indeed?"

They had only one question for Kieran Rider this time: from where on his body was the man bleeding?

"The stomach area," they were told. "Maybe stomach and groin, round there."

Back at their desks, the Loftys agreed on this much at least: a man sitting down, leaning against a wagon, might feasibly sustain such injuries in such an area - but it would have to come into the category of outcomes traditionally labelled by accident investigators as UFU: Utterly Fucking Unlikely.

"He was already bleeding when the wobbly cyclist hit him," said the younger Lofty.

"Got to be," said his partner. "That wasn't a bike wound - that was a knife wound."

"Or gun shot."

Lofty shrugged. "Maybe. In any case, that's why the body disappeared - his mate in the wagon took it away with him."

He took out his phone again, and called the science unit which had been examining the junk from the pond. "Sorry to call you so late," said Lofty, who wasn't.

"No problem, actually - I was just about to call you."

"Great. Listen," said Lofty, who wasn't, "did you search the items from the pond for invisible blood?"

"Not invisible, no. Looked for visible, sure, but there's so much stuff, we couldn't put it all under a microscope, could we? Besides, you gave us no indication of a possible violent - "

"I know, absolutely, but we've got new evidence. If you could do that first thing in the morning, it'd be a great help."

"All right, if you say so. Now listen, you want to hear this."

"Go on, I've got my notebook out," said Lofty, who hadn't.

"One of our blokes had an idea. There's a video machine amongst your lot, right? Dated 1990s, circa. Well, our guy loves all these old TV shows - cop shows, you know?"

"Yeah, I work with someone who can't get a girlfriend, too," said Lofty.

"Piss off, granddad," quipped his partner.

"*Listen*, Serious Crimes - this is good. Something they did in those days - our bloke saw it on an old show - the police had a campaign to get people to mark their belongings with their details."

"We still do something similar today," said Lofty, "in case you hadn't heard."

"Something *similar*, yes - but they didn't have the technology we've got, did they? So what they did, was write on their property in invisible ink which showed up under ultraviolet. And that's why I'm still here, on a Saturday night. We've managed to botch together a kit to read the ancient runes. Not easy, though I say so myself, because the ultraviolet fades over time, but we've done it, using nothing but our genius."

"You're not telling me you've got one?" Now Lofty was listening. He even stopped arm-wrestling his partner for the final bun.

"I am in fact telling you that, as it goes, in the event that you're even remotely interested. That video machine? It's only got a bloody surname and post code on it."

Lofty punched the air. He'd have preferred to punch the other Lofty, but until they'd matched the ultraviolet details with a living person, it seemed prudent to keep his celebrations in check, so as to avoid hubris. "Gawd bless ancient technology!" he said into his phone. "And Gawd bless ancient television - and Gawd bless your mate's non-existent girlfriend, and all."

Catherine couldn't get that bloody caravan out of her mind. She couldn't help thinking - ridiculous, of course, but she couldn't help it - that the whole thing was more her fault than it was the DI's fault, because she was a woman. And the DI wasn't. Somehow, she thought (or felt, to be strictly accurate, rather than thought) that she should have known the woman at the door of the caravan with the imaginary ill husband was a phoney. A woman should know when another woman is acting. 'It takes one to know one,' was the expression she was carefully not saying to herself.

Anyway, it was on her mind, and she was halfway home that evening when she suddenly thought *How did Kim Nottle get into that van?* And Catherine had to sit down in the cool of the nearest greenspot and think about this.

When she and Greg had realised that the woman at the caravan was Kim, they'd asked the Cornish police to go and check if she was still there. They'd reported back to Gerard, and she could remember what he'd said: the Cornish had checked all the vans, breaking in where necessary.

Right. Step by step.

She phoned DC Vaughan, their contact in St. Ives. Vaughan checked the reports. The van in which Catherine and Greg had failed to recognise Kim Bradley belonged to Sanj and Karly Owen. Yes, it had been locked when Uniform had arrived, and they had broken into it to check that it was now empty. Yes, they had needed to break into all the vans other than the McFarlanes', and one other for which the McFarlanes kept a spare key. And finally, no, the Owens' caravan showed no signs of having been broken into already.

Next, Catherine phoned the Owens. They had, of course, been informed that their holiday home-from-home had been brutally violated by the police, and had been assured that it would be repaired and rendered secure again, without delay and at the police service's expense. Mrs Owen, answering the phone to another police detective, was understandably suspicious. Catherine's regret that she did not have time to explain why she was asking a series of daft-sounding questions did little to allay Karly Owen's fears.

"Do you leave a spare key to the van under the mat, or under a flowerpot, or - "

"Certainly not!" Mrs Owen interrupted. "We don't want to start our holiday by clearing out all the used condoms and empty cider bottles from half the teenagers in Cornwall, thank you very much. What's this about, anyway?"

"So, what happens if you lose your key, or forget to bring it, or - "

"Well, we'd get the spare of course."

"Absolutely," said Catherine, "I should have thought of that. And where do you *keep* the spare?"

"We don't. The people from the neighbouring caravan - they're local, you see - they keep it for us. The McFarlanes. They're very helpful. Look," said Karly Owen, "is this the bloody government trying to get out of paying our insurance?" But she said it to a severed connection.

Catherine rang Greg. She explained as succinctly as she could.

"The Cornish police had to break into the Owens' van - but there was no sign of previous breaking-in, so how did Kim get in there? She had a key. Where did she get the key from?"

"From her cousins, the McFarlanes." She heard Greg groan. "They tried to stop us going down there, didn't they? Mrs McFarlane - she told me I needn't bother, because they'd already checked."

"I suspect," said Catherine, "that the McFarlanes think of Kim killing Brad as a kind of justifiable homicide."

"I don't care what they think," said Greg. "They are going to be prosecuted for aiding and abetting a fugitive."

"Thing is, I was wondering - where would Kim go next? Well, how about to somewhere we've already searched?"

"I'll call you back," said Greg.

Less than an hour later, in St. Ives, armed police entered the home of Andrew and Alicia McFarlane, and there arrested Kim Nottle on suspicion that she did murder her husband, Bradley Nottle, some time in the first week of July, in the present year, at nineteen Beech Lane, Sudbury, which was contrary to the Agreement of the People.

CHAPTER SIXTEEN

"Nice to see you again, Mrs Nottle," said Greg the following morning, once Kim had been escorted back to London, had her breakfast, and been safely installed in the main interview room.

Catherine Blake smiled at that, but Kim Nottle didn't.

"I didn't kill him," she said, as she had been saying every few minutes, to anyone who would listen, and many who wouldn't, from the moment of her arrest in Cornwall. "It wasn't me. I didn't kill Brad." She looked pretty awful: her eyes red from crying, her skin grey from hiding, her flesh shrunken from loss of appetite. She'd already been examined by two doctors - a police doctor in Cornwall, and a police doctor in London - and shortly she'd be examined by a third, summoned by her lawyer.

"All right, Kim," said Greg. "I promise you you'll have every opportunity to tell us the whole story. Why don't we start at the beginning?"

But Kim wasn't interested in starting at the beginning. She had only one thing to say, and that was that she was innocent of the murder of her husband. She had come home from a walk on Sunday and found him dead.

"Did you call the police, on making this terrible discovery?"

"No," she said, her voice hoarse, painful to the ear. "You know I didn't."

"Why didn't you?"

"I just ran. I had no idea what I was doing. The horror of it all, the shock ... I believe I was in a fugue state."

"Is a fugue state," Catherine asked, "the same as a blind panic?"

"That," said the lawyer, "is a question for the doctor, not my client."

Through almost an hour of questioning, Kim Nottle stuck to this simple tale: she had no idea who'd killed Brad, except that it wasn't her. She had found him dead, and had fled the scene for reasons which she couldn't properly explain.

After a break, Greg changed the subject. "What happened to your furniture, Kim?"

"My furniture? I don't know what you mean."

"Your house is almost empty. Almost all your possessions have been stripped out. We wondered why."

He was watching her carefully, and he could have sworn she looked genuinely puzzled by this development. On the other hand, they had already had evidence of her acting skills. "I'm sorry," she said, "I don't know anything about that."

"Can you imagine anything which might explain it?"

She pulled at her bottom lip. "A burglary, I suppose. The house was empty, after all."

"A burglary," said Greg. "Yes, perhaps so. We'll have to get our CID colleagues to look into that for you. Tell me about the other body, Kim - the one buried under the drive."

The lawyer opened his mouth - to object to his client being questioned about a crime other than the one for which she'd been arrested, Greg presumed - but his client beat him to it. "I know nothing about any other body," she said. "All I know is someone's killed Brad, and you're doing nothing about it. I don't even believe there is another body, you've just made that up to trick me."

Over the next twenty minutes, her condition - her apparent condition, is the expression Greg would have preferred - deteriorated noticeably and rapidly. Her voice became huskier and harder to understand; her limbs took to shivering, and her face to twitching. Eventually, Greg and Catherine conceded defeat, and Kim's lawyer took her to see her third doctor.

"Not fit to interview," said the doctor, a young woman specialising in mental health crisis care, who Greg had met several times before, and had still not quite got round to asking out for a drink. This was probably not the moment. "I gather both your police doctors said she was borderline fit?"

"They said she was fit to interview," Greg corrected her. "Whether borderline or not, their conclusion is what we go by."

"Of course, I'm not criticising. I'm just telling you - if you ask the police doctors now, they'll agree. Her condition has deteriorated. I suggest that recent events - seeing her husband's dead body, no matter who killed him, and then fleeing the scene and hiding - have tipped her from a rational state to a largely non-rational one. Being arrested and interviewed has, quite naturally, made matters worse. Any further interrogation at this stage could prove extremely damaging and, in any case, any information gathered during such an interrogation would be inherently unreliable."

"She seemed pretty bloody rational a few days ago in Cornwall, when she was impersonating someone else in order to evade capture," said Greg.

The doctor shrugged. "I didn't examine her then, Greg. I can't say what state she was in then. I can only go by what my examination today reveals, and that is what we doctors call a woman with bits dropping off her."

"Could she be faking?" Catherine asked.

"Certainly she could, if she's a good actress. But I'm not going to take that chance. Sorry."

"All right." Greg smiled. "Thanks for coming out so quickly, Anjika."

"My pleasure." At the end of the corridor, she turned round. "Greg - I believe your son's team is playing my nephew's next week. Maybe we'll bump into each other at the game?"

"Yes," said Greg. "Maybe." He reviewed what he'd just said, and decided it could do with an edit. "That'd be nice," he added.

Catherine made a disgusted noise in her throat. "Well, she's a fat lot of help."

"Just doing her job, I suppose."

"And stopping us doing ours. Do you really think Kim's cracked up? More likely to be faking it, surely?"

"I don't know," said Greg. "Killing your husband - finding out he's killed your lover - that'd be enough to drive anyone a bit loony, wouldn't it?"

"So how do you explain her behaviour at the caravan?" Catherine demanded.

But Greg was bored with this pointless conversation. It wasn't like Catherine to chew on things, like this, to no purpose. "I don't explain it, Catherine, I'm not interested in explaining it. We are where we are. For the time being, we can't interview Kim. Even if we could, be honest - did she look like she was about to confess?"

"Not really," Catherine admitted.

"We need Rosie Liddle and her bloke. If they did obtain the gun for Kim, and help her clear out her furniture afterwards, they're our best way in. If you've got three suspects, all worried which one's going to start talking first, it generally speeds things along. *Shit.*" He lit a roll-up, and scratched at his neck, as if its itching were the source of his frustration. "If we'd carried on, I was going to ask Kim about Rosie. If I could have got her to admit knowing the woman, even, that might just possibly have given us enough for a search warrant at the boyfriend's furniture place. On the other hand, they might have nothing to do with anything. We now know they weren't sheltering her while she was on the run, after all."

"The boyfriend," said Catherine. "What's his name - Upsall?"

"Ed Upsall."

Catherine frowned as she thought. "You've actually de-listed Rosie and Ed as official suspects for accessory after the fact, have you?"

"Haven't got round to it," said Greg. "But I'll do it later today. Have to, after the phone records came back blank."

"But right at this moment, they're still listed?"

"So what? You got something?"

Catherine was quick to shake her head. "No, sorry, Greg - nothing exciting. No rabbit from the hat. I was just thinking, this Ed Upsall is listed separately from Rosie, he is a person in his own right, so presumably we're entitled to have a look at his phone records, too?"

Greg blew out his cheeks. "Might as well, yeah. Why not? Can't do any harm."

It didn't do any harm. In fact, it turned out to be what Ginger Thom was later to describe as "a bit of a hat-rabbit." Two hours later, Greg and Catherine were looking at a screen display which clearly showed seven calls around the previous weekend from Ed Upsall's phone to Kim Nottle's.

On the doorstep of her flat in Cricklewood, Greg took considerable pleasure in telling Rosie Liddle that he had brought her good news. "You'll be relieved to hear that we've found your old friend Kim Nottle. She's alive and unhurt and currently under arrest."

"That's funny," said Catherine; they'd been rehearsing this all the way over. "You don't look very relieved. We'd like you and Ed to come and answer some questions, please."

The Loftys showed the squat, red-faced man their police identity cards. "Ah, now," he said. "Representatives of the vulture state. What a pleasant surprise. Well, I'm not dead yet, as you can see, so you'll have to wait to get your hands on my property."

Despite what might sometimes be heard from Radio Free Europe, and other propaganda sources, not one person had ever been kicked out of their dwelling by the Process. It was thought that any policy of direct dispossession would be Contrary to Good Order. On the other hand, in a country in which every square foot must, by necessity, be productive in the public good, in one way or another, it was clearly impossible to allow large houses, and large areas of under-utilised land, to remain for very long in private hands. The compromise which, for the moment, held this contradiction at bay had led to the creation of a class of people generally known as 'the fading rich.' Example: Mr Ramage, owner and sole occupier of a handsome pile named the Manor House, near Potters Bar.

Mr Ramage was legally entitled to keep possession of his multi-roomed home, so long as he was never absent from it for more than a set number of days in a row; absent, that is, for any reason whatsoever, including death. When that absence did finally occur - as, in the way of mortal affairs, it eventually must - the house would be compulsorily purchased by the nation. Properties above a certain size were non-inheritable.

A person's own home was one thing; the land attached to the Manor House was another. Although it remained Mr Ramage's property, regulations determined what could and could not be done with it. Thus, the two acres of landscaped lawns which had one surrounded the house itself had mostly been replaced by polytunnels in which disease-free vegetable seeds were raised for sale to the patio-farming trade, while the former game shoot, once the pride of the Ramages, was now set aside as a wildlife conservation area.

"We're not here to do with the house, Mr Ramage," said the younger Lofty, with rather more respect in his voice than his partner would have wished. "We just need to ask you a few questions on another matter."

"You can't come in, unless you've got a warrant."

"We don't need to come in, sir," said the older Lofty. "It's a nice day - we can talk out here just as well."

The man was obviously disappointed at having his battle taken away from him. "Well, go on then. I'm very busy."

"Of course. Mr Ramage, have you had a burglary here lately?"

"No. Wouldn't bother calling you lot if I did."

Lofty took a VCR out of his wheeled bag. Bloody heavy thing; no wonder they'd gone extinct. "Is this machine yours, do you know?"

Ramage peered at the defunct gadget. "No idea. Why?"

"Eight, nine, ten," said Lofty.

"What?"

"Nothing, sir. This item is marked in invisible ink with the name Ramage, and the postcode of the Manor House." He pointed to where he knew the inscription to be; malicious thing to do, of course, but young Lofty's respectful tone had wound him up. Why would you respect someone for inheriting a big house? It wasn't even as if he'd won it in a duel.

"I can't see anything," Ramage snorted, and then his already red face reddened further as he realised what he'd said. "Could be, I suppose. We had an outbuilding full of junk we've only just got round to sorting out, dates back to my parents' time. We just got rid of it a few days ago."

"When you say 'got rid of,' sir ... ?" said the younger Lofty.

"One of the men who works on the land loaded it all up in his wagon and drove it into town to the recycling. I said he could keep anything he got for it, not worth my bothering about a few pounds here and there."

"Very generous of you, Mr Ramage," said the older Lofty, on the grounds that he knew the thing was going to be said, and he'd rather it was said in his teasingly sarcastic tones than in the kid's sincere ones.

"Come to think of it, he was supposed to come back for a second load, but he hasn't yet, lazy sod."

"Not come back?" said Lofty.

Ramage's lack of surprise for the fecklessness of the lower orders was painted across his face. In red, mostly. "Phoned in sick, apparently. Sore throat. Well, he was perfectly well last time I saw him!"

"One more question, in that case: did any other wagons go out from here that day?"

Ramage thought about it. "There was one, yes - carrying a load of first grade tomato seed to the packaging centre."

"Worth much? In financial terms, I mean?"

"Worth plenty!"

"And it got there all right, did it? The tomato seed?"

"Of course it bloody got there all right," said Ramage. "What are you talking about?"

"Bloody hell," said the younger Lofty, softly, as if to himself. "The wrong wagon."

His partner, ignoring the red-faced man, turned to him and nodded. "Hell of a thing to get killed for, eh, kidda?"

While Greg, Catherine and two uniformed officers were taking Rosie Liddle and Ed Upsall back to Kentish Town for questioning, another team, led by Bob Lemon, was executing a search warrant at Ed's furniture store. One of Ed's two employees was present on his boss's behalf, to make sure, as Bob explained to him, "That the uniformed guys don't nick more than is strictly necessary." The man took his duties, of safeguarding his employer's interests and property, about as seriously as one might expect an employed person to take them: he sat on a ratty sofa in the office, drinking tea and reading a magazine about bicycle racing.

"What are we looking for?" asked Erin, having tied up the horse outside. Rover now stood with his saddlebags ready to receive any items found in the search which might need to be rushed back to the officers interviewing Rosie and Ed. Obviously, Rover didn't know that, but that didn't matter because Erin did.

"The DI is rather hoping that'll be obvious," said Bob. "A carpet covered with blood, or a sofa full of bullets, a Spitfire rifle - something along those lines."

"They'll have got rid of anything like that, won't they?"

"Quite possibly," said Bob, "though it's not that easy to dispose of bulky items, no questions asked. You'd really want to burn them, and if you try that without the proper paperwork, you're going to have everybody jumping on your feet from the street committee, through the police and the fire brigade, all the way up to the Re and the pollution panel."

Erin had an idea. "You could dump it in a pond!"

Bob smiled. "Good point. Make a note - if we do have to go looking for missing evidence, we'll put the Loftys in charge of the underwater search. The thing is, whatever they've done with the stuff, they're not forensic experts, so they will have left traces.

Doctor Minto and her team are due here any minute - if there's anything to find, they'll find it."

Ed Upsall's removals business was not a large enterprise - it owned just two carts and one large van - but it was housed in a rambling, nineteenth century building, which included two sizeable storage areas and a stable block. It was going to take some searching, as became obvious two hours into the process when nothing of interest had revealed itself - either to the naked eye, or to Doctor Minto's various instruments.

Bob phoned the squad office. "What's the latest word from the interview room, Gerard? Any hints about what we should be looking for?"

"Our guests are saying nothing, last I heard," Gerard told him. "Just sitting there drinking our tea and eating our biscuits and staring at the walls."

"No theories yet, then? This is definitely the Nottles' stuff, that's confirmed, so it must be here for a reason."

"But you don't think it looks like a clean-up job?" asked Gerard.

"I've been thinking about that. It never really made much sense, did it? I mean, unless Kim Nottle chased Brad all over the house shooting at him - or he was wounded, running away from her, leaking blood everywhere. Otherwise, why virtually clear the whole place out? Why not just take the bloodstained sofa, or whatever it was, and leave the rest?"

"To make it look like a burglary?" suggested Gerard.

"Or maybe," said Bob, "they didn't actually know what they were looking for, so they had to take the lot. What did they actually leave behind?"

"Hold on." Gerard checked the notes. "Yeah, just a few big items - dining-room table, some bookcases, things like that."

"In other words, items that you can't hide anything inside, or that are easily searched in situ. So we could be looking for something quite small."

"All right, Bob, I'll pass a note into the DI, giving him all this.

We're all agreed that there must be *something* there, yes? They haven't shifted all that furniture just for practice. So I think I know what the DI's going to say."

"Keep looking," said Bob.

"Keep looking."

"The trouble is," said Bob, "if I'm right, and Rosie Liddle and Ed Upsall didn't know what they were looking for - "

"Or knew what they were looking for, but didn't know exactly where it was?"

"Either way - we don't know whether or not they found it, do we?"

It would be wrong to say that hope was fading in the search for the missing child, Sarla Brown. The fact was, hope had never been high. By the time the Squad was called in, all likely possibilities for finding the girl alive and unharmed had been exhausted - that's why the Squad was called in, after all. From the time they became involved, most officers acted on the assumption that Sarla was either dead, or otherwise beyond them.

They still had to find out who'd put her there, though.

For the two Serious Crimes officers assigned to the case, hearing of progress being made in the Nottle murder investigation did nothing to lift the gloom.

"Are you going cold on the granny, then?" Dahlia Kotane asked Phil Kale. Surveillance of Felicity Cook had produced nothing. She seemed to have no contact with anyone other than her daughter and her doctor. She went nowhere. She was just about the single most bloody unhelpful suspect Dahlia had ever dealt with.

Phil shook his head. "It's still her. She did it. She's clever, that's all. I'm just agreeing with you, the father is definitely odd, and I want to know more about him."

Dahlia agreed. "It would be nice, if only for the sake of completeness. But who can we talk to? His workmates say they hardly know him, he doesn't seem to be a member of - well, of anything. He doesn't play sport, he's got no hobbies, he doesn't go to union meetings, or street meetings ... " She spread her hands in a gesture of surrender. "His wife's got nothing to say about him, his cousin was no use, and his - "

"The cousin's wife," said Phil, standing up. "She must know John Brown pretty well, if her husband's been his best mate since childhood. And with any luck, she won't be blinded by excessive loyalty."

"The cousin didn't want us to see her, did he? She had bad nerves or something."

"The cousin," said Phil, "doesn't need to know. Phone his work, make sure Johnny Costas is there today, and find out when he gets off. And make sure they understand he's not to know we've been asking after him."

"Sarge."

"I'll look up his address while you're doing that, and we'll get straight over there. No need to ring for an appointment, I don't think."

"What if she's not at home?" asked Dahlia.

"Then we'll go to where she is," said Phil.

But in fact it was Tressa Costas herself who answered the door to them, at her detached house in Hendon. Set well back from a quiet road, and with a good-sized front garden, it offered a charming picture on a summer day.

Tressa's own charms were, Dahlia could immediately see, well hidden beneath a thick layer of worry and fear. Phil hurried to reassure her. "Not bad news, Mrs Costas - don't worry."

"No news at all, actually," Dahlia clarified. "We just wanted a bit of a chat with you, if that's OK?"

It was a rhetorical question, of course; about as rhetorical as you could get. When you're a Serious Crimes detective looking for a missing child, and you ask someone if it's OK to talk to them, you are merely obeying form - you're not actually asking. But Tressa seemed to be seriously considering Dahlia's request. She made no move to invite the police officers in.

"Mrs Costas ... ?"

"Actually," said Tressa, "I have got ... " She tailed off. Dahlia remembered what they'd been told about her nerves, and hoped this visit wasn't about to go unpleasantly wrong. Perhaps they should have made an appointment, after all.

"You have got ... ?" Phil asked.

And then, quite without warning, Tressa Costas stood straight, stood aside, and told them: "Please come in."

The first thing they saw inside the house was a man's bicycle in the hall. The second thing they saw was a ponytailed man, framed in the doorway of the living-room, the look of horror on his face tinged, Dahlia thought, with both embarrassment and defiance.

"Mr Molloy," said Dahlia. "What on earth are you doing here?"

The American refugee said nothing. It took Dahlia a moment longer to see it all; then, she looked across at Phil and saw from his expression that he'd been a second or two ahead of her. He began bounding up the staircase.

"Stay with these two, Dahlia." At the landing, he paused, and spoke quickly, over his shoulder. "We haven't got a search warrant, Tressa. You're not going to tell me we need one, are you?"

"No," said Tressa, her voice surprisingly strong.

DC Kotane took her two prisoners into the living-room, and told them to sit at either end of a long sofa. After only a couple of minutes, she heard Phil call down from the landing.

"Dahlia? Up here."

She went out into the hall. "What shall I do with these two?"

Phil lowered his voice. "Cuff the fuckers. But out of sight, all right?"

She handcuffed the silent man and the softly weeping woman to each other, and followed Phil up to the second floor, which looked like a not terribly well-made twentieth century extension of the first. There were only two doors on this floor; Phil knocked on one of them, and then opened it slowly.

"It's me again," he said. "Can I come in? This is the friend I told you about."

Phil opened the door wide, and ushered Dahlia into a pretty, freshly decorated bedroom, containing a large, pink bed, a good selection of toys and books, and a little girl with confused eyes. Dahlia pasted a smile on her face, but she was a cop; her open eyes did a quick stock check. No visible injuries, no restraints, natural movement in the limbs, the girl's hair, clothes and face were clean, and she hadn't been raped. Dahlia knew what that looked like on a child, and it didn't look like this. She'd only seen it once, but it was something which, once seen, could not be mistaken. She glanced at Phil, and gave him a slight nod. "This is a nice room," she said, her voice unmistakeably cheerful and unconcerned, and she saw such a sagging, draining, physical force of relief flood through the DS that from that moment on she considered him the finest officer on the Squad, and she would bite the head off anyone who implied otherwise in her presence.

"Dahlia," said Phil, "this is Sarla - you know? Daughter of Chloe and John, who we met the other day? Sarla, this is my friend, Dahlia."

The two of them nodded at each other, and Sarla did the thing that a lot of the kids had taken to doing in place of a handshake - she patted her heart, two sharp taps, with her right hand. Where did that come from, Dahlia wondered; did someone invent it, or did it just evolve?

"Pleased to meet you, Sarla. We've got a quadcycle outside. Shall we get you over to your mum's?"

"Actually, I think we can do better than that," said Phil. "Have you ever been in a motor car, Sarla?"

"That would be nice," said Sarla. "If Mum says it's all right."

"Of course," said Phil. "We'll phone her from outside."

He insisted on holding the girl's hand in his own gloved fingers as they went downstairs, which clearly embarrassed them both - she was seven, after all, not three - but Dahlia knew exactly how he felt, because she felt exactly the same. They'd found one, found one alive, and you couldn't help the horrible fear that it was a mistake, quite conceivably due to be rectified by a tumble down a staircase.

"Is my little holiday over, then?" Sarla said as they reached the hall.

"Yes, love, that's right," said Dahlia. "Home-time now."

"I'm quite glad," Sarla whispered, "it's a bit boring here."

"Is it?"

"But I'd better thank Auntie Tressa, though."

"She's a bit busy in the other room at the moment," Dahlia explained. "I think it'd be OK if you just call out to her."

"Thank you for the little holiday, Auntie!" Sarla shouted. "I had a lovely time!" She seemed quite unconcerned that there was no reply.

"Good girl," Phil told her. "Very polite."

"Granny says manners are next to godliness."

"Manners are certainly important," said Phil. "Dahlia - could you check on Auntie and her friend, please? And perhaps call some other friends to come and join them? Sarla and I will just have a bit of a stroll round the back garden, and she can phone her mum."

Dahlia waited with the two prisoners until the uniformed officers arrived to take them into custody. When they'd gone, she joined Phil in the garden. Sarla was just finishing her phone call. She looked puzzled.

"Mum seems very upset."

"Oh, I don't think so," said Phil, with such an unconvincing air that Dahlia almost wanted to laugh out loud. "I think she just missed you while you were on your little holiday."

Sarla digested that. "I expect so," she said.

CHAPTER SEVENTEEN

Ginger found it. He wasn't looking for it - except in the sense that they were all looking for the same thing, none of them knowing what it was - but as luck would have it, he knew it when he saw it.

It was inside a carved wooden trunk, which was inside a plastic packing crate. DI Wallace had ordered a fingertip search, so Ginger took the trunk out of the crate, and took out of the trunk an album of wedding photos. The album looked sadly ignored, its pages sticking together. Remembering Greg's frequent advocacy of thoroughness, Ginger removed the photographs from their sticky backing sheets one by one, and set them aside. Halfway through the album, he uncovered a sheet of paper. It was just an ordinary piece of A4, folded once along the middle, but as he looked it over, Ginger's heart began to beat a little faster. He reckoned he had an idea what it was.

A few pages further on, there was another sheet, similarly hidden; and then another and another ...

"I don't get it," said Bob Lemon. "Something to do with bees? It's all technical stuff, I don't know what it means, do you?"

"Not in detail," said Ginger, "but enough to tell that it's a report on the design, construction and siting of artificial bumblebee nests for rooftop gardens. That's what Kim Nottle's work is all about."

"So," said Bob, "why shouldn't she have papers about it in her house?"

"These were hidden," Ginger pointed out. "If you hide something, you hide it for a reason."

"All right ... "

"You remember that call I attended a few days ago? At the potato research place? The one Counter Terrorism took off us."

"Christ," said Bob. "The inside job."

"Exactly," said Ginger.

The bumblebee papers travelled in Rover's saddlebags to Kentish Town. There, copies were made of them, which Rover and Erin took to the Ministry for Bees, with a request for an urgent comment on their contents.

Meanwhile, Ed Upsall was returned from his cell to an interview room. Catherine reckoned, and Greg agreed, that Ed was a likelier talker than his girlfriend, Rosie Liddle.

"We found the bumblebee stuff," Greg told him, without much preamble. "It was hidden in Kim's wedding album. I suppose you'd have found it eventually, but it was pretty well hidden."

"Don't know what you're talking about," said Ed.

"Quite possibly," Greg allowed. "I'd be willing to believe you - except that you're refusing to tell us things that you *do* know about. For instance, how the Nottles' property comes to be in your furniture store. You see what I mean?"

Ed pushed his lank, sandy hair off his forehead. He chewed at a hangnail. He looked at his lawyer. She shrugged. Greg and Catherine waited. "All right," said Ed, after a good minute and a half of chewing. "I don't know what you're talking about - bees. I don't know anything about bees. Is that understood?"

"I understand what you're saying," Greg replied, carefully.

"I had nothing to do with the bloke who died, either."

"Fair enough. But the furniture ... ?"

There was another minute of silent chewing, then Ed continued. "This Kim - she's an old friend of Rosie's. She rang up on Sunday in a terrible state, she'd had a row with her husband. He was a bastard, by all accounts - knocked her about and that, you know? Violent, drunk, the lot. They'd had a row, she'd killed him. Rosie ... well, Rosie persuaded me that Kim didn't deserve to go to prison for that, so she got me to help her shift all their stuff out of their house."

"Not all their stuff," Catherine interrupted. "Most of their stuff."

Ed looked annoyed. "I don't know, most of it - all right. We didn't have much time. She just wanted to mess up the crime scene, you see? So you lot couldn't tell what had happened."

"Who did?" Greg asked.

"What do you mean, who did?"

"Kim or Rosie?"

This time, the answer came without delay. "Kim, of course! What do you mean, Rosie? Rosie was just trying to help her friend."

Greg stood up. "OK. Thanks, Ed. That'll do for now."

DC Vaughan rang Catherine from St. Ives, to confirm that Kim's cousins, the McFarlanes, had been charged with aiding and abetting a fugitive, and had been bailed. Kim had arrived at their place hours after Brad's death, saying only that 'something terrible' had happened, and that she needed somewhere to hide. They'd given her the spare keys to their caravan - which shared a key ring with the spare keys to the Owens' van - and she had hurried to the beach, refusing all further offers of help or comfort.

When they'd heard about the body being found at Beech Lane, the McFarlanes had assumed that Kim had finally killed the husband who'd ruined her life. If so, they were entirely on her side. After her encounter with Greg and Catherine at the Owens' caravan, she had returned to the McFarlanes' house and they, hoping that they were no longer under surveillance, had taken her in. They were convinced that she had suffered a breakdown and their plan, they claimed, was to persuade Kim to see a doctor, see a lawyer, and turn herself into the police - in that order.

DC Vaughan reckoned they would get community service when their case came to trial. Catherine hoped she was right.

One of the things you had to take into account when you were designing a serious crime squad's base was that, given the precise nature of the work, there would be days when several cells and several interview rooms would be required all at the same time. The person who'd designed Kentish Town had done his or her best, and couldn't really be blamed for today's overspill, but it did mean that they ended up interviewing Sarla's Auntie Tressa in the comfortable room usually reserved for traumatised victims.

Phil and Dahlia were about three minutes into the interview, when they had to break off and, on the basis of new information, make one further arrest. Four people, in all, were now in custody in relation to the abduction of Sarla Brown, and associated matters.

"Of course it was madness," Tressa told them, when they resumed. "I know that and I *knew* that, do you think I didn't know that?"

"Well, if you knew it - " Phil began.

"I didn't know what they were doing until they'd done it." She leaned forward across the table, willing them to take her proximity as token of her sincerity. "Once it had been done, how could I do anything without putting my husband in prison? You can't ask anyone to do that!"

"Actually," said Phil, "I think you can. If the alternative is going along with kidnapping, I very much think I would expect any half-decent person to do exactly that."

"Kidnapped?" wailed Tressa. "You can't say kidnapped - she was having a little holiday, that's all, she didn't even know she was missing."

"Her mother knew she was missing," said Dahlia.

"I did what I could," Tressa insisted. "I spent all day every day begging them to take her home. I was working on them, you see? Wearing away at them, trying to get them to see sense. I did all I could!"

"You didn't do all you could, Tressa," said Dahlia. "Because what you could have done is picked up the phone and called the police. And you chose not to."

Next, they spoke to the latest arrival - the last to be arrested - John Brown, Sarla's dad.

"Explain your plan to me, John," said Phil. "I just need to be sure I've got it clear. OK?"

John looked surprised that anyone should need something so obvious explained, but his expression also suggested that it was no skin off his nose. If the slow-witted copper needed it explaining, then fair enough.

"My cousin Johnny's got a bicycle with a covered sidecar - uses it to carry his tools in. This job he's working on, they have to take frequent breaks, dust-breaks they call them. He parked his bike round by the greenspot where they go for their dust-breaks."

"But how did he know exactly when Sarla would be coming out of the house?"

"He didn't." John sounded scornful. "How could he? He went round there several times over several days. He knew roughly the times she was likely to be going out to play with her friend, or going to school, or going to her clubs - "

"And eventually he got lucky?" asked Dahlia.

"It's not luck," John told her. "It's probability. I could explain the difference, but - "

"No, that's all right, John," said Phil. "Did Johnny ride right up to the house?"

"Of course not. He could have been seen. He stopped down the street a bit, and when he saw Sarla coming along the pavement, on her own, he called her over. Told her he'd arranged with me and her mum to have a little holiday with him and Tressa. She was pleased - she loves staying at their place. She calls them Auntie and Uncle. They've got no children of their own, they spoil her, she likes that."

"How long was this ... little holiday going to last?" asked Dahlia.

"Until the witch died," said John. "Only a few months - less, with any luck. Then Sarla could just come home again. Chloe's mum was filling my daughter's head with all sorts of religious nonsense, you see. Horrible stuff. It had to be stopped, as I'm sure you can understand." Even now, he didn't seem at all worried. As far as Dahlia could tell, it simply hadn't occurred to him that he might be in trouble. "People are always lecturing me about consequences," he continued. "Always have done, since I was Sarla's age. Well - with this plan, there weren't any, were there? Sarla would spend some time being well looked after by her loving relatives, and then she'd come home, and everything would be fine again." His smile, as he concluded, was three parts complacent to one part smug.

"What about the consequences for your wife, John?" said Dahlia. "All the worry, all the - "

"No, no, no." His exasperation at her lack of comprehension was clear. "Don't you see? Sarla *hadn't* been kidnapped, she *wasn't* murdered, so in the end, there was no harm done. Yes? Nothing to worry about. Consequences aren't temporary - that's what I've always been told. Well, Chloe's worry was temporary, so it doesn't count."

"John," said Phil, "what were you and Johnny going to say, after your mother-in-law died, and you brought Sarla back home - what were you going to tell your wife, to explain where the girl had been?"

John looked at him in astonishment. "Tell her?" he said. "I was going to tell her the truth, of course."

They sent him back to his cell. Both detectives needed a break after that.

"A dust-break," said Phil.

"So it was a rescue, after all," Dahlia couldn't resist pointing out. "But a rescue from religion, not by religion."

Phil just grunted, and Dahlia wished, after all, that she had resisted. On the other hand ... she had no use for faith herself, but she did feel quite strongly that you couldn't paint all religious people from the same pot. She knew someone who was a devoted churchgoer, and who spent all his time helping other people. He was the kindest man she'd ever met, and a committed and very practical patriot. And she'd never in her life heard her beloved brother give anyone a sermon, or even so much as a hard word.

There was something approaching a festive air in the canteen at Kentish Town that afternoon. The place was full of Serious Crime detectives, along with officers from several other branches of the service, all coming and going, creating a feeling of bustle and achievement. The missing girl was back with her mother. The Beech Lane killer and her accomplices were at least in custody, if still some way from being charged. The Loftys were looking unusually pleased with themselves; they'd announced to DS Emmett that they were now available for reassignment, and that they would shortly be giving a public explanation of the Mystery of the Pond ("In all frankness," said the older one, "we're holding out for a classier audience. We'll wait until the DI's amongst us.") Ginger Thom said he had one more small errand to perform, later that day, after which he too hoped to have a tale to tell. All around, the tea flowed like water, the fragrant smoke billowed with each arrival or departure, and the cake vanished almost before it landed on the tables.

Bob Lemon was briefing Catherine Blake on a new case, just that hour received by the squad. Someone had tried to burn down a pub. What had initially seemed like a straightforward arson investigation had become complicated by the identification of a suspect - an ex-businessman who had strong family links to a cartel that, a generation earlier, had made a fortune buying up former pub sites.

"I haven't gone through all the details yet," Bob said, "but it seems it was no secret that this same company had a big hand in lobbying for some of the legislation that caused the pubs to close in the first place. Now, go forward a couple of decades, and you have a lot of very rich investors squealing that they've been ripped off when parliament passed the Reestablishment of Community Pubs Act. Anyway, CID want to know whether this is just revenge, or is it some sort of conspiracy?"

"Sounds like a juicy one, Bob," Catherine congratulated him. "You'll enjoy that."

Erin Smee, who'd arrived in time to hear the end of the conversation, asked Catherine: "You didn't have pubs when you were young, did you?"

Catherine wasn't sure where to begin with that. Perhaps a simple answer would suffice. "We did have them, and then we didn't, and now we've got them again."

"My mum says the old government closed them all down?"

"Well ... " Catherine didn't want to publicly contradict the girl's mother, but she also wanted to give an accurate answer to an important question. "Sort of. It's true that governments over a period of time introduced a number of laws which had the effect of closing most of the pubs."

Erin nodded. "Because they didn't want people gathering in public, right."

"Ah ... " Was this another of Mum's pronouncements? "A lot of people today believe that to be the real motivation, yes, but what they said at the time was that they were doing it to protect people's health."

"*Protect* people's health?" It was obvious that Erin thought the older woman had got this bit wrong. "By stopping them socialising?"

"Um ... " began Catherine, but then Bob came to her rescue.

"In those days, Erin, people were obsessed with what was called 'healthiness,' because we didn't really have much control over our own lives. The political and economic set-up was so different - you basically spent your life being blown this way or that every time the wind changed."

"Right," said Erin, who - Catherine had noticed - seemed to listen raptly whenever Bob spoke. She just hoped Bob hadn't noticed.

"Now, one thing that any psychologist will tell you - or is it psychiatrists?"

"Or is it blokes in pubs?" said Nasser, from a neighbouring table.

"Well, any head doctor," Bob went on, "will tell you that if people don't feel they have any control over the big things in life - their job, their home, their environment, war and peace, the economy - then they will compensate by trying to get control over trivial things. Things that don't really matter, or aren't even real, but which they can hope to have some power over."

"Like adolescent girls cutting their own arms?" said Catherine.

"Self-harming, exactly. You could say that the healthiness movement was just a socially acceptable alternative to self-harm. Or, at the more benign end of the scale, there's things like feng shui. People got themselves all worked up about all sorts of largely nonsensical, self-contradictory, micromanagement of imaginary health risks and benefits."

"At one point," said Catherine, "some schools banned Marmite, because it was considered too salty."

"They banned Marmite?" For Erin, it seemed, an interesting historical discussion had just become personal.

"Marmite." Catherine nodded. "On the same list as switchblades and heroin."

"That's right," said Bob. "It all became very competitive - who could go furthest, either as an individual, or corporately."

"Yeah, but why did the government get involved?"

"I think it goes back to the 1980s," said Catherine. "There was this new ideology which said that governments shouldn't interfere with running the country. All that - the economy, housing, jobs, even health and education - should be left to the free market to sort out. But of course, government still existed, we still had politicians. They just didn't have anything to do - everything had been privatised."

"But they had to do something all day other than snooze," said Bob. "And nature abhors a vacuum, so they devoted themselves full-time to telling people what they could and couldn't eat, how much of each food they were allowed per day ... "

"Like rationing?" said Erin.

"*Nothing* like rationing," said Catherine as Bob laughed. "They told us how and where we could drink or smoke, how much exercise we had to do ... "

"These days - whether for better or worse - we all have much more control over our everyday lives. Political and economic power has been devolved and collectivised, most people work in co-ops, not for big corporations, so they're actually in direct charge of their working days. So all that healthiness stuff has just faded away, along with feng shui and numerology."

"That's true, I hope." Catherine sounded thoughtful, even to her own ears. "Maybe as a society, we're no longer cutting our own arms."

"*We* don't have more control," Ginger objected.

Bob frowned. "How do you mean, we?"

"Us!" Ginger poked himself in the chest. "Coppers. Tell you what, if someone ever comes up with a co-op police force, I'll join that."

"I like it," Bob agreed. "Dividends paid on every arrest!"

"It's very simple, Rosie," Greg Wallace said. "Whoever gives us Brad Nottle's murderer first will win a note to the judge. You know what that means?"

Rosie Liddle smoked and said nothing.

"It's a note in the file, written by the investigating officer, saying that this person has cooperated with the police investigation. The judge is permitted to take this into account during sentencing. Now, your boyfriend is talking to us - and so far, you're not. As things stand, it looks like you're going to come second."

Rosie's lawyer tried to whisper in her ear, but she brushed him away. "Inspector, I've got something much more valuable to bargain with than the mere death of a wife-beater."

"Have you?"

She stubbed out her cigarette. "In exchange for complete immunity for myself and Ed, I am willing to give you everything I know - which is a lot - about an industrial espionage organisation operating in this country."

Her lawyer looked astonished. It always amazed Greg - and, as a copper, delighted him - how much information people in trouble routinely withheld from the only person who was actually paid to help them.

"And how do you happen to know all about this, Rosie?"

She smiled. "Guess."

"As your lawyer will tell you," said Greg, "the idea of total immunity is absurd. The charges are far too serious. Besides, plea-bargaining is illegal in this country. I can only repeat my previous offer of a note to the judge. It is reasonable to suppose that the value of that note would increase with the value of the information you gave us."

She looked at her lawyer. "Well?"

"What the inspector says is true."

"Shit!"

"However - Mr Wallace has left out one aspect of the matter which I think is of some interest."

Here we go, thought Greg.

"What's that?" said Rosie.

"If your information is as ... *exciting* as you suggest it is, then the security services might wish to take you into their custody. In such an event - "

"Never mind the legal crap," Rosie snapped. "You mean they can make deals that the police can't?"

"Not deals as such, but - "

"Yes or no?"

The lawyer was evidently uncomfortable with such a binary question. "More yes than no," he eventually admitted.

"Is that true, Inspector?"

"It's feasible," said Greg, sounding more reluctant than he truly felt. If Rosie wanted to spend the next ten years or so in a safe house, helping Counter Terrorism with their inquiries, perhaps even being run as a double agent, just to avoid a trial and prison sentence, then she was welcome to her fate.

"All right," she said. She had clearly been rehearsing her statement for some time, since what followed was fluent and concise. "Ed and I have been for some years involved with an organisation which uses various methods to persuade scientific researchers - especially those involved in the field of food security -

to keep some of their most promising research from their employers."

"One of these persuaded people is Kim Nottle?"

"Correct. When the day comes that your Process is overthrown - either because of humanitarian intervention from the USA or Europa, or because of the British people themselves rising up against it - the network, as it calls itself, will register with the new authorities as a legitimate business, and will be able to market such research to whoever wishes to buy it, quite legally."

"Legally?" said Greg. "You've just said yourself the stuff is stolen property."

"I don't think a new regime, committed to free enterprise, will see things that way, do you? Your Commonwealth's concept of 'patriotic property' will disappear on the same day as your Commonwealth disappears. Why should talented people work all their lives for no reward?"

"Other than their wages," Greg pointed out, "and bonuses, and prizes, and sundry other incentives and recognitions, and of course the big bonus - survival as a nation. So, what do you get out of this?"

Rosie waved the thought away with an impatient hand. "Ed and I get modest finders' fees, and there'll be a royalty after the research is sold. But I am doing this out of principle, Inspector. I am doing it to stand up for the principle of private property. Even if you do succeed in putting me in prison, I am confident that world opinion will adopt me as a prisoner of conscience."

She was probably right about that, Greg admitted to himself. Some world opinion, anyway. "I'm glad you told me you were a free enterprise martyr, Rosie. If you hadn't, I might have got the mistaken impression that you were a greedy cow. Now, tell me about the murder of Bradley Nottle."

"Never."

"Why on earth not? How can it be worse than what you have just told me?"

"Brad was a violent bully, Inspector, and Kim is a gentle woman who was pushed too far. No." She shook her head. "No matter what it costs me, I will not be party to sending that poor woman to prison."

At going-home time, Ginger Thom stood outside the quadcycle factory with a tally counter in his hand. Every time an employee came out, Ginger clicked the clicker.

It didn't take long for the manager, Mr Doyle, to appear.

"I understand you've been questioning some of my employees, Constable?"

"I have, sir," said Ginger, carrying on clicking. "And now, I have one simple question for you: how many employees have you got?"

Doyle, apparently transfixed by Ginger's clicker, said nothing.

"Only," Ginger continued, "it's harder counting like this than you might expect. I make it fifty-one, yourself included. Does that sound about right?"

Doyle took out a cigarette, lit it, took two drags, cursed loudly, and threw the cigarette away almost un-smoked. Ginger made a surreptitious mental note of where it landed, in the hope that he might grab it later.

"So," he carried on, "with a nightwatchman, that would have been fifty-two."

"Oh for God's sake," said Doyle. "There's bloody laws for bloody everything. I'm just trying to run a business."

"We'd better continue this at the police station, sir. I'm afraid there might be some formalities."

Doyle admitted it all, without much further pressing. After a cup of tea and a piece of Jade's cake, he became quite philosophical. "Well, that's it, then. A moderately successful career in management finally comes to an end. Why should I care? No-one else will give a toss, that's for sure. My wife and kids will piss themselves laughing. At least in prison I won't have to count anything."

Prison? thought Ginger. "So, how did it go wrong?"

"I just cocked up. Simple as that. It's a very stressful job, you know, running a private company. It's not like a co-op - you've got no-one to help you, you're on your own."

"Right, it must be tough."

"It is. A lot of stress. I'd forgotten to make a proper note of several employees who were on study sabbaticals. The government forces us to give people - "

Ginger interrupted, to stop the rant before it could get going. "I know, sure. So you already had the maximum number of staff, but you didn't realise it?"

"I needed two new tool fitters, so I took them on. And that put me over."

"But then half your problem disappeared with the sudden resignation of the roof garden nightwatchman."

"I couldn't believe my luck. One down, one to go. I wasn't that worried, to be honest - staff turnover's pretty high in our sector."

"So I've heard."

"I didn't think it'd take long to balance out."

"But meanwhile, you couldn't hire a replacement nightwatchman. Why didn't you appoint someone internally?"

"There was no point, was there? I needed to lose someone, not shuffle them around. Anyway, we've never had a theft from our gardens before, not ever."

Yes, thought Ginger, *that's possibly because you always had a nightwatchman before.* "And you couldn't organise a staff rota to cover the night watch on the garden, because you didn't want to draw attention to the fact that you hadn't got a nightwatchman? You knew the staff wouldn't be happy about that."

"Well, yes, and also because if I'd admitted we had a vacancy for nightwatchman, one of the staff would be bound to say 'Oh, my neighbour'll do that,' or 'My brother in law'll do that,' or 'That's just the sort of job my sodding auntie's been looking for,' and then I'd have had fifty-three bloody staff!" He lit a cigarette to calm himself down and, to Ginger's disappointment, smoked it properly this time. "As it is, I had to agree to a rota once there'd been that theft - and

I'm running out of excuses as to why I haven't managed to fill the vacancy. I tell you, it'll be a relief to give it all up."

"But how were you hoping to get away with it? Surely someone official was going to notice soon enough?"

Doyle tapped a cunning finger against an old hand's nose. "*Not* soon enough, was my hope. Believe me, all my years in management, I know that things take time to work through a system, whether paper or computer. And that was all I needed, wasn't it? A bit of time. I just hoped one more of them would bugger off to become a miner before the discrepancy came to light." He sighed, and slumped in his chair. "How long do you suppose I'll get? Longer than a bloody rapist, probably, the way things are these days."

"Well," said Ginger, "it's not a fine, I can tell you that."

"Hah! Didn't think it would be! Not community service either, I'll bet?"

"No," said Ginger. "It's a written warning."

Doyle waited for the DC to finish. After quite a long time, he realised he had. "A written ... a what?"

"I looked into it the other day, Mr Doyle. It's all on-line, if you ever need to check. Open government, you know?"

"I thought - you know, any excuse! I thought they'd bang me up as soon as look at me. I thought they'd nationalise the company, seize the assets."

Ginger shook his head. "Not even a fine until the second offence. First offence, written warning, and your business is given a statutory time to sort the problem out. I read somewhere that some economic historian worked out that what determines whether or not a new system succeeds is whether it manages to get higher productivity of labour than the mode of production it replaced. It's not in the nation's interest to see your business go under, Mr Doyle."

"Written warning? God almighty, man, I haven't slept for three weeks! I'm on bloody pills from the doctor."

It was at that point that Ginger decided, in his mercy, not to pursue a charge of wasting police time against Mr Doyle - and also not to tell him that the business with the tally counter this afternoon had been all for show. Ginger reckoned he was better at counting than Doyle was, but even he couldn't successfully count an unknown number of people who were on holiday, sick leave or sabbaticals simply by standing outside a factory with a thing that went click.

CHAPTER EIGHTEEN

It had been a slightly dodgy phone call to make, which was why Catherine Blake had insisted on making it herself, rather than allowing the DI to do it. The thing was this: classed as unfit for interview, Kim Nottle had been transferred from the police cells to a secure hospital. Greg and Catherine were pretty certain that - distressed as Kim no doubt was - her unfitness was, to put it politely, largely voluntary. All the same, the police were not allowed to initiate contact with her; the next move had to come from the doctors, when they decided that their patient was sufficiently recovered.

Which was quite right, of course, and as it should be, because otherwise what was to stop police officers wringing false statements out of people who didn't know what they were saying? But it was also irritating in this particular case - and yes, Catherine was perfectly well aware, although she was no veteran, that every case was always 'this particular case,' and therefore an exception to the rules, but all the same ...

They had heard back from the Ministry for Bees (she couldn't help it, the title made Catherine giggle; they should call it the Ministry About Bees; it wasn't a ministry *for* bees, was it? They didn't go there to get their little visas extended, did they?), and the buzz was (Greg's joke; Catherine laughed quite a lot) that Ginger had been spot on about the papers hidden in the wedding album. They were, indeed, stolen documents relating to Kim's work, and it was, certainly, a criminal offence to remove them from the workplace. More to the point, as a noisily tearful colleague of Kim's had told Ginger over the phone, these papers explained why Kim's career had not come up to expectations. Simple answer: it had. She had, some time back, made a significant breakthrough in her research concerning artificial nesting sites for bumblebees in elevated locations (which was, apparently, terribly important stuff, for reasons which Catherine really couldn't be bothered to wonder about), but she had kept it to herself.

The Ministry Concerning Bees (*that's better*) didn't know why she had done such an extraordinary thing, but the detectives did. She'd done it for money. Future money, admittedly, and money that might never arrive, but then if greed was rational you wouldn't need a special name for it. Those involved in the network exhibited the signs of pathological greed, an unstoppable force with which every police officer was sadly familiar.

The point of all this was, Greg and Catherine were sure that once Kim knew that they had her on the bumblebee business, she wouldn't bother denying the murder any longer. She was never going to be released from prison, once the judge had finished totting up the tariffs for espionage, treason and sabotage, so why bother pretending she hadn't done her husband in - especially since the said husband sounded as if he'd been begging for it.

In other words: if Kim knew what stage the game had reached, she'd talk to them. Get it over with. But the doctors were hardly likely to accept that she was compos mentis just a few hours after they'd found that she wasn't. Apart from anything, it would make them look silly, something which doctors, as a species, tend to be very frightened of.

On the other hand, you couldn't stop someone talking to their lawyer. Anywhere, any time, under any circumstances, that was one of the most basic of all rights. The lawyer wasn't going to go and see her, though; Kim would have to summon the lawyer. Hence the dodgy phone call.

An old friend of Greg's ex-wife's sister worked at the secure hospital. Catherine phoned her and, after spending about five minutes introducing herself ("My boss is your friend's sister's ... "), she managed to persuade her that it was in the patient's interests that she talk to her lawyer urgently because "The police know all about the bees."

"The police know all about the bees," repeated the boss's ex-wife's sister's old friend. "I shall be awake all night trying to figure that one out."

It worked, anyway; the sister's friend talked to the patient, the patient called the lawyer, and the lawyer called the detective inspector, who told him all about the stolen papers. The lawyer then visited the patient in hospital and spent over an hour with her, during which she gave him the full and frank statement which she was currently unable to give to the police. The lawyer went straight from the hospital to the police station, in order to convey his client's statement to them.

The first thing he said to the detectives when he got there was: "You think you've been very clever, but you're not going to like this."

"The sooner you're able to explain to us your role in this matter," Phil said, "the sooner we'll be able to process you, and perhaps get you bailed."

"I've nothing to hide," said Austin Molloy, though his constant smoothing of his ponytail with his sweaty hands seemed to Dahlia to belie the confidence of his words. "I've done nothing I'm ashamed of."

"I'm pleased to hear it," said Phil. "So how did you get involved?"

"I know Tressa Costas well from work - she's done the covers on many of our books. She phoned me in a terrible state. She said your lot were on the verge of arresting her husband's cousin for abducting his own child. She was absolutely certain that this guy John, who I've never met, was innocent, but that the police had got it in for him."

"Why did we have it in for him?" asked Phil.

"Tressa said he had a few minor convictions, long time ago, so you'd fixated on him." He gave them a disapproving look. "Believe me, I know how that works."

"But you believed her when she said he was innocent?"

"I've worked with the woman, I trust her judgement. And I trust *my* judgement, in knowing she was someone whose word I could take. If she said he didn't do it, that was good enough for me."

"And Tressa suggested a way in which you might help?"

"That's right. She said the little girl's mother - Chloe, is it? - had heard some American accents round about when the girl was taken, but that the police were refusing to take her seriously. If I were to come forward saying I'd also heard those voices, that would force you to stop wasting your time persecuting this guy John, and concentrate on looking for the evangelicals who'd really got the girl. I was proud to help."

"You were proud to waste valuable police time," said Phil, very slowly and very quietly, "during the hunt for a missing child?"

"Are you really *so* anti-American?" said Dahlia. Phil looked at her, shock written on his face, and she realised with embarrassment that, just for a second, he'd thought the question was addressed to him.

"Listen, young lady," said the American, leaning towards her. "I don't expect you to understand this, or even try to understand it. But anything I can do - anything - to get the complacent people of this country to understand the real and ever-present threat that religious Yanks pose to your way of life, I will do it."

"Anything you can do to whip up racist hysteria, you mean?"

He spread his hands, and leaned back. "You want to put it that way, I'm not going to argue with you. I'm happy with that description. Anything it takes, to put this country on its guard. Think about it - if the Yanks invade, what do you suppose is going to happen to people like me? The kindest fate we can hope for is a bullet in the back of the head."

"You've no time for Distraction Theory, I take it?" Phil asked. "The idea that the Yanks are so preoccupied with natural disasters and unrest at home, water shortages, the soil wars, secession and all that, that they haven't got the time or resources or will to go around invading well-defended countries like Britain?"

"Damn it!" Austin banged both fists down on the table in front of him. "I hear that single word, 'Distracted,' chanted like it was some kind of charm to ward off evil. Listen - empires are at their most dangerous when they're dying. You don't believe me, then go ask the Burmese, the Indians, the Kenyans, how they got on in the last days of the British Empire. They're still digging up the mass graves to this day." He took a long drink of water. "Look, I'll take what's coming to me, but don't expect me to apologise for what I did. You want to condemn me, first you walk a mile in my shoes."

"Or," said Dahlia, who felt that Phil and the suspect were becoming a little too chummy here, "you could try walking a mile in Chloe Brown's shoes - the mile she walked while she tried not to imagine what was happening to her kidnapped daughter."

"Look, I didn't know Tressa and her husband had the kid. I swear to you, I had no idea."

Much to Dahlia's disappointment, this appeared to be true; it was what Johnny and Tressa Costas were saying, anyway.

"In that case, why were you at their house today?"

"Just called round on the off-chance, to offer them my sympathy, my support. When you two came through the door, I thought I'd had the shock of my life. Turned out I was wrong - when you came downstairs with the missing girl, *that* was the fucking shock of my life."

In the canteen, a little later, Dahlia said: "You reckon all four of them will go to prison?"

"Sure of it," said Phil. "Unless they get sent to a secure hospital."

"You think that's a possibility?"

Phil sipped his tea. He took his pipe out of his pocket, put it in his mouth, put it back in his pocket. "Let's face it, they're all mad in their own ways. John for thinking this was a sensible solution, cousin Johnny for going along with it, Tressa for thinking she could control it - and that Yank bastard for ... well, he just is, isn't he?"

"But one way or another, they'll all be locked up?"

"I can't see why not. The fact is they're guilty of, variously, lying to the police, wasting police time, causing distress to the mother and others - and they did conspire to kidnap and falsely imprison a child, even if the child didn't know she was kidnapped."

"Phil," Dahlia asked, "they won't send Austin Molloy home, will they? Him being a refugee, I mean."

"God, no," he said, and he put a hand on her sleeve, in a clumsy, obviously unpractised, but much appreciated gesture of comfort. "Our legal system might be a long way from perfect, but rest assured - we have at least moved on from those days."

It was a very full statement, and it seemed to start promisingly enough.

The lawyer was provided with the most comfortable seat in DI Wallace's office, and with a pot of tea and a plate of sandwiches, as he had happened to mention in passing several times that it was several hours since he'd eaten. When he was feeling a little revived, he lit his pipe, and began.

Much, he allowed, was as Greg and Catherine had already surmised. Kim had been having an affair with the lodger, Nathan. Her husband Bradley had found out, and was both heartbroken and enraged. He had confronted the lodger, unfortunately when both of them were the worse for drink. There had been a physical struggle, or tussle, which had ended in the manslaughter of Nathan Ackery.

"She only has her late husband's word for that version of events?" Greg interrupted.

"Indeed, but she believes his account."

Brad had buried the lodger temporarily in the garden, until he was able to dispose of him properly. He told Kim nothing - neither that he had found out about her infidelity, or that he had fought with Nathan. By claiming to believe that his lodger had absconded to avoid paying his rent, he allowed her to believe that her lover had absconded to escape from her. He persuaded her that they should move into number nineteen "temporarily," and the first thing he did was pave the drive, ostensibly to make the place easier to sell.

Kim spent the next several years constantly begging Brad to move from Beech Lane - a house and a neighbourhood for which she had never felt any affection - until finally realising that he never would. She could never understand why - he only ever told her that it wasn't the right moment to sell, or it wasn't the right moment to buy - and in her frustration and perplexity their marriage had all but died.

Why did she never leave her husband? Simple: because she still loved him. The affair with Nathan had merely been youthful lust - and curiosity; other than Brad, she had never slept with another man before Nathan.

She often wondered, on the other hand, why her husband didn't leave her. He seemed to have no feelings for her at all. She convinced herself that it was because, at some sunken level, he did still love her, and that one day ... who knows?

"Did she really not suspect anything, when her lover disappeared?" said Catherine. "Or did she just not suspect because she chose not to suspect?"

The lawyer - who was clearly getting into his role of storyteller now - was equally clearly annoyed at the interruption of his narrative. "A fascinating question indeed, DS Blake, but one with which we should perhaps not trouble ourselves overmuch, since we cannot possibly hope to know the answer. If I may continue ...?"

As she now knew, of course, Brad didn't dare move; whoever occupied the house after them might well dig up the driveway, and expose his crime. And so their dead marriage - their empty lives - continued. They had no children, by unspoken mutual agreement, and no friends. Brad's reclusiveness, Kim now believed, was the result of living with the guilt of what he'd done, and living with being a hypocrite.

"Her exact words are: 'He couldn't stand the stink of himself, didn't want to see other people in case they smelled it on him. That's why he loathed me - because I loved him. He despised me for that.'"

No-one ever came looking for Nathan, and there he stayed

beneath the drive. But Brad could never have imagined, back in the late 1990s, that one day the state would order him to dig up his paved driveway.

"More tea?" Greg offered, at what seemed like a natural break in the statement.

"Actually," said the lawyer, "what would really go down well would be a glass of cider."

"Would it?" said Greg. "I expect you'd like me to get one of my officers to pop over to the pub and fetch one for you, would you?"

"Oh, that would be most kind. Thank you, Detective Inspector."

"Right," said Greg, with roughly a ten-second pause before the word.

Once tea and cider had been procured and drunk, the lawyer went on.

Brad Nottle's refusal to comply with the re-greening order on his drive was a slight puzzle, even now, to his wife. Was he burying his head in the sand, refusing to confront a problem he could no longer bear thinking about? Was he endlessly hoping for an opportunity to move the body, which never arose? Or was it simply that he just couldn't face the body again after all these years?

"We'll never know," said Catherine pointedly.

Whatever the truth, he simply refused to discuss the matter of the re-greening, with Kim or with anyone else. She was so used to this way of life by now, that she thought nothing of it. However, the day came when the exhumation could not be delayed any further. The community council served notice on Friday that the drive would be compulsorily dug up the following Tuesday. And at last, after a lifetime, Brad made his confession to his wife.

"And she killed him," said Greg.

The lawyer smiled, and put his finger to his lips.

Far from being angry, Kim was delighted. This was the happiest day of her life - the happiest day in decades, at least. Now, suddenly, her life made sense! Brad hadn't stopped loving her, it wasn't her fault, there wasn't some failing in her that had ruined their marriage.

There was a reason - a proper, external reason - for all the years of unhappiness, and now it was out in the open, they could start again.

But if they were to start again, it must be with no secrets. And so she told him about her involvement with the network. Naturally, he was horrified. Who wouldn't be, on discovering that his wife was a traitor and a criminal. He did, however, realise that he was in a poor position to make moral judgements.

"Does your client explain why she allowed Rosie Liddle to recruit her into this network?" asked Greg. "Is she some sort of beefeater?"

"She claims no ideological basis for her actions," said the lawyer. "Rather, she says that Rosie caught her at her lowest, when bitterness and depression clouded her judgement."

Rosie's scheme had seemed to offer the apolitical Kim some future hope - one day, under a new regime, she'd be rich, and her husband would admire her again. She'd win him back through her success.

At that time, she had recently produced some results in her work at the Ministry for Bees which were highly promising. Instead of presenting it to her colleagues, she gave them a faked set of results, which showed that course of research as being a dead end. Meanwhile, she smuggled the real work out, registered it with the network, and kept it hidden in her house, in a place where she knew Brad would never chance upon it. She used printouts because she had no idea how long it would be before she could sell the documents, and paper is the only form of data storage that is never rendered obsolete.

"She 'registered' it?" said Catherine.

"The people behind this so-called network preferred their - what shall we say? Vendors? They preferred their vendors to keep the documents themselves; to lessen the risk to those in charge, I presume. You see, the data was of no immediate commercial value. The network couldn't sell it, because it'd be too obvious where it'd come from - everyone in such fields knows what everyone else in their area of speciality is working on."

Instead, the documents which would ultimately be sold - after the counter-revolution which Rosie and her colleagues confidently awaited - were registered with the network, as if with a legitimate agency. When the Commonwealth fell, the network would go down the list, call on all its registered vendors, and collect their research ready to place it on the open market. Meanwhile, the network itself was funded by an international data brokerage company which planned to be the main broker of 'liberated' data in the post-Commonwealth gold rush. Some of the research, inevitably, would become out of date and worthless during the wait, but not all of it - and presumably, stocks were constantly being replenished.

Kim told Brad all this, and they agreed to put everything behind them.

"Oh," said Catherine. "Not going to turn themselves in, then?"

They would find a way, together, of removing Nathan's remains, and also of feeding Kim's withheld research back into the system. Neither task would be easy, but now that they were reunited they were confident they could manage them.

Eager to begin their new life, Kim rang Rosie to explain that her involvement with the network was at an end.

"A little naive," Greg noted.

"This my client now acknowledges, but she says that she had not previously realised that the network was a big business - she had supposed it was just Rosie Liddle and a few likeminded friends."

That Sunday evening, Rosie and her boyfriend, Ed, turned up at Beech Lane to explain to Kim that withdrawal from the scheme was not an option. Rosie was friendly, cajoling, reassuring, flattering and optimistic. Ed was silent, standing behind his girlfriend, with an old, leather cricket bag at his feet. Rosie was eloquent, but Kim and Brad were not to be dissuaded. After more than two hours of stalemate, Rosie gave her old friend a sad look, and nodded to Ed.

"Oh, hell," said Greg.

"I did say you weren't going to like it," said the lawyer.

Rosie left the room, and they heard her leave the house. Kim thought she'd at last understood that their decision was final, and that this part of the nightmare, at least, was over. Brad grasped what was happening rather more quickly. He threw himself on Ed, and almost overpowered him - almost, but not quite. Ed managed to remove a Spitfire rifle from his cricket bag, and shot him once.

"How old was the cricket bag?" Greg asked.

The lawyer stared at him. "What? I don't know. Old, my client said, with Ed Upsall's name painted on it."

"The name 'Ed Upsall'?"

The lawyer tutted. "Honestly, Inspector. Wait a moment." He flipped through his notes. "No, just the surname. Any more questions about the bag? Do you need to know where it was made?"

"Please, carry on."

Seeing her lost-and-regained husband fall to the floor, Kim snatched up a heavy ornament and brought it down on Ed's neck. He, too, fell to the floor, apparently unconscious.

"And your client?"

"Ran. Out of the back door, across the garden, and away. She took a bus to Paddington, and a train to Cornwall. Inspector, she was not running from the police."

"No?"

"She was quite sure that the gang would send someone else after her. She was hiding from them. She was in hiding for her life. She had no long-term plan: merely survival, from minute to minute, and hour to hour."

Greg smiled. "You can try that on the jury if you like, but we all know why she couldn't go to the police for protection, don't we? Because she had committed, of her own free will, a major crime for which she will spend the rest of her life in prison."

CHAPTER NINETEEN

The Loftys at last got their full canteen audience, late in the afternoon. Even the DI was there, taking a break between interviews, when the older Lofty received a message from Scientific: blood traces, matching those on the bicycle tyre, had been found on two items of junk recovered from the pond, and on the ground surrounding the pond.

The older Lofty knew how to tell a story in a busy police canteen: start telling it quietly and confidentially to the person sitting next to you, and let a natural tendency amongst detectives for eavesdropping do the work for you.

"A gang of hijackers," he explained to Dale Emmett, "planned to steal a wagonload of first grade tomato seed - worth a decent bit of money on the black market, especially if you can somehow get it out of the country and sell it abroad. But two wagons set out from the Manor House that day."

"And the hijackers got the wrong one," put in the younger Lofty. "Presumably they didn't know there were two loads going out. The other one was a pile of old junk for recycling - nothing to do with the seed business itself."

"It was the driver of this second load - a worker at the Manor House - who got killed," said his partner, and now everyone in the room was listening. "Whether the hijackers always planned to murder the driver - "

"Or maybe he fought back, and got killed that way," the younger Lofty interrupted. "Or they might have killed him out of sheer temper, when they realised they'd stolen the wrong load."

The older Lofty raised his voice slightly as he completed his sentence, but otherwise gave no sign that he was aware of his younger colleague's presence. " - we can't know. In any case, they've ended up with a wagonload of junk, which they need to get rid of. They daren't turn it in for recycling, so they decide to dump it in a flood pond. Perhaps they planned to get rid of the driver's body at the same time, or - "

"More likely," said his partner, "they'll have disposed of the wagon, its contents, and its driver separately, so as to confuse the police. Once the wagon's empty, they can take it somewhere deserted and burn it out."

"They're halfway through emptying the wagon into the pond, when wobbling round the corner comes a drunken cyclist."

"This is your hospital accountant?" asked Greg. "The one who's in love with a prostitute?"

"That's him, chief. Kieran Rider. Now, he rides his bike straight into a man - we presume, the poor driver - who's sitting against the side of the wagon."

"Sitting," said the younger Lofty, "or more likely propped up against. The gang have put him there, awaiting disposal."

"Wait a minute," said Bob Lemon. "Is the driver dead at this stage?"

"Possibly not," said the older Lofty. "Kieran, the accountant, is adamant that the man he ran into was bleeding heavily. So maybe he's dying rather than dead - his stabbing or shooting has only just happened - and the gang plan to finish him off when they've finished getting the junk into the pond."

"Or chuck him in the pond still alive," suggested the other Lofty, with youthful relish, "and leave him to drown."

"Perhaps he tried to escape while the gang were unloading," said Bob, "and that's when he got stabbed."

"Quite likely," said the older Lofty, nodding to give the false impression that this idea had already occurred to him. "Anyway, the cyclist panics - believing himself to have just killed a man, he hurls his bike into the pond, getting rid of the evidence, and decamps at whatever speed he can manage, on foot."

"Why don't the hijackers kill him?" asked Bob.

Lofty shrugged. "Perhaps they realise that another killing is really pushing their luck. They don't want the dead bodies piling up all over the shop, do they? But I reckon they panicked, too. Everything's gone wrong for them today - especially if we assume that they didn't set out to kill anyone. For all they know, the cyclist is going to sober up any second, realise what he's done, and call 999."

"They've got to get out of there," said Dale. "Chuck the driver's body in the back of the wagon, along with however much junk is still in there, and flee the scene as fast as their horses can go."

"That's what we reckon," agreed the older Lofty. "They sent a message to the driver's boss, saying he'd fallen ill and wouldn't be in for a few days. Gives them a bit more time, before people start looking for him."

"So the investigation's continuing," said Greg. "Hijacking and suspected murder. Do the local CID want us on it, Lofty?"

"They don't think it's worth our while, Chief. Either the gang had an inside man working at the Manor House, in which case they're confident they'll find him easily enough. Or else, the wagon will turn up eventually, or the driver's body will, and there'll be plenty on either of those for Scientific to look at."

"Or they do it again," said Bob, "and this time they manage to steal something that someone actually reports missing."

"But at least," Lofty concluded, "we can tell our accountant that he's not a killer - he's just an idiot. Oh, and also that he's under arrest for going with an unlicensed prostitute."

"And for giving a false statement to police," added the other Lofty, "and for failing to report an accident and for riding a bicycle while intoxicated. And polluting a flood pond."

"And buying expensive gifts for a tom," said Nasser Agarkar. "Surely that's covered by the Pratt Act?"

"Food theft and murder," said Greg. "Your polluted pond turned out to be very much in Serious Crimes territory. But how did you Loftys know to keep pursuing it?"

"Oh, you know, Chief," said one of the Loftys, modestly. "You get a nose for these things."

"Nose," agreed the other.

"Right, I thought it must be something like that," said Greg, finishing his tea and rising from his seat. "Anyway, Lofty, a tale well told - you have hidden talents."

"Oh, you've got to keep your talents hidden, Chief," said Lofty. "You never know who's watching."

He planned to interview the furniture man, Ed Upsall, next. But first, Greg had needed a word with Bob Lemon, who'd been lead officer when the search warrant was executed at the furniture store. He'd wanted him to check an item on the property list he'd been in charge of compiling, and - if he found it - to ask Rover to run it round to the laboratory. While he was waiting, Greg refreshed himself with a cup of tea, and the famous Lofty cabaret, in the canteen.

Then he rounded up Catherine, and had Ed Upsall returned to an interview room. It had been a long day in a long week, but he reckoned it was nearing its end now. This shouldn't take long.

"You got rid of the Spitfire rifle, Ed," he told his prisoner, "but you kept the cricket bag. We found it in amongst the Nottles' belongings in your warehouse."

Ed Upsall, who looked as if he'd aged ten years in the last ten hours, just stared at the DI for a moment, the frown on his face more confused than worried. He had reached that stage - Greg had seen it in interview rooms hundreds of times over the years - when the mental processing of data slowed right down.

And then he got it. *The cricket bag.* His face fell, and with it his remaining resistance. "Oh ... damn."

"I get the impression your cricket bag is pretty old. Your father's?"

"Grandfather's. He played for Cambridge University."

"I understand." Greg nodded, sympathetically. "A family heirloom. I'll ask Scientific to be careful with it. Mind you, the officer who checked it for me says if you stick your head inside it you can smell the gun residues. Hardly need the lab to confirm that."

"I was going to take it over to my brother's," said Ed, his delivery slow and flat. "Leave it with him. Just didn't get round to it."

"Well, you had a lot of details to take care of, you couldn't help forgetting one or two," said Greg. "Mind you, Rosie's going to be furious."

"Oh God ... "

"You know what she's going to say, don't you? That she can't possibly be blamed for anything that happened after she left the room."

Ed's lawyer whispered in his ear. Ed nodded.

"Not terribly fair," Greg continued, "but that's what she'll say. I'd put money on that. She didn't know you were going to shoot anyone, she just intended you to - "

"At this stage, Inspector," said the lawyer, "my client would like to amend his earlier account of events."

"Do you mean some of the earlier details were incorrect? Do you hear that, DS Blake?"

"Hard to credit, sir."

"You carry on, Ed."

"It was all Rosie's idea. I was just her bloody stooge."

"Noted," said Greg. "You arrived at Beech Lane with a stolen rifle in your granddad's cricket bag - were you planning to kill them all along?"

"No, no," said Ed, looking shocked and even offended at the very idea. "Oh no, not unless it was completely necessary."

"Can't say fairer than that," said Greg.

"Rosie was going to talk them round. You know - bigger promises, bigger threats. Get them to change their minds about leaving the network."

"But if they refused?"

"Well - to be fair, we couldn't risk leaving them alive, could we? I mean, they might have gone to the authorities, or anything." He stopped, and wrinkled his brow as if trying to recall something. After a few seconds his face cleared. "Anyway, we're political dissidents, aren't we? We've got a right under international law to protect ourselves from persecution by the regime." He smiled, obviously proud to have remembered his lines. His smile vanished as his lawyer again whispered urgently in his ear. "Oh. Right. Not that I am claiming any ideological motive for my part in these events. I was simply the unwitting tool of a manipulative personality."

Greg wrote on his notepad. "I'm ... just ... a ... tool. Right, got that, Ed. So you shot Bradley Nottle, and Kim knocked you out. Is that right?"

He nodded. "When I came round, Rosie was standing over me, slapping my face. I felt a bit rough, to tell you the truth. But she said we had to hurry. She didn't think Kim would go to the police, but we had a lot to do. We buried the bloke in the garden - made a neat job of that, so he wouldn't be found unless someone was looking for him." He scowled. "Of course, we had no way of knowing there was *another* sodding body, under the drive."

"Pure bad luck," Greg agreed. "Did you search for Kim's papers? The stuff she was keeping for the network?"

"We started looking, but then Rosie said - this is a waste of time. We could be here for a week, and not find them. The idea had been, if necessary, to make Kim tell us where the papers were, before we ... " He trailed off.

"You were going to offer to swap her life for the papers - or her husband's life - and then kill them anyway?"

"Well, whatever, that wasn't going to work now. So, Rosie had this idea - she sent me home to get the furniture van, while she searched the structure of the house itself. The loft, the cistern, all that. Then when I got back, we loaded everything up and took it home, so we could search it in safety. If anyone caught us moving it, we were going to say Kim and Brad had split up - he'd stormed out, drunk, she was scared of him, so she wanted to get all her stuff out of the house and away to a friend's before he came back. That bit was my idea."

"Very clever," said Greg. "And what did you do with the rifle?"

"Chucked it in a pond on the way home."

"Did you? Well, you'll be charged with that as well, then. Very serious offence, polluting ponds."

When they arrived at their usual table in the Coach, Catherine and Greg tucked themselves in next to Phil Kale and Dahlia Kotane and lost no time in getting involved with the sandwiches that Jade's customary foresight had made available to them.

"So we arrested Kim Nottle for the wrong offence?" said Dahlia, while Phil took a phone call.

"We did," Catherine agreed. "She never killed anyone in her life. But she was guilty of stealing her own research work."

"Doesn't make a lot of difference in the end," said Greg. "All three of them will go to prison forever."

"I just wish Brad Nottle could join them," said Catherine, to general murmurs of agreement.

Phil put his phone away. "Well, that's a little bit of good news. Just been speaking to Chloe Brown. She's told her mother she can't ever be alone with Sarla again, and that if she makes any further attempt to infect her with religion, Chloe'll send her packing - terminal illness or not."

"John Brown's secular rescue worked in the end, then," said Greg.

"You could say that," said Phil.

"That reminds me," said Catherine. "Jade gave me a message for you, Phil. Muswell Hill have finally traced the 'north American voices' the mother heard on the day Sarla was taken."

"You're kidding? I thought they'd stopped looking?"

"They had, but someone came forward." Catherine smiled. "Two members of a New Zealand football team, visiting nearby relatives on their day off."

"New Zealand? Oh, for ... " Phil slumped in his chair and stuck his unlit pipe in his mouth.

"There's an oddity," said Greg. "Why did your American refugee say he heard a man and a woman with American accents, when he must know that in all the stories, evangelical rescues are carried out by two women?"

Dahlia rolled her eyes. "He threw that in, he told us, to make it sound more realistic - less like something from an urban myth. He's quite proud of that touch of subtlety, believe it or not."

"Good heavens," said Greg Wallace. "What a horrible mess."

Catherine looked at him in surprise; that didn't sound a very Greg-like thing to say. But then she saw that he had opened up one of his sandwiches, and was peering at its contents. "Mutton?" she asked.

He nodded miserably. "Mutton. Horrible. Oh well, can't waste it."

She put a restraining hand on his sleeve, as he lifted the sandwich towards his mouth. "Hold on, Greg. I think I can solve that little dilemma for you. Erin!"

"Yes, Sarge?" came the eager voice from the other end of the table.

"Come over here a second, would you - the DI wants a word."